Unhallowed Rites

Allegra's skin burnt like a molten flame. But
the worst of the punishment was countered
by her overwhelming awareness of the young
priest's appetite. She wanted him to want her,
indeed she wished she could command him to
kiss and lick the painful results of his labours.
She guessed he must be wildly throbbing
beneath his robe; struggling in a private agony
of violent lust.

Unhallowed Rites
Martine Marquand

BLACK LACE

Black Lace books contain sexual fantasies.
In real life, always practise safe sex.

This edition published in 2004 by
Black Lace
Thames Wharf Studios
Rainville Road
London W6 9HA

Originally published 1998

Printed and bound by Mackays of Chatham PLC

ISBN 0 352 33222 0

Chapter One

*T*emptation. Allegra knew it had been sent to try her virtue. What sin would it be? To steal, to covet or only to spy?

Allegra lifted the key; she knew it to be the means of entry to the one room in her guardian's rambling palazzo that she had not seen. The room that was always kept locked. And unlike the other, rough cast and heavy keys that the servants carried about to unlock chests and store rooms, it was very fine: a twisting loop of brass, like the elegant treble clef on the musical scores she practiced each day in her room.

The key to her guardian's private room must have been left out quite by accident. Each day, before he set off for his day's duties at the Senate, Signor Pietro di Rivero carefully locked the heavy oak door of his favourite chamber and hid the key away, she knew not where. Today, for some reason she could not fathom, he had left it untidily out on the table where they breakfasted. But then again, in this Godless household, anything might happen.

Her mind fluttered like an escaped butterfly; today there would be some relief from the stifling boredom of life in Palazzo di Rivero. Each day now, for the last three months, she had woken late and breakfasted alone after an hour of prayers in her room. What was there to do next? True, she practiced her instrument, she sewed, she watched from the window. But the walls seemed to stifle her, with their crumbling shields and rusty swords all testifying to a greater, more glorious age. There was no suitable chaperone in this household mostly of men, so the answer for a young woman like herself was simple. She must not leave the house.

Allegra jumped as she heard the scuffle of boots on the polished stairs outside. Instinctively, she thrust the key inside the muslin of her bodice. But it was only Paolina, her guardian's surly housekeeper, who thrust the door aside with an impolite kick.

'Has my guardian left now for the Senate?'

She thought Paolina gave her an odd look, but it was difficult to tell from such a coarse and swarthy face. Even the servants here were unpleasant, Allegra had decided. She missed her old nurse, Francesca, and the old estates in the country with the rows of cedars which glowed green as emeralds in the evening light. Her parents though, despite her fervid prayers, were growing ever more distant in her memory. They had both succumbed to the fever which drifted in from the marshes each autumn and she had not seen them in those long and lingering final weeks. Now she felt lost between two different states: the carefree life of childhood and this new, uneasy state of adulthood which brought with it only boredom and confinement.

'He has left, signorina,' Paolina mumbled, picking up the remains of bread and coffee.

'And his son?' Allegra would not call him cousin, as her guardian would have liked. Leon was a sallow, bony kind of lad, who followed her movements with the pale eyes of an eel. The first time she had seen him he had been eating his supper; he had fixed those sucking eyes upon her and carried on chewing his meat, unconscious of the spittle collecting at his mouth. He had not

2

even had the manners to use a handkerchief to wipe his chin.

'I have not seen him, signorina.' Again, it seemed the woman bowed her head to avoid her eye. The servants disliked her in their turn, considering her too cold and religious. On arriving at Palazzo di Rivero, she had been appalled to find that her guardian allowed the servants to miss their religious devotions; it seemed that no one attended a daily Mass. She had chided him about the dangerous risk to their souls and reluctantly he had insisted that they all find time, after their usual chores, to walk across the city to her favourite church of the Virgin of the Assumption. That way she could keep track of their devotions, for Father Lorenzo would whisper all that happened to Allegra, over the counting of her rosary.

So where was Leon? At this hour he could be any-where – hanging around the coffee houses, drinking spirits or worse. She had a dreadful fear that he had more than a familial interest in her. For where his father was elegant, despite a certain coarseness of dress and speech, the son was simply loathsome. It was clearly some novelty to have a young woman of some breeding in the house at all.

At dinner he left a trail of crumbs and spills and dribbled soup down on his clothes. Once she had come across him in the garden without even a shirt on. She had seen his bare body, all white and hairless in the sunshine. She had dashed away, pulling her veil of lace down over her eyes. But he had laughed, she had seen it, he had turned towards her without shame so that she saw his private parts like a little bunch of pink grapes. No, she had said to herself, if my guardian were to try to inflict him on me, let my dowry go to a convent. At least then she would be preserved from his spidery fingers. She would be happy as a nun. There would at least be some honour in pursuing a life of virtue.

Now that Paolina had left, Allegra wondered at herself.

3

Was this taking of the key a sin? The cold curls of the key pressed hard against her breast. She would not steal the key, only use it this one time. No one would ever know but herself. Paolina would be busy in the bowels of the house, preparing food for the evening. She had already seen the manservant on the canal outside. So no one might ever know.

It was too late now, anyway, for she was eagerly walking up the broad staircase. Her guardian's room was hidden high, in the very eaves of the house. It was not his bedchamber; that was on the first floor, overlooking the walled garden. No, this was a room he kept for another purpose, he had made as much clear to her when she had first arrived. Little had interested her; the place was gloomy and dusty, sadly lacking the ordered touch of a gentlewoman.

'Behind this door is my own private apartment, my dear. You may have the run of the whole house, but this room I prefer to keep locked.' He had ushered her past it, and she had thought she smelt a scent of cedar and spice waft from beneath the heavy carved door.

'Is it where you keep your papers of state?' she asked solemnly.

'Let us say it is where I keep important papers,' he laughed. He laughed a great deal, her guardian, in an open-mouthed way she did not like. 'Important papers about life and its strangeness.'

Of course she had not cared about the room at first. It was only after she had examined the whole palazzo the next day, from the wet cellars where the canal water washed away the stone and rotted the wood to pulp and turned the metal to rust, to the highest eaves of the low, dusty attics where pigeons cooed and nestled below the roof, that she began to wonder. Whenever she passed the low wooden door, inscribed with classical carvings of half-naked nymphs and goat-hoofed satyrs, she hesitated a few moments, trying to guess what lay inside.

Now the moment had come. Allegra stood before that

4

familiar door, breathing hard. Cautiously, she strained her hearing to detect whether she was truly alone. Oh, if anyone knew, it would be too terrible – the shame and the mortification. No one must ever guess that she could be subject to the same whims and prying as less godly mortals. But no, there was not a sound but her own heartbeat. With a slightly trembling hand, she pulled the long brass key out of the stiff fabric of her bodice. For a long moment she stared at its glistening curves, feeling the warmth of her own body where it had been absorbed into the metal. With a sudden twist, she plunged it into the narrow hole and turned the handle. Then carefully pulling it out, she slipped it into the woollen pocket at her waist. With a quick glance behind her, she slid into the room.

The door opened to reveal a sumptuous apartment of crimson velvet and dark, carved furniture. The high windows overlooking the Grand Canale were covered with gently nodding blinds in a soft yellow colour which cast warm shadows into the chamber. At the centre of one wall lay a couch, piled with cushions in oriental patterns of blue and green silk. Above the couch hung a large painting; it represented a naked woman lying in a state of extreme abandon. I might have known, Allegra said to herself as she studied the details of the painting. The woman was very fair, very much the Venetian type, with coils of plaits and curls falling down her back. Luxurious jewellery studded her hair: lengths of pearl, and stars and coils of precious jewels. But at her neck, her wrists and ankles, the jewellery was more strange: a golden collar was set about her narrow neck, and similar bracelets clasped her wrists and ankles. The fine chains which ran from these, she had collected in her right hand. The effect was of some sumptuously chained animal which now offered its naked self to the spectator.

Allegra looked more closely at those parts of the female anatomy she knew only slightly from her own newly blossoming body. She had no sisters or close friends and now, indeed, no mother. With care she studied the milky white breasts, where the pink nipples shone erect like stiff little rosebuds. Below, the woman's stomach was studded with a single glittering diamond, and below that, her legs were spread to reveal a wide, hairless vulva with the crimson lips gently opened by the fingers of her left hand. Inside was revealed another diamond clasped inside the very centre of her sex. It was very strange, Allegra felt, and very discomfiting. She really wished her guardian did not like such things. She even wished there were no such object in the house where she was forced to live. No virtuous person would want to look at such a thing.

Reluctantly, she pulled herself away from contemplation of the painting and began to look around other parts of the room. On the desk was that symbol of the modern man, a newly-made globe of the world showing the New Americas as well as the Old World. Spinning it, Allegra found what she always considered to be the centre of the world – Venice, and its outlying empire. There was the lovely symbol of Venice, a woman with blonde curls, shield and nautical crown. But much of the empire had passed away – the islands of Crete, of Malvasia and Arcadia. It seemed to her, as ever, that the better, more noble times, had all passed.

For a moment she looked again at the naked figure in the painting. Was it perhaps a political allegory of Venice? For certainly, the theme appeared to be submission. But no, this creature's submission was willing; that was the point about the chains. So did her guardian believe that a woman would give herself willingly in such a way? Maybe a whore who was desperate for money. She had seen such low-bred women hanging around on the quaysides on the few occasions she had travelled about the city. They were brazen, spectacularly-dressed creatures who lured men to their doom. But not her. She was formed for better things. She had a spiritual nature.

But this was disappointing – where were these documents which needed to be kept so private? Carefully, she scoured the room. The only promise lay in the rows of dull-looking books which lined her guardian's shelves. Picking up the nearest volume, Allegra caught her breath, and then slowly, not removing her eyes from the image inside, carried the book to the desk where she might sit and study it further.

The first picture she gazed upon represented three figures. They were set in a fashionable boudoir hung with long gilt mirrors and pretty paintings. A naked woman was squatting on all fours like a dog, her breasts hanging pendulously downwards. Her clothes were hanging on a hook at her side; they were fashionable petticoats and hoops and not the poor clothes of a street whore. At first, Allegra could not understand the gymnastic muddle of the scene – one man stood behind her and one before, so at first she thought they might be harming her, or even engaged in a wrestling match. But no, the man behind had mounted her, was astride her spread buttocks like a male dog, pushing his long red penis inside her. The man at the front was being pleasured too; for as he stood before her, his swollen member was pushed inside her mouth. Allegra studied it awhile; it was unlike anything she had ever seen before. The woman appeared not to be a passive recipient of attack by the two men; undoubtedly, she was enjoying the whole business. How strange that must feel, she allowed herself to think for a second. But how impure!

That's what the artist would have us think, she snorted. It is some fantasy of a lunatic man. So, turning the page, she found another. This was of a quite different type. It was a line drawing only, quite roughly sketched. Here were a peasant couple, the woman dressed almost in rags. She was sitting upon a wall; there was very little detail. Her shift had slipped and a pair of very heavy breasts with large nipples spilled over her bodice. The

7

peasant man was upon her and a penis larger than any she had ever imagined was sitting up stiff before the woman's outspread, hairy cleft.

'My goodness,' Allegra mumbled. It was horribly crude, but also uncannily lifelike. She could even see the veins standing hard and knotted on the man's member, and the rounded top. She had never actually seen a proper grown man's penis in its fully hardened state. She had seen young boys, of course, on the farm estates, and had known full well for years of the differences between boys and girls. And from the farm animals, she also knew how a baby animal was made. She had even watched her father's stallion service one of his mares, with his massive heavy tube of crimson flesh.

She thought again of that day – she had been very young, but even then the sight had oddly thrilled her. There had been the massive thrusts of the stallion's hindquarters, and the slapping of his massive testicles against the mare's trembling rump. If she were to see it now, it would be quite overwhelming. The peasant in the picture – she could imagine the rapid thrust of his gigantic member as he entered that gaping fissure.

She felt very queer. Breathless and uncomfortable, as if her clothes were suddenly too small for her. Queer, but still angry. What kind of artist was it who imagined women agreeing to such loathsome acts? She herself was better, made of purer, rarer matter. There was more, of course. Quickly she rifled through the whole album of pictures. She could not help but linger over a few. There was the woman dressed only in the tightest stays and stockings who bent her bare behind for the attentions of a cleric in black who swiped a long, quivering switch. There was something about the plump cheeks of the woman's behind, and the hint of a crimson slit below, which made the drawing strangely powerful. But a priest – who could believe it?

A sudden cry from the canal awoke her from her reverie. With fearful rapidity Allegra shuffled the draw-

8

ings back into the folder. She must have been here for nearly an hour. Now there was another sound – maybe a footstep on the stair. Her heart pounded so hard she could barely hear herself think. Please, God, let no one find me here, she prayed. With a final glance at the lady in chains above the sofa, she crept to the door. Thankfully the corridor was clear. With a head spinning with guilt and confusion, she hurried back to her own room and cast herself down on to her bed.

It felt good to be back in the familiar quiet of her room; here was her narrow damask bed, her breviary and prayer book. Thankfully, she looked around and was glad to be alone.

Well, now she knew more of her supposedly respectable guardian. The dirty old goat. It troubled her to think of him, poring over those drawings alone in his room. What secret thoughts lay buried inside people's heads? Maybe if respectable people knew of his interests, they would say he was not fit to care for a young virgin such as herself.

It was hard, now, to stop herself thinking of the images she had seen. Oh, the impure thoughts that had been sown in her hitherto innocent head! What was she to do? She needed to confess to something, she decided. But then the idea of confessing such impurities to Father Lorenzo made her shiver. Yes, she must go to confession somewhere else, maybe find an odd little church where no one would know her. But first of all, she had to change from these clothes and wash. Her clothes were sticking to her skin.

Eagerly, she poured some water into her basin and began to tear at the laces across the front of her bodice. With a sense of relief, she felt the tight garment fall to the floor. Next there were her stays, hard leather panels which failed to flatter, but were at least modest, such as virtuous women wore. With a pant, she freed her flesh from the restricting confinement which flattened her

9

breasts and stomach. Next was the sequence of long overskirts and petticoats which fell rustling to the floor.

At last she stood before her glass in a thin shift and stockings. She was not esteemed beautiful, she knew that. But with her long brown hair and heart-shaped face the hue of palest porcelain, she knew that she was pretty enough to attract unwelcome attentions. And however much she tried to hide her newly blossomed curves beneath plain dresses of grey silk and unfashionable corsets, still she could not disguise a tall and pleasantly rounded figure. Now, beneath the thin shift, she could see the nipples of her swelling breasts poking through the gossamer fabric. It was hard, as she lifted the garment over her head, not to compare her own twenty-year old body with those she had seen in her guardian's library.

Her breasts were not quite as large, she saw, as those in the drawings. But the nipples were stiff; she knew they stiffened when cold, or when she rubbed them. Then they felt strange – uncomfortable but thrilling. Standing in front of the glass, she cupped each fleshy breast in turn and rubbed gently on each pink areola until they grew as hard as little red buttons. The strange feeling was growing inside her now, in the pit of her stomach. Gently she rubbed her stomach, wondering if it were some kind of illness she had brought on herself, like the blood curse which came each month because of the sin of Eve.

But as she rubbed, she found herself thinking once more of the peasant woman with her eager cleft. Was that the source of it all, then? Setting the looking glass into the middle of her room and padding over to lock the door securely, Allegra settled down on the edge of the bed. Yes, she liked to have her stomach rubbed, but then afterwards she felt even more unsettled. So, stretching her thighs out wide, she inspected the interesting prospect of her own womanly sex. The lips gleamed redly in the mirror, framed in a bush of curly brown

10

hair. Inquisitively, she prodded the inner lips, thinking suddenly of the peasant's large and broad stemmed member. The sensation was delicious. She imagined the huge, veined penis brushing against her vulva, prodding to gain entry. But surely this was wrong? What if she were to ruin herself for a future husband? Then she remembered. No husband need ever see her. She was going to be a nun.

Luxuriously, she probed the slippery lips, stopping each few moments to admire her breasts in the mirror and pinch them back to pert, erect fullness. Certain bits of her felt wonderful when rubbed, like gliding through a bath of warm syrup. But when she closed her eyes and remembered the strange drawings, when she brought them to life in her imagination, she felt she might burst with desire.

Feeling stranger than she had ever done before, she watched her fingers rub against the glistening lips of her sex, lifting her legs wide to gain a better view of the tiny hole she now saw growing slack and wide. This, she knew, was the heart of all pleasure with a man. If only she could try it! How big was a man? At first she attempted only a long, slender, index finger. It slid in easily enough, soon disappearing up to the very end. It felt good as her muscles gripped the digit. She closed her eyes and let her head roll back, rubbing her breasts with her free hand. If only it were bigger, like that massively endowed peasant with his great shaft of heavy flesh.

Cautiously, she tried slipping in the next finger. That stretched her aching entrance and was delightful. She remembered the stallion and began to thrust her fingers back and forth. This is bliss, she thought, imagining a swarthy, ragged peasant forcing his fleshy stem inside her innocent little hole. If he was to force her to do it – if she couldn't fight him off . . . Just the thought made her push faster. Opening her eyes, she watched herself, as if she were watching some strange girl in one of her

11

guardian's drawings now sprung to life. The girl in the mirror's breasts jiggled back and forth as her hungry opening rubbed itself wildly on the upheld fingers. Suddenly Allegra's breath became loud, and she moaned out loud, rapt in pleasure.

To her absolute horror, a wheezing gasp answered from behind the tapestry at her bed head. In horror, Allegra stared at the hanging, appalled at anyone watching this most private of moments. But it was too late to stop. Her body had a power of its own. She could no more stop her fingers frigging herself to her first climax than stop the progress of her heart itself.

In the space of a few more thrusts she had reached the crest of this wave of passion. Alarmed, she watched herself bury three fingers deep in her slippery entrance. An image came into her mind of a thick red penis buried hard in her, thrusting and pushing her into a wild oblivion. Uncontrollably, she pinched at her own elongated nipples, spreading her fingers out wide to fill herself to the point of frenzy. In a sudden spasm of excitement, her internal muscles gripped her fingers like a vice. There was no control left, only the explosive fire around her slippery fingers. With a long moan of release, she felt her entire body tingle with excitement and relief. Exhausted, she collapsed back on to the bed, pulling the cover over her nakedness.

It was some time later that she stirred, her limbs heavy with the luxury of spent desire. Slowly she washed the swollen lips of her sex and her thighs, which were streaked with salty juices. Putting on a loose robe, she remembered with a catch of her breath the peculiar gasping sound which had emerged from behind the tapestry. Perhaps it had been a trick of sound, or a hallucination brought on by the odd contagion which had struck her. Certainly, she had not been her usual modest self today.

Timidly, she approached the faded tapestry which

covered the wall at the opposite side of the room. She had never had any occasion to inspect it before; now she found it hung a full hand's breadth from the wall. It showed an old hunting scene, the moment when the hounds first spy the fox. Allegra gently ran her fingers over the greying wool, finding nothing of any interest. Then she carefully lifted the hanging up, revealing the bare wall behind. It was there. A hole the size of a ducat coin was set in the plaster at about the height of her own eye. A matching hole had been carefully cut into the fabric, disguised in the tapestry by the pattern of a panting hound's hungry eye. Allegra's heart froze. Someone had watched her – had watched her perform that undignified act! She blushed crimson all the way down to her panting breast. How could she ever claim to be virtuous again?

I must confess, she repeated to herself, I must make amends for my sin. But to whom could she confess? She could not ever speak of this to Father Lorenzo. And even a strange priest, even some itinerant cleric in a lesser church – how could she bring herself to whisper what had happened, through the grille? And if she did, if she described the events of the day in its depraved detail, how could any man remain unmoved? For she had decided that it was some strange, physical contagion. Her guardian's sick imagination had bred it, and unwittingly it had passed to her.

Flinging herself on to her bare knees she prayed for forgiveness until dusk. As the shadows grew, she imagined the penances which might allow her to remain silent. But even as she strove to return to a state of purity, impure thoughts returned to haunt her tingling sex. When she imagined subjecting herself to useful charity, she saw once more that ragged, eager peasant. And when she promised herself the cleansing pain of the whip, then it was the curious cleric she recollected, beating a naked woman for reasons she only now began to guess.

13

Chapter Two

*A*llegra emerged from an uneasy sleep in a state of frantic suspicion. Her comfortable apartment was still the same: the long green drapes across the gothic windows, the glitter of jewels and gold at her prayer book and breviary. But all was changed. To someone used only to the daily round of prayer, musical practice and sewing all was turned upside down. Who might the secret voyeur be?

She had believed her guardian to be at the Senate that morning, yet might he not have returned? Certainly the contents of his apartment suggested that he had such indelicate tastes. She had already found him unsettling, with an overly courteous manner combined with coarse, immodest banter. But even Allegra knew there to be a large chasm between the private enjoyment of salacious pictures and the breaking of all taboos of civilisation by spying on a young woman under his personal protection.

Was it Leon? He had often bothered her with importunate staring from those round, fish-like eyes. But somehow, she did not feel he had the courage to make such sophisticated arrangements to spy upon her. That left only the manservant, whom she had earlier seen out on the canal, or Paolina herself. Indeed, so strange was the sudden gasping sound from behind the tapestry that she could not discount any man or woman. Finally, Allegra was left with the most comforting solution of all – it may indeed have been an hallucination, a phantasm of guilt, inflicted upon her by her own disturbed imagination.

But this latter notion was confounded when she further explored the architecture of the house. Behind her bedroom wall was a storeroom. It was a small space containing only a few old brooms and summer awnings. There, below the coin-sized hole bored into the wall, was a disturbance in the dust where shoes had clearly twisted from side to side as the owner sought an even better view of her room. Standing on her toes and setting her own eye to the hole, Allegra squirmed with embarrassment. She could clearly see the length of her bed, her wash stand and the tall looking glass. On the floor by the looking hole was a bundle of old rags; she could not bring herself even to poke at them.

The day passed as slowly as a snail sliding across the great piazza of San Marco. As the bells of the City rang, tolling the doleful hours, she wondered how it could be that time was now suspended. Each time she encountered another inhabitant of the house she found herself blushing deeply, unable to look straight into their eyes. The mere thought that someone had seen her made her curl up inside.

But her greatest trial occurred when, after a silent supper of quite paralysing embarrassment, her guardian called her over. With her veil pulled low across her eyes, she approached him. He was sprawled as ever in his great chair at the fireplace, his long patrician wig discarded to reveal short curls clinging damply to his skull.

'Allegra. I am sorry to disturb the quiet habits of your evening. However, I must have an audience with you. Would you kindly proceed to my private apartment at the quarter hour?'

15

Allegra glanced into his face with apprehension. It was perfectly blank; quite as placidly amiable as if he had merely asked her to play him a piece on the harpsichord. 'Your private apartment?' she asked, in a tone very close to a whisper, so little breath seemed within her to answer him.

'Yes. For since the key has disappeared, it is no longer quite so private.'

It was impossible to hide the tumble of emotions which broke within her at the mention of the key. Where was it, then? In horror, she remembered that it must still be lying in the woollen pocket of her dress. Her hand had flown involuntarily to her face. She had gasped quite audibly. Surely he must know.

'I would rather not, sir,' was all she could manage.

He was looking at her keenly now, his intelligent face resting elegantly on his ornately beringed hand. His wrinkled eyes were quizzical. 'Allegra, there is not much I ask of you,' he said with a new firmness. 'But one thing is obedience to the simple requests of your legal guardian. I repeat, I expect you on the quarter hour.'

Flying downstairs to the privacy of her room, she was aware of the entertainment she had caused. She had experienced a fleeting glimpse of Leon, laughing into his stupid, clumsy hands as she passed. And Paolina, who had just then cleared a plate of food, stopped dead on the stairs to watch.

Back in her room, Allegra searched. And there it was, the wicked source of it all, the sinuous brass key. Hastily she hid it in her sleeve and once more climbed the stairs to the heavy carved door. This time she knocked: a timid little knock, as if she wished not to be there.

Opening the door, her guardian ushered her in, directing her to stand in the centre of the room. Still, she could not resist a glance upwards at the painting of the lady in chains and, feigning never to have seen it before, she shook her head scornfully and turned to Senator di Rivero with a cold little glance of reproach. He mean-

16

while sat at the desk, only recently relieved of his long blue procurator's gown, relaxing in his ordinary waist-coat and breeches.

'To get to the point quickly,' he began, drawing on a long clay pipe which he kept at his desk, 'I have a little mystery to solve. My private room,' and here he waved about the walls of the chamber, 'is generally locked, as you well know. And yet, I do believe that yesterday someone took the key in order to get a closer look at my personal possessions. Do you know of this?'

Allegra froze with fear. She managed only a very quiet and meek answer . 'No.'

'I am sorry you say this, Allegra, for I believe you confound your theft with lying. You see, I know that you were here. You were seen.'

'By whom?' she demanded, anger suddenly rising in her throat. 'I would ask, sir, if it were someone you would trust above me? For as you know, I am a good, pious girl. And this is indeed a serious charge you put. One that perhaps you might discuss also with my spiritual guardian, Father Lorenzo.'

Signor di Rivero rose, knocking the ash from his pipe into the fireplace. The coals glowed red as hellfire for a long moment. Allegra waited for the effect of her speech; it seemed once more to wrap her in the warmth of sanctity. But her guardian approached her, shaking his head sadly. 'Allegra, this will not do. I tell you, you were seen. How would you feel if I told Father Lorenzo that you had lied to me, had stolen my private key?'

'But you,' she began, burning with emotion at his trapping her, 'you are nothing but an old sinner! I need only tell him of what it is you look at here. You disgust me, you and your filthy pictures! You are no more fit to care for me than the old men in loose drawers who hang around the brothels in the Calle de Paradiso.'

He took her hand gently, though she struggled to free it. Shaking it out of his grasp, she stared defiantly at

17

him. No, she would not be weak, she would not expose herself to him.

'My dear, no one condemns you but yourself. It was idle curiosity, I am sure. But now it is out, you must admit that you were wrong to steal and then lie.'

'I will not,' Allegra maintained, rubbing her fingers in pretence that he had hurt her. 'I hate you all and I wish to leave this place.'

She felt abnormally hot, trapped as she was by her guardian's eloquence. She did hate him – oh, how she longed for the quiet sanctity of the cloister. If only they would leave her in peace.

'Very well. Your desire to leave brings me quickly to a second matter. Often you claim you wish to leave – mostly, I hear, to take the veil. That is an irreversible step, Allegra. Think of what you would miss. A pleasant home, the warmth of a husband in your bed and, in time, the blessing of children. Why should a convent of dry old nuns get your dowry when many a young man would honour a healthy and clever girl such as yourself?' He shook his head at her obstinate expression.

'What I am saying is that often these fits for religion in the young are five-minute wonders. In a few years you will go to Mass at the regulated times but will have other interests too, and other means to express these violent emotions. Indeed, as one who aspires to be an enlightened philosopher, I do believe that those who suffer the most powerful transports of mysticism are often those whose true natures are most thwarted. What do you say? You are a clever girl.'

Throughout this speech Allegra had grown more and more distressed. So her guardian was also a heretic, a rationalist, a twister of truth into dark, wicked ways. 'I cannot answer such a speech. I believe in my faith above all other.'

'But Allegra, listen to me,' he begged. 'There is Leon, for example. He has formed an attachment to you, but the lad is too shy to come forward.'

So that was it. Yes, it would suit them, wouldn't it, to get hold of her dowry? 'I feel nothing but revulsion for your son,' she stormed. 'I could never marry him.' She carried on, unable to stop. 'I cannot live here. I cannot live under this heretic roof.'

Her guardian retreated angrily, picking up papers and dropping them again on the desk. When he spoke there was a new harsh tone to his voice. 'You are certain of this? I say to you again, do not make a rash decision. There will be plenty of leisure to regret your choice from behind the convent grille.'

'I am entirely fixed, sir. I have had it with you and your lecherous son. If he thinks I will submit to his fawning, he is mistaken. It was he, was it not, who claims to have spied on me?' But still she could not bring herself to mention the eye-hole – then she might have needed to explain what the boy had seen later. And no one must ever know that.

'I admit it was. And I know he tells the truth.'

Allegra turned on her guardian proudly. 'So you would put the word of a spy and a lecher above my own? Yes, for I can guess now who it is he has inherited his interest in young girls from. Your reading matter disgusts me, sir. I wish to leave now.'

'Well, leave, then!' he bawled, unable any longer to contain his pent-up spleen. 'Never did I guess I had taken such a poisonous viper into my bosom.' He marched straight up to her in the centre of the room, peering so closely into her face she could see his eyes twitching with white rage. She flinched, knowing that she had gone too far. 'I will arrange you a convent, madam, one which may yet teach that proud spirit a harsh lesson or two. For there are places in this city where submission can be learnt and wicked pride flogged from out of young girl's hearts. So tomorrow I shall see you packed off, to have your fine clothes removed and your jewels confiscated. And talking of lessons, you must not think I will allow your girlish sins to be passed over. You have incited me, signorina, and now you must bear the cost. Get over to the table.'

I have overstepped all boundaries, Allegra thought. What was it he would want from her? Her signature perhaps, to sign away her dowry. But no, he had the glowering complexion of someone able and ready to administer a punishment. She considered running for the door.

'Get over there, this instant.' His face was bloodless as she had never seen it, though his eyes burnt dark as little beads of black coal. Slowly Allegra did as she was bidden; his will drew her slowly over to the long, flat table.

'Now, madam, I will do as you wish tomorrow and we may never meet again. But for one last night you are my legal charge, sheltering under this hospitable roof. And I have found you guilty of two crimes against my person. I intend to punish you as I would punish any charge, boy or girl, within my care.'

Allegra stood before him, trembling with apprehension. She dare not even ask what punishment he intended. She only fumbled in supplication at his waistcoat and murmured, 'Please, please, signor . . .'

'No. For is it not written, "spare the rod and spoil the child"? And you are spoilt, my little madam, that I have observed from the day you first arrived. Well, you have chosen your proverbial bed. You may lie on that hard, cold slab all your days. For now, fetch me that rod from the corner.'

'I will not.' She could not help herself. Submission was not in her nature.

'Shall I fetch the servant then? Or Leon? Come now, do you not at least wish this to be a private matter?'

Unaccountably, she fell on her knees, grasping his sleeves. The humiliation – it would be too much to bear. But with a sudden lurch, he pulled her to her feet. She felt like a lifeless creature, bent to his will.

'Fetch the rod, or I will call the servant.'

20

It was no use. Heavily, she turned to look for the rod he asked for. With knees almost buckling, she searched and found a long, flexible switch propped up by the corner of the bookcase. It looked cruel and pliant, as if it had a strange animation of its own. She could hardly bring herself to touch it, she felt so ashamed.

'You cannot, sir,' she moaned weakly. But her guardian was past reason. In a few moments he had his waistcoat hung upon the chair and the sleeves of his linen shirt rolled up to his elbows. He motioned her to stand before him.

'Now, are you truly sorry?'

I cannot submit to this, she thought. I cannot admit I did these things. So she answered, 'No.'

'You make it worse for yourself, stupid girl. I only hope this is a lesson which will stay with you all your life. Your pride must be curbed in some way. Now bend across the table. You may grasp the other end.' He motioned her to stretch the whole of her upper body out across the smooth wood. It was too much of an indignity. Never, in all her life, had she been so mistreated.

'No, I cannot, sir,' she mumbled. 'It is not becoming.'

'Maybe it will be more becoming in front of Leon? I shall call him.' And, flexing the long switch in his palms, he sauntered towards the door.

'Stop,' she called desperately. But it was no use. His hand moved to the door handle. 'Very well,' she whispered at last, feeling almost faint. Reluctantly, she lowered herself across the polished wood, and her guardian fixed her hands to grip the far end of the table. She felt both stupid and ridiculous.

'Now,' she heard his voice continue from above, 'I am afraid because you are not contrite, the punishment must be taken on the skin.'

To her utter horror, he began to lift her skirts up around her waist. 'Stop, stop!' she cried, rising and attempting to pull them down again.

With a violent tug he had them up around her waist,

21

and grasped her wrist tightly in his free hand. He had her pinioned like a vice. 'You may struggle, but it will only be worse. There will be more pain if you move, and if you try to escape me I will ask Leon to hold you still.'

'This is a diabolical,' she cried, staring at the smooth wood. 'I shall tell the nuns of your impertinence.'

'Oh, I am sure they would want to hear,' he laughed dryly. 'Especially the details.'

He appeared to take a small step back. Allegra caught her breath. She could not believe the events of the evening. The affront to her dignity was incredible.

'Now I am going to administer fourteen strokes – seven for each of your sins. Again I ask if you are sorry?'

'No,' she sobbed, but they were tears of rage now. He had lifted her skirts above her waist, revealing her naked backside. She was shaking at his damned impertinence, staring as he did at her. With a sudden movement he patted her rear. The feeling was like a flame, scorching her cool skin. She wriggled defiantly.

The first blow made her cry out; it came fast with a whistling swish on to her naked cheeks. The pain was fierce, like a rod of hot steel which stayed burning long after the switch was removed.

'Please,' she begged, but it was too late. The next blow fell. Again, he grasped her rounded rear to pull it back to centre. Horribly, as his fingers touched her flesh, another emotion smote her along with the pain.

She never knew if she would have found the enterprise so exciting, had she not seen that strange drawing of the corseted lady and the cleric. For suddenly, as the image of a bound, submissive woman and a shadowy, domineering cleric returned to her mind, she felt very odd indeed. Where her own fingers had explored before, she again felt a burning heat, each blow from the switch seeming to push her to a higher level of fierce pleasure.

Utterly confounded, Allegra tried to hide the effects of her guardian's well-intentioned punishment. But when he asked her after seven strokes, if she was now sorry for lying to him, she had to struggle to speak.

'No,' she whispered, the shadow of a pleasurable groan making her voice sound thick and sultry. Quite consciously, she twisted away from the first of the next seven blows, and so again he had to grasp her buttocks, almost pushing her on to the table with an alarmingly pleasurable effect upon the sensitive front of her sex. As the rod whistled through the air and the stroke fell, she let herself be thrust forward on the table edge.

With what little senses remained to her, she was aware of an increasing slide towards that oblivion she had brought on herself with her own fancies and three stiff and busy fingers. As the next stroke fell, she again let herself be thrust back and forth, now aware of her nipples stiffly growing hard against the fabric of her stays and being massaged back and forth against the leather. She knew without looking that her sex was swollen and juicy with desire. She had to fight not to cry out with some indelicate phrase of encouragement.

At last the final blow fell. Allegra lay some time, feeling the burning weals across her soft flesh. She wished that her guardian would go away, so she could be alone to explore again the strangeness of her own, obstinate anatomy. But he was not moved as she was. He spoke to her now with some remorse, his anger spent on the beating.

'I am sorry, Allegra; I have hurt your skin as well as your pride. It was not my intention to mark you, though when you enter a convent, such marks are seen as trophies of the soul. Here, let me administer some ointment to your weals.'

With the delicate fingertips of a woman he traced the outline of her punishment, kneading the cool salve into her skin. It stung and yet was thrilling. She wanted him to rub harder, to knead and massage her buttocks, her slit, even her hot and aching entrance. No, this would not do.

Rising, she pushed him away and let her skirts drop over her burning shame. 'Thank you sir, for your admonishment.' It was strange but she did feel both grateful and somewhat more sorry now, for what she had done. 'I will retire now for the night. Goodnight.' And so, with some fears yet that he might see more than mortification in her reddened cheeks and shortness of breath, she escaped him, walking somewhat stiffly to her room.

Alone at last, she lifted her skirts and threw her aching body down on the bed, letting her burning rear end cool in the evening air. And thank the good saints she knew that she was alone, for she had carefully stitched a patch to the hole in the tapestry and put a bung of plaster in the eye-hole. Again, she wondered what contagion this was, that so easily inflamed her senses at the slightest touch. She felt hot and sore and very restless.

Tentatively, she let her cool fingertips explore the raised marks across her skin. That felt good, she thought, gently stroking the slippery ointment round in lazy circles. But it was still sore. Tentatively, she pulled a cushion down, beneath her stomach. Now her throbbing buttocks were raised in the cool air, luxuriously spread with her lips pulled pleasantly apart.

It was like a sickness; uncontrollably she remembered the delicious edge of the table and its stimulating properties. Gently, she began to rock back and forth, squeezing the massive cushion between her thighs. There is something I need, she inwardly groaned, but I hardly know what. As she rocked, she thought again of her guardian's pictures, and again of that great stallion whose penis was as large as the great wax candles used on long winter nights. He had thrust into the mare, giving his full, knotty length, working in and out of her like a great pointed bellows.

Eagerly, she pushed the cushion further up, so it bunched and pushed at her suffering, slippery lips. The relief was coming, she knew, as the fabric compressed damply to form a stiff wedge against her throbbing sex. Her mind became a riot once more, of tumbling images of the great erect penis of the peasant with its hairy base and swollen balls, of the woman being taken and pleasured at both ends.

As she arched her back in pleasure, a silky caress slid up the inner skin of her thigh. That was good too, she thought, only push higher – yes, part my thighs to their limits. She wanted to be completely open, surrendered, exposed. In a second, reality shook her back to the airless room. There was someone else there, behind her, touching her legs. With a stifled scream, she struggled to raise herself. But her position, straddling the cushion, made it difficult, especially as now two hands were gripping her thighs like a vice.

'Who is it? Let go! Get off me!'

But even as she squirmed the grip grew tighter.

'I will scream,' she announced. But still her assailant remained silent. Now he began to pull her downwards, off the cushion towards the edge of the bed. With a blaze of revulsion she kicked out against the soft body she was being pulled against. She felt the warm flesh of a human torso, and there, something prodding her thigh, something pliant and hot.

'You must not go, Allegra,' Leon's thin voice whined. 'You must stay here and marry me. After this, you must stay.'

Leon! Allegra kicked out again, aiming the heel of her shoe at his groin. He swerved and redoubled his attempt to mount her from behind. He had a strong grip around her legs and now one shaking hand moved intemperately to find the source of entry for his bucking penis. She could feel it now, rubbing horribly against her thigh, searching for its goal.

'You will be hung for this. Get off me now, or I will scream and tell your father.'

'No!' he cried, and reaching forward slid a hand

around her mouth. Allegra was burning with fury now. He would not have her.

'I know what you need, Allegra,' he spluttered in a passionate whisper. 'I have seen your need for a man. Now I bring you my manhood. Feel that?'

He was edging his stiff member upwards towards her juicy, receptive sex. And he too was close to climax; she could feel a twitching in his penis and a damp leakage on to her skin. No, it could not be like this! Somehow she had to lull him into a false state. In a few seconds he might take her. Anything but that, to be deflowered by Leon.

She began by protruding her tongue against the cupped palm which covered her mouth. As she tickled the skin with little wet strokes, he loosened his hold. Feigning a groan of pleasure, she said, 'If we must play, let us do it properly. Let me turn around so you can see me as you deserve.'

'You will not try to escape?' he asked incredulously.

'No,' she assured him with a sigh. Rolling on her back, she lifted her thighs to let him see the full glory of her thighs and glistening vulva. He was kneeling at the bed edge, fully dressed save for his small, reddened penis standing up like a little horn of flesh amongst his linen. He looked dazed with desire, his eyes muddled with incomprehension at her new, compliant attitude.

'Oh, it's not so big, Leon,' she complained, casting a reproachful look at his manhood. 'Here am I about to give you the supreme moment of my life and that's the best you can do. Can you not make it larger?'

He glanced down apologetically at the slender wand of flesh. 'If you will permit me,' he said, and slid his hand about the base. In a few moments he was rubbing it vigorously.

That is something at which he is skilled, Allegra thought. 'Do you not desire me?' she asked, rubbing her hips against the sheets. The salty smell of desire was heavy in the air; he could see the lovely flower of her

26

sex, plump and ready for a man. Seductively, she rocked her hips, watching his face drain of colour. His hand continued to work on the knobbly flesh, working the foreskin back and forth. He was breathing hard now; it could not be much longer.

'Allegra, I think soon – ' He could barely talk, but he could not take his hand from his cock. He looked longingly down at her spread thighs and the way her most private lips pouted wetly. Tentatively, he reached down with his free hand.

She slapped him back. 'No, it's not big enough yet. When it is larger. Tell me, did you watch me, Leon?' she asked. 'Did you wish it was you?'

He nodded emphatically. He did look stupid, rubbing away on his own penis. He was jiggling it about now, massaging the glistening round end.

Slowly, she dipped her index finger in her mouth and covered it with saliva. He was panting, just watching her. First, she rubbed it against one of her free nipples. Soon it was wet and very hard, a rigid bead of crimson flesh. He was feverish now, cupping his little balls in his other hand. As a *tour de force*, she let her finger slide down her bodice and over her bare stomach. His eyes were bulging with excitement.

With a lingering movement, she traced the outline of her sex before travelling into the inner sanctum of delights. Poising her stiff index finger above the loosened entrance, she raised her hips so he could get a closer view. 'Do you wish that was you?' she asked almost innocently.

His reply was explosive. With a cry of frustration, his hand reached a prodigious speed. Groaning, he spent himself liberally, shooting a small fountain of milky semen over his own linen. She found it hard not to laugh as he staggered at the violence of his climax.

'Leon,' she reprimanded him sternly, pulling down her skirts. 'Could you not wait? Now you have spoiled it. Now I must go tomorrow and be a nun. And I will still be a virgin, you stupid boy.'

Chapter Three

*P*ulling back the heavy curtain of the gondola, Allegra felt a shaft of sunlight pierce the gloomy interior. Outside, the whole of Venice seemed to dance in the warm July morning: the light glinting across the rippling waters of the lagoon, the crowds of visitors thronging on the quayside in costumes of crimson, blue and green, and above all the fluttering sails of the great galleys as they bobbed and curtsied at their moorings by the Palace.

The surly gondolier from the convent of Santa Agnetha had carefully guided his craft through the network of narrow canals around the Palazzo di Rivero; at that point Allegra had felt profoundly relieved to be on her way. At least then she would no longer have to feel the weight of her guardian's sardonic gaze as he bid her a grave farewell, nor cast her eyes away from Leon's sheepish smirk. With a sense of delight at being alone she had settled down in the darkness and sighed out loud to be away from them at last.

Then the shaft of sunlight had peeked in through the brocade and she had lifted the curtain. With a stab of regret she watched the city drift past her: the pink elegance of the Doge's palace, the distant domes of the

Basilica, all shining in the sun like jewels beneath a lamp. Her life till now had been sequestered, spent within walls, rarely experiencing the splendours of the glorious Serenissima; indeed, until now she had often publicly scoffed at its wild reputation. Suddenly she realised that she knew far too little of her home and had indeed taken its beauty and glamour entirely for granted. Surely it was, as many said, the greatest city in the world, a wondrous meeting of east and west, of dreams and commerce, of land and ocean?

The black gondola slid out towards the Lido, soon leaving the amber-sailed fishing craft behind and plowing mostly against the streams of high-towered galleys of the great Venetian navy. Leaning from the window, she gazed back towards the shore, noticing at first a delicious sweet scent rising on the breeze. Searching, she saw for the first time a wide vista of pure whiteness stretching across a broad inlet of the lagoon.

For a second, she wondered if it were snow – but there could be no snow in July. Then she recollected from what that whiteness was formed; it was a lily-white carpet of flowers, all collected and spread across a bridge of small boats to celebrate the great feast of the Redentore. That very night at dusk the Doge and his Senate would cross the waves on a bed of flowers, to celebrate mass in gratitude for the passing of the terrible plague which had threatened the city. The happy crowds would linger for the lighting of hundreds of coloured lamps strung across the waters and then to marvel at the skies lit by an exploding rainbow of fireworks.

Here at least, corruption had been vanquished and the purity of the lilies reigned. In her heart Allegra longed to stay, just once to be witness to one of the great city's festivals. There were so many wonders she had not seen, so many marvels undiscovered. A small voice within her asked why it was she should leave the world so young and deny herself a full and varied life. But then she turned from the spectacle with new resolve and faced

29

the choppy grey waters of the lagoon. There was her sacred duty to perform. She must not be weak as others were, but carve herself anew from harder and stronger material.

Soon the Isle of Santa Agnetha loomed ahead of the craft: a craggy upthrust of rock, upon which stood one vast and solitary building. Surrounded by a curling wall of stone, the convent was a building of some three storeys falling away from a central bell tower. It had perhaps once been a building of some grandeur. Now, however, it displayed alarming signs of a lack of general repair. The triple arches across its facade were crumbling and the shutters swung unevenly from their hinges. Moreover, the whole exterior of the convent had a dark, sea-battered hue which contrasted sharply with the glittering palaces of holiness back on the mainland.

In Venice, convents and monasteries were places of ease and retirement: centres of art where the greatest composers and artists fought for commissions. Allegra had fancied herself to be a companion of rich and comfortable widows or talented younger daughters. In her mind's eye she had fancied herself draped in a habit of virginal white, striking a contemplative pose before some elaborate jewelled icon. Now a shiver of fear troubled her heart as she let the gondolier help her up to the quayside. With a grunt, he jumped back in the boat and disappeared out of sight. Alone, she gazed up at the unwelcoming vista of her new home.

There was nothing to do but venture onward, and so Allegra found her way up a steep drive to the heavy studded doors of the building. As her fingers left the bell, she lifted her veil and turned around and gazed back across the water. Still twinkling in the July heat, the city hung like an apparition in the air: far, far, across the haze of water. Where then is Heaven? she wondered. Must I turn my back on all that is lovely and bury myself here in this miserable old ruin?

It was too late. With a groan which could only indicate

a lack of frequent use, the door swung open. An unwholesome looking servant squinted out at her; then, with a lack of grace, ushered her inside.

Within the convent walls it would have been hard for an inmate to know of the fine summer day outside. There were no windows in the passage Allegra travelled down, only yellow tallow candles flickering in their iron sconces. They met no one and she saw little; a few wooden statues and an occasional image of a saint lined the way, but she saw none of the great artistic works of the soul she had imagined herself throwing herself beneath. At last they stopped. With something akin to a shove, the vile little servant opened a small leather door and pushed her inside. Allegra was inside the Prioress's office.

'Ah, Signora di Vitale.'

The room was gloomily lit with long, thick candles set about the corners. Allegra peered into the shadows and identified her new spiritual mother. The crone was sitting spinning wool by a smoking fire and looked very old; her face was knitted into a mesh of wrinkles. But instead of suggesting the gentility of old age, the woman peered out of that face with hooded eyes which spoke of the cool appraisal of a huntress. In her heavy black habit and veil, she looked malevolent rather than holy as she cast her eye coldly over Allegra and bade her come closer. Fearfully, Allegra curtseyed and felt herself crumple beneath the woman's scathing appraisal.

'So, you wish to be a nun.' The Prioress's voice rasped like wind through trees in the Autumn. Allegra nodded, staring at her own shoes.

'And are you then a virtuous girl?'

'I am,' Allegra answered warmly. 'That is why I am here, to protect myself from sin.'

'But these walls cannot protect you, signorina.'

Allegra looked up and quickly wished she had not. The old lady's face had not the usual benign weakness of a nun. It was cold, sharp and merciless.

'What I mean is,' Allegra stammered, looking at the fire, 'your convent will keep me from the earthly temptations of the world.'

'Will it?' the Prioress asked. 'Perhaps temptation is a state of mind.' Her words hung in the silence and Allegra watched the embers shift in the grate.

'Look at me.' Reluctantly she turned once more to the Prioress's terrible, ancient face, wherein the eyes burnt brighter than two raging coals. 'I will test you. I will see into your heart, your desires, your masquerades. Your moral dilemmas have travelled with you. These walls cannot protect you from yourself.'

'Myself?' Allegra felt her hackles rise. What were these riddles, these accusations? The impertinence of all of this struck her. 'I have no need of protection from myself, I assure you. My violators are back there, in that city of deathly pleasures. I thank God for the watery chasm between us.'

The old woman laughed, which Allegra hated all the more. It was a rasping, vicious sound. The young girl suddenly noticed the slackness of the Prioress's mouth: as if it had once been wide and sensuous but had since drooped wetly.

'Very well,' she croaked at last. 'Let us imagine you safe enough here. Let us imagine it all to be a trick of geography. So now we must assist you in leaving that terrible past behind.' She showed Allegra a paper from her desk and equipped her with ink and quill. 'This paper,' the Prioress said, 'bestows on myself as head of this house, all of your worldly goods in the form of dowry from your guardian, inheritances and gifts. Is that what you wish?'

This was not a possibility which had struck Allegra before; she had expected perhaps to sign a vague contract of will, but not to sign her inheritance away. However, such was her obstinacy to show the old woman her determination, that she immediately agreed.

Lifting her head from the document, Allegra thought

she saw a momentary flash of greed illuminate the Prioress's eye. She scarcely knew how much money she had just bestowed upon this strange old woman. Perhaps it was hundreds, even thousands of gold ducats. Money had never concerned her before. For indeed, she had never before felt the lack of it.

After ringing the servant's bell, the Prioress sat back in her chair, continuing to watch her new charge. Perhaps Allegra was mistaken, but a glimmer of malice seemed now to lurk behind her heavy lids.

'Very soon you will leave your old self behind,' she said. 'And there are new and arduous tasks for your new self to master. Our order is strict and does not allow weakness. Only the strong pass our tests. What say you to that?'

'That I will succeed,' announced Allegra.

'Will you?' At this the old woman suddenly reached out and grasped her hand. It was all Allegra could do not to pull back in fear. The woman's hand gripped her tightly; she could feel the bone of the fingers under the brown spotted flesh. With a sudden repugnant gesture she tickled the young girl's palm with her nails. Allegra shuddered at the strange sensation, pulling hard to free herself from the odd caress.

'You are sensitive, that's good,' she laughed, showing the spittle sticking to her mouldering teeth. But Allegra could not tell if this really were a joke or not. Her palm still tingled in the spot where the old woman had made the strange, impertinent caress. At this moment the servant returned.

'Ah, at last. Take Sister Almoro to meet Silva. She is waiting for her.'

Allegra looked at her, surprised.

'A new name, for your new self.' She laughed unpleasantly again. 'For now you are neither man nor woman. Instead, you are ours. We shall call you Almoro. Allegra is no more.'

Glad to be free of the Prioress, Allegra hurried to

follow the servant down yet more labyrinthine corridors. At last they reached a high and spacious room, covered from floor to ceiling with painted tiles depicting scenes of the Orient. Here, Allegra was left with another woman whom she assumed to be the waiting Silva: a swarthy creature in a coarse shift whose sturdy arms and neck flexed with unfeminine muscles.

With a nod of her heavy head, the woman indicated a large, dusty chest which was standing in the centre of the floor. On the lid was pinned her name, her real name: Allegra di Vitale.

'What do I do?' she asked. The woman merely grunted and stared. She was to take off her clothes and deposit them in the chest.

Nervously, Allegra looked about her. It was a large room and somewhat chilly. At the one end was a high gallery but all was deserted and silent. The July sunshine now seemed very far away. Still, this was what she had come for: to strip her past life away. Somewhat reluctantly, she began to unfasten her veil, which hung from a comb down the back of her head. Unused to dressing her own hair, her fingers fumbled with the elaborate pins her maid had inserted that morning.

With a grunt of impatience, Silva shook her head, tapped her foot – indeed, made every sign bar speaking that she would not wait around like this. At last the veil slipped down; relieved, Allegra passed it to her. With a look of disdain, Silva motioned to the chest. Carefully, Allegra folded its yards of finest black gossamer lace and put it away. Next she began to unlace the front panel of her stomacher.

Again, Silva shook her head and shifted from foot to foot. Finally, as Allegra wrestled with the tiny hooks and eyes which held the ribbons criss-crossed against her breast, Silva swept over to her and snatched the ribbon. As quick as lightening, she had the bodice open and was pulling it roughly over Allegra's shoulders.

'Stop that!' she cried. 'You are hurting me, you fool.'

34

But it made not the slightest difference to the surly woman; she had thrown Allegra's fine taffeta bodice on the floor. Allegra stood, shaking with rage as she allowed the woman to unlace her stays. Without the patience to carefully loosen each silken eye-hole, Silva tugged and pulled on the pink cords, eventually producing a small knife and cutting the cords with a breathless grunt. With a savage gesture she threw the lovely French stays of silk and delicate whalebone to the floor.

'I will not stand this!' Allegra whirled round and faced the brutal woman.

She, in her turn, bared her teeth and grimaced like a pug dog. It was too late. The woman's anger was raised and she was by far the stronger. Suddenly grasping Allegra's loosened hair, with the other she unloosed the cord which held her skirts and petticoat. Struggling caused only pain; the woman tugged on her thick hair whenever she resisted. Soon Allegra stood only in her thin shift, shivering in the cold air.

With a gesture intended to be harsh and bruising, Silva roughly grasped the shift and dragged it over her head. Then, with a look of grim satisfaction, she stood back to survey the product of her work. Again, there was a strange look of appraisal as she took in the girl's narrow shoulders and full breasts, the creamy skin across her stomach and her long limbs. Allegra was trembling now with cold. Trying to cover even some of her nakedness with her unloosed hair, she glared back at the uncouth creature into whose care she appeared to have been placed.

With no more than another grunt and gesture with her hand, Silva indicated that the girl was to recline on a block of marble set in the centre of the room. Set by the slab was a bowl of water and the implements of washing. Undoubtedly, Allegra thought, they must bathe all who arrived to ensure that no distempers were brought into the place. But nevertheless, the thought of this rough-mannered servant touching her filled her with repugnance.

Seating herself delicately at the edge of the block, Allegra pointed to the sponge and washing bowl. 'I will wash myself,' she announced. 'You may go.'

But again she had not taken into account the ill temper of the woman Silva. With a brusque shove Silva pushed the young girl down on to the cold, hard slab. Trying to raise herself, again Allegra was restrained by Silva's broad, muscular arms. There was no point in struggling; she may as well endure it.

'Very well,' she muttered. 'Only do be quick.'

As if responding to a challenge, Silva was instead painfully slow. She began by rubbing a foamy lather across Allegra's shoulders, her back and arms. Silva knew her work well and, despite her mood, Allegra began slowly to relax, feeling the hard fingers press and smooth her tense flesh. Cold as she had been, now the heat of the masseuse's hands created a silky fire which burnt dully in her sleepy mind. Slowly, Silva's hands reached her waist and then her buttocks. Again, the warm magic spread across the twin arcs of her flesh, gently lifting her body and then fractionally dropping it on to the cool slab. Next, her thighs were massaged, and finally her calves and the delicious soles of her feet.

With an impatient bark Silva ordered her to move over on to her back. Again, Allegra was soon drifting beneath the lulling caresses of those strong hands. But now as she unwound, her mind drifted to more pleasant surroundings. The hands squeezed her shoulders, blissfully delivering ease. Next, the slippery lather was dribbled on to her breasts; one hand rested on each, kneading the twin orbs. If only, Allegra thought, it were some strong and handsome man who worshipped her body thus. As each nipple was simultaneously squeezed between slippery fingers, she pictured beside her an ardent man, a man with a strong and muscular body made to please a young woman, a man with endow-

36

ments of such a proportion, she might say, that every inch of her would be satisfied.

The fingers drifted on, caressing now the pit of her stomach, which fluttered excitedly at the thought of this generous young man teasing her thus, kneeling between her legs, his manhood swinging and ready. The fingers reached the line of her pubis, and it was all she could do to restrain a gasp of sudden pleasure.

With a harsh shove, Silva grasped her thighs, pulling them apart. For a second, Allegra blinked her eyes open, remembered, and then shut them tightly to forget. Soon her visions of her lover returned. Again, the soapy suds were being dribbled over her, on to the most sensitive mouth of her sex. The sensation was delicious as runnels of warmth trickled into her most secret crevices. The fingers were at work, massaging her tangle of hair, brushing it back to reveal the swollen lips, probing, prodding, rubbing. She imagined the young man, yearning and gentle, lowering his handsome face to kiss the moist pink lips then teasing them with his tongue, flicking and sucking.

The fingers became yet more intrusive, gently squeezing the glorious swelling of pleasure, parting the lips wide and rubbing deeper towards the gap at her centre. It felt empty, gaping, trembling to be filled. Very gently, the fingers traced the outline of the rim and a violent fire erupted within her. In her mind she saw the young man pressing himself hard against her slippery emptiness, a proud, purple phallus guided by his hand which he threatened to jab inside her and deliver her from this lust. She wanted to moan out loud, to buck downwards on to the fingers and push her greedy sex right over them.

No, no, no. In a spasm of fright she opened her eyes and recollected where she was. It was a wrench to awake from such a daydream and find the vast tiled room around her. The brutal Silva was washing her still, seemingly unaware of the violent effects of her ministrations.

Without a pause, she began to lather Allegra's thighs and then finish soaping her legs. Desperately, Allegra fought the sensations of desire which still flooded through her body. She was aching now; she longed for the man of her daydream to finish his task, to take her, impale her, have done with her.

At last, it seemed, the soaping was done. For a few moments Allegra lay in trembling silence as Silva fetched fresh water. She felt sticky and restless and very ashamed. It was then she heard voices; from above it seemed, and tinkling laughter. Lifting her heavy head she peered across the room, and to her astonishment saw a group of three girls standing on the balcony. Hurriedly, she tried to rise to cover herself, but Silva stopped her in an instant, pushing her backwards with a reddened fist.

Through half-opened eyelids Allegra watched the group, mortified that they had seen her, but intent that they should not realise she had in turn seen them. Two girls were whispering and laughing together, their arms about each other's waists and their heads close together in seeming conspiracy. The third girl stood apart. She was leaning on the rail of the balcony, watching Allegra with an intensity that was most disturbing. Slowly Allegra felt herself blush hotly at being watched naked, even at this distance. Besides, there was something alluring about the girl; she was tall and slender with fair hair tucked haphazardly beneath the white cap of a novice. The way she leant dreamily against the rail, her elbow on the metal and her solemn face in her hand, touched her.

The next moment her reverie was shattered. With a pail of freezing water Silva rinsed the soap from her body; then administered another soaking and then still more. Finally, she set to her task with a large spiky sponge, rubbing the soft skin of Allegra's breasts and stomach and scraping every scrap of lather from Allegra's newly-moistened skin.

'Get off; get off me. That hurts!'

Again, it was no use. But worse than before, she now had the sound of idle laughter tinkling in her ears as she wriggled about, trying to escape the rough spikes of Silva's implement. With a fierce grunt Silva lifted her palm, as if to strike her. Furiously, Allegra settled back and lay still, gritting her teeth to bear this last indignity before she might finally escape.

With an air of eager retribution, Silva finished her task, scraping and grazing her calves, her thighs, her buttocks. As if leaving the best until last, she grunted as she again approached the delicate area at the top of Allegra's thighs. With the stiff sponge she set to, rubbing the soft pink skin which had so recently swelled like a budding flower beneath her sensual exploration. It was painful and sore – but so recently had Allegra been aroused, it was also fiercely intense. Where before the fingers had been tender, the masseuse now rubbed the strange bristles back and forth, driving Allegra to a new plateau of burning discomfort. Again, she wished that it could go on and on, if she could only drive that bristling mass deep and hard into the centre of her being.

With a groan of pleasure only just contained within her lips, Allegra again dragged herself back from the brink to the tiled room. With a momentary blink of her eyes, she quickly glimpsed the balcony. The two girls had disappeared, but the solitary girl stood there still. But now she was even more languorous, leaning expectantly against the railing, both hands gripping the metal as she watched with her mouth a little apart and her hair falling across her watching eyes. For a second the two girls' eyes met, and Allegra felt her head swim as the sponge stroked up and down her throbbing centre, on and on and on.

'Stop, you evil creature. I have had enough!' With a fierce shove, she untangled herself from Silva's grip and jumped up on to the floor. 'You have done your work. Be off.'

With a look of unmasked hostility Silva picked up her

goods and marched away, muttering beneath her breath. Slowly Allegra turned to the balcony, hoping to call out to her fellow novice. But she too had disappeared.

Sighing to herself, Allegra dried her poor, raw skin on a sheet and began to dress in her new clothes. Her old costume lay on the chest, still shaped around the curves of her body as it had fallen. For the first time she noticed how fine her taffeta dress was and how exquisitely the silver thread embroidery traced the outline of her bodice. Even the shift was of finest lawn, edged in scarlet flowers and lace from Bruges.

As for the poor costume she must now wear as a novice – it was penitent stuff indeed. The stays were of stiff, unyielding leather which pinched and rubbed her ribs and breasts. The skirts and bodice were of a dull brown serge, with a coarse kerchief and cap of grubby linen. As for her shoes – her fine Morocco shoes with the red heels were to be replaced by shabby, tough boots worn over knitted stockings. Such was her costume to be until she was admitted to the order.

So this was the attire of the novice Almoro. It was not the sublime virginal white of holy visions and beautiful transports of the soul. The dreams of the old Allegra must lie discarded, like her clothes lying scattered on the tiled floor. With no other place to go, Allegra walked to the door, resigned to make her new home here in the heart of this strange and cruel house.

Chapter Four

*A*llegra waited restlessly in the room. The long afternoon was fading as shadows lengthened on the
stone walls of the narrow chamber. She had taken her
evening meal in silence with the other novices, glancing
around at their grave faces as she ate the simple meal of
maize porridge and fruit. Two of the sisters had led
them to chapel for a brief session of prayer, after which
one had silently led Allegra to what was undoubtedly to
be her room. There she lay waiting, pondering the
narrow bed which was the twin to her own.

It had not occurred to her that she would share her
room. All the books she had seen about visionary saints
pictured them alone in their cells, accompanied by no
more by way of a companion than a single tame dove.
The other bed lay neat and empty, along with tell-tale
signs of recent occupation: a jar filled with flowers, a
pretty book of hours and a candle, tinder and snuffer all
laid out on a natural stone shelf.

Outside the summer's day was melting away into a
warm, balmy evening. The room was well situated, its
arched window overlooking an open quadrangle which
was partly filled by low shrubs and plants. Now, as she
breathed in the sweet air, she became aware that this

was the convent's kitchen garden, a scented collection of herbs and flowers grown for use indoors.

There was a tap at the door. Startled, Allegra sat up on the bed, pulling her kerchief tight around her shoulders. 'Come in.'

It was the girl from the balcony. She looked less dishevelled now; her hair was neatly held beneath her cap. She smiled shyly. 'Hello. My name is Celina. We are to share this room.'

'And I am Allegra. Sorry – Almoro.' She shook her head at her own forgetfulness. 'It is hard to lose one's own name.' She reached out her hand to take Celina's fingers and then thought twice. Perhaps any physical contact was banned in this place. Quickly, she withdrew her hand. But Celina would not let her; with a darting movement she had grasped Allegra's fingers. Suddenly laughing together, they both shook hands most courteously.

'You need not concern yourself about your noviciate name,' Celina added. 'I have been given the name of Dorico but only the sisters call me that. I like Celina. It is my true name.'

In a most friendly manner, Celina sat herself carefully on the edge of the bed. Suddenly Allegra felt happier. In setting herself the task of becoming perfectly holy, she had felt some small worry about never sharing human companionship again. It would surely be more pleasant all round, to pursue her vocation but also have charming friends such as Celina with whom to spend the empty hours when she could neither be at prayer nor pursuing good works.

'But you must surely give up your first name when you join the order?'

Celina laughed. 'Oh, I suppose so. If I must. I hope the day never comes.'

She had a pretty pout. But Allegra was somewhat disturbed. 'What do you mean?'

'Oh, I am happy as I am. Who wants to be a nun anyway? It's unnatural.'

'Not to me,' Allegra asserted hotly. 'I cannot wait for the day I leave the cares of this tawdry world behind. I am only sorry it will take a full year.'

'I apologise,' Celina said quickly. 'I didn't realise anyone ever actually wanted to be a nun. I am only here at the convenience of my family. You see if I were to marry, the family's fortune would be split. And there is not the money for me to live an independent life. Most of us girls are in such a position. The old families of Venice need to preserve their wealth – or what is left of it. If there were more money left, I might at least have been sent to a more comfortable nunnery. But as it is – well, the little amount that was scraped together for a dowry only bought me a place here.'

For a while, Allegra contemplated this speech, feeling her heart beat fast. Where had her guardian sent her?

'What is it? I've not upset you, have I? Oh, me and my loose tongue.'

'It is just,' she began at last, 'that I have a vocation, a strong vocation to live my life as nun. But you see, I am rich. I am sure I might have gone to any convent I might have fancied.'

'Then who was it chose this place?' Celina's pink face puckered with concern.

'My guardian chose this place. I cannot believe it, this must be a joke of his.'

'A joke? It seems to be in poor taste.'

'That would suit his purpose. To teach me a harsh lesson.'

'But why ever would he want to do that? You seem such a good person.'

Allegra sighed and stared dully at the ceiling. 'Precisely. It is precisely that he seeks to test.'

Celina suggested she showed her new companion the lie of the place. So, with more pleasant sensations than she had before encountered at the convent of Santa Agnetha, Allegra went forth with her new friend. Beyond the kitchen garden was a walled area where simple crops were grown. Celina explained that a few working men came over from Murano to help till the fields and manage the boats and animals. Some dusty outhouses held squawking chickens, a goat and a gentle-eyed donkey. Passing through a rusty gate, it was surprising to find a shady, wooded area around a small freshwater lake.

'This is where we wash the clothes,' Celina said. 'And also bathe in the long summer months. When the sun beats down on this little rock, we are glad enough of somewhere to retire and shade ourselves.'

All was still at this time in the evening; beneath the towering branches the air was scented and cool. Celina paused and kicked off her boots, walking on slender bare feet along the sandy path. Envying her freedom of manner, Allegra felt unable to follow suit. It was only her first day, and her recollections of the Prioress were still potently strong. Suddenly they left the roof of branches and emerged on the sea shore. The island was deceptively small; they had traversed it in less than a quarter of an hour.

'What is your opinion of the sisterhood here?' she asked carefully.

Celina swung her boots over her shoulder and began to walk in the shallow rivulets of sea water which trickled over her feet. 'I should not like to speak ill of them. Only they seem a strange choice for someone like yourself to join. You see,' and here she looked quickly over her shoulder, 'they take the harshness of their role somewhat seriously. A few of them – well, take it more seriously than could be believed.'

'What do you mean? The Prioress, she talked of tests. What are they?'

But it was too late. A sudden cry from the direction of

the convent drew their attention. There, by the wall, was a figure in black, waving them back from the shoreline.

'Mary and the Saints, we are in trouble,' Celina muttered, scrabbling to get her boots back on to her wet and sandy feet. 'It is Sister Ino.' Allegra stood still by her side, letting her lean on her waist to gain her balance. Slowly then, they walked back to the waiting figure.

As they approached, Allegra made out a sister whose cowl hung about a wide, red veined face. Pent-up anger suffused her broad features. Though she stood motionless, a wild agitation could be detected in her expression. Fearfully, they both drew near.

'Sister Dorico. I am appalled by you.' The nun's round eyes inspected the girl's leaf scattered costume and sand encrusted boots. 'What are you? Are you not a wanton slut?'

Celina cast her eyes to the ground and nodded. Allegra felt herself curl up inside with shame for her new friend. 'I am sorry, sister.'

This seemed only to antagonise the blustering, red-faced woman more. 'I assure you, you are not. Not so sorry as you will be! To drag our new novice about in the undergrowth, setting the worst example possible. What are the words of discipline?'

Without looking up, Celina chanted, 'Through discipline is purity. Humility by pain.'

'Exactly. You will come to my cell after Compline. Understand?'

'I obey.'

'Very well. To your room.'

With a new weight hanging over them, the girls retraced their steps to the chamber by the garden. Once inside, Allegra shut the door and breathed easily. 'What in heaven's name was that about?' she asked.

'Oh, it's nothing,' Celina replied evasively. 'I was trying to tell you earlier. Some of the sisters can be a bit – harsh.'

'But why? She sounded cruel. Where do you have to go?'

Celina took her hand and guided her to the bed so they could sit together, far from the unlocked door. She spoke gently, smiling sadly. 'It is simply the way of the order. Just as our founding Saint, Agnetha, punished herself for loving others in her sisterhood too devoutly, so do our sisters believe in the punishment of the flesh. They believe such pain is cleansing to the soul. What she will do is of no account. It is just that some of the sisterhood, such as Sister Ino, take their task rather too much to heart. One might almost say there is a secret pleasure for them in the pain they administer.'

'Oh, you poor creature. And it is all my fault.'

'Indeed it is not, Allegra. For if you had not been here, I would still have taken that walk tonight.'

It took some time to convince Allegra she was blameless. Finally, Celina took her hand and squeezed it generously. 'Come, let us be friends. It will never do to fall out so quickly. Give me a kiss and then it is all done.'

Allegra believed she had never had such a friend before; so sweet and kind and self-sacrificing. With a pleasant laugh, she leant towards her, letting her lips brush Celina's mouth, feeling a damp softness as their lips met. At the same time, Celina reached to catch her hair. As Allegra turned away, the other girl's fingers momentarily lingered, catching her neck as if indeed she wished very much to let that kiss last much longer. However, the next second she jumped up and Allegra wondered if she had imagined the intended caress.

'It is time to light our candle.'

As Celina lit the little chamber, Allegra paused at the window, watching the remains of the sunshine turn to dusk over the bobbing heads of lavender and rosemary. She wondered for a moment about the festival of the Redentore, far away across the water. Soon the coloured lamps would be lit; the crowds would be gathering for merrymaking. But she held her tongue from describing

46

the events to Celina. Unlike herself, the poor girl had no choice but to be here. She was almost a prisoner in this strange place.

'Here. It is almost cosy now. Let us get into bed and then we can talk into the night quite comfortably.'

'Oh, you will never be a nun, will you?' Allegra laughed. 'What about your prayers?'

'My friend Magdalena used to say the same thing,' Celina pouted. Again, Allegra could not help but be struck by how disarmingly pretty she was. As the girl took off her cap, her fair hair fell in waves over her shoulders. 'Magdalena shared my room before you,' she added, and Allegra was surprised to feel herself flinch with something like a pang of jealousy as the girl spoke. 'How I have missed her. You cannot imagine how dreary it is to sleep alone here, with no one to keep me company.' She began to unlace her bodice, and though Allegra tried not to watch, her eyes occasionally flickered in that direction every few seconds.

Celina chattered on. 'You see, she was my very best friend and we were so very fond of each other. But at last her family found a cousin who would accept only a tiny dowry for her and she left. She was so excited to be going back to the city and getting married and having a new dress and jewellery.'

'So she was not suited to being a nun either.' Allegra could not help but appraise her friend as she said this. Celina's bodice lay tidily on the bed now, and beneath the filmy shift Allegra could see the rounded outlines of two firm breasts pushing against the fabric.

'Is it not wrong – ' She swallowed and began again. 'Sorry, was it not wrong, to have a special friend in that way? I thought the Patriarch forbade such close relations?'

She found herself watching again, as the girl undid her skirt and at last she could see the shadowy outline of her whole figure, with all its delicious curves and swellings.

47

To her alarm, Celina came over to her dressed only in her shift and sat again on the bed, reaching for her two hands. 'What could be the harm, Allegra? Can we not be fond of each other too?'

Her eyes were very round and beseeching. Slowly she caressed Allegra's hands, stroking the palms in a sudden echo of the Prioress's oddly lewd touch.

'I – I don't know,' she said with a dry mouth. 'I thought it was wrong, that's all.' She flinched and turned away. 'So. We must be going to bed.'

Allegra had begun to understand that the girl represented an appalling temptation. Whilst no doubt completely artless and innocent, her loveliness was all too close a snare to one who had sworn to renounce all fleshly things. Even as she sat, clutching her hands, Allegra could smell a sweet, salty scent rising from her, where the stays had just recently released her plump flesh from their tight compression.

'Let me help you,' she offered, as Allegra rose to begin unloosing her hair.

'No need,' she began, then as she fumbled, said, 'Very well. Just my hair. It is not fair to use you as a maid.'

And so the girl sat behind her on the bed and begun to pull the pins from the coils of chestnut hair which Allegra wore beneath her cap. As she worked, she could feel her struggle with the fastenings and press against her back.

'I do not mind being your maid at all. Just tell me if there is anything you want me to do.'

The girl's breasts pressed into her spine as Allegra sat, stiff as a statue, grimly fighting the beginnings of desire which awoke in the tingling pit of her stomach.

'You have beautiful hair,' Celina said, and rapidly fetched a brush to stroke across the waves of unleashed tresses. Slowly she brushed the long hanks of hair, stroking the roots in a deeply soothing manner. 'Now, while I'm here, I'd better unlace you.'

'No,' Allegra replied, alarmed. Standing, she turned to

the girl, knowing her face to be flushed with confusion. 'I can manage it all myself, Celina,' she said with some command. But having said so, she had to begin. Pulling the kerchief off, she was aware of a flush across her throat and breast and hoped Celina could not see it in the candlelight. Next, she pulled at the rough cords across her bodice. Suddenly she was all fingers and thumbs, unable to undo the knots and find the ends of the laces.

'Here,' Celina laughed from below her on the bed. 'I know how to do it.' In a second she was eagerly unwinding the cord until it fell loose. Then, smiling, she pulled the bodice backwards so it slipped back and off Allegra's shoulders. With a look of some satisfaction she eyed Allegra in nothing but the leather stays over her thin shift. 'What a horrible corset. There must be a more comfortable one somewhere. Is is rubbing against you?'

'Only a little.'

'Here, let me help you.' Again, Celina expertly unlaced the heavy leather stays, allowing Allegra at last to feel some relief from heavy pressure on her ribs and breasts. With a deep sigh, Allegra let the corset fall open, leaving nothing but the gossamer shift to cover her modesty.

'Here, I'll soon make it better. Sit down and turn about.'

'In all honesty, Celina, I don't need it.'

'Go on. You will sleep better.'

'Very well, then. Only we must go to bed soon.' With some reluctance Allegra sat on the bed once more, with the girl behind her. Deftly, Celina began to rub Allegra's shoulders through the thin fabric and all the stiffness in her muscles seemed to ebb away. Soon Celina's attentions moved down her back.

'Your back is chafed by those things. Soon you will be in agony. Is the front reddened too?'

Allegra duly turned round on the bed, ready to suggest they retire for the night in a moment. But in a trice Celina had parted the front of her shift and was

49

inspecting the flesh at her waist where thick red marks were evidence of the pinching of the new stays. Allegra flinched at the chasm of flesh now open to her friend's gaze; glancing down, she could see the silky chasm between her pale breasts and the rising curve swelling on either side. But Celina seemed blind to these distractions and attended only to the marks at her waist. Slowly though, Allegra noticed, she was pulling the opening of the garment apart, until finally her ministrations forced the cloth to pull back revealing one bright and swollen nipple.

'I think I must sleep now,' Allegra announced wriggling away from the girl's gentle fingers. 'Surely we must be up early.'

Celina looked up slowly; it seemed she was now growing sleepy and languourous too. She certainly noticed the disarray of Allegra's shift and her eyes lingered on the single rosy point of the escaping breast.

'Goodnight then, my friend,' she murmured. At that moment Allegra surprised herself by feeling both relief at the end of this ordeal and a tinge of disappointment at such an unsatisfactory ending. 'Let me kiss you goodnight, then.'

Leaning forward, Celina did this time brush the hair from Allegra's throat and let her fingers linger there on the soft skin as her mouth delivered a long and passionate kiss. As their lips met, Allegra surrendered utterly, drowning beneath a tidal flood of pent-up desire. Her senses were overwhelmed with the sweet sensation of caresses at her throat and neck and the exquisite pressure on her mouth from the other girl's succulent lips. There was no relief: the kiss went on and on.

Suddenly the girl's hot tongue darted into her mouth and Allegra felt she might faint away with bliss. Unable to control her physical movements, her mouth fell apart, slack and greedy, wanting to suck and nip that stiff little tongue, wanting it to fill her mouth. Still the fingers lightly played around her face and under the heaviness of her hair, driving her wild with pleasure.

Slowly Celina let herself drop on to her prone friend, until soon she was pressed down hard on Allegra's arching body. Still they kissed in long deep kisses, exploring each other's hot mouths and cheeks and throats. Soon Allegra became aware of her shift falling apart at the opening and nervously tried to pull it back. But Celina gently restrained her hand, kissing the soft inside of the wrist as she did. With her own breasts uncovered, Allegra became aware of the gorgeous sensation of her friend's breasts now pressing against them. Where before she had felt excited, now she experienced a trance-like thrill. Unable to resist, she felt Celina pull her own shift apart so that her breasts too, rose naked and swollen to rub and knead against her own. With their tongues intermingling, so did both pairs of jutting nipples rasp intensely one against the other until, losing all control, Allegra's mouth opened with a moan of pleasure.

'Yes,' Celina whispered. 'Let me show you pleasure. Let me do as I please.' Glancing down, Allegra could see her own breasts rising larger than she had ever seen them, like milky spheres which pressed into Celina's smaller breasts. Celina's were more pointed and pert but similarly swollen. Her nipples were pinker, like elongated rosebuds set in a pale circle of swollen pinky flesh.

With a deliberate movement, Celina left her mouth, kissed her throat, her chest, and finally settled her pretty mouth on the rigid crimson spike that Allegra's own nipple had become. As Celina's lips slipped around it and sucked, Allegra's head swam dizzily, coasting on a wave that was close to complete release but inevitably hung on the distant edge of physical satisfaction. With small flicks of her tongue, Celina teased the poor swollen nub of flesh, even nipping gently with her teeth to transport Allegra to the very rim of pleasure.

Unable to control her gasping breath, Allegra moaned

with abandon now, allowing the girl to seek out her other breast with her fingers. There, Celina simultaneously tweaked and rubbed and rolled the twin nipple, so that Allegra felt double rapture, flinging herself with arched back across the bed with her glistening breasts high and stiff and exposed to pleasure.

With a subtle movement, Celina slid her leg between Allegra's, parting her thighs so they hung loosely. Slipping between them, the girl pressed as hard as she could, crushing her groin into Allegra's. The effect was explosive. Allegra became aware of a rising heat in her loins which every second of pressure from the girl's grinding pubis increased. With an assurance belying her earlier innocence, Celina began to grind her pleasure spot expertly against Allegra's, pushing her thighs ever wider until her victim felt her shift grow wet and slippery against the tangle of fabric and hair.

With a sudden wail of impatience, Celina lifted her hips and pulled up both their shifts around their waists. With a shock of pleasure, Allegra saw the girl's long, creamy thighs and curling thatch of reddish hair. She was aware of herself with her legs spread indecently wide and both girl's vulvas stretched and distended as they craved the friction of one against the other. Unable now to stop, her hands clutched Celina's shoulders, frantically pulling her deeper into that slippery gorge. Again the girl thrust, faster and faster. Her movements now were involuntary; she too was gasping wordlessly, driving her bony sex against Allegra's in a frenzy, pushing her thighs apart as widely as possible. Driving each other to complete abandonment, they squeezed each other's breasts, feeling a rising quake tremble in their hearts.

All at once, Allegra became aware of her lips overflowing with salty juice, of the crimson bead of pleasure at her centre bursting with lust. With a hoarse scream, she rammed herself against the girl's juicy vulva and the bubble burst in a spasm of rippling waves, her body juddering against Celina's pubis, her own lips spilling spurts of juice as the walls of her aching hole pumped again and again.

It took some time for her heart to stop racing. The room began to settle down around her where before it had spun; her breathing slowed and the rhythmic throbbing between her legs pulsed ever more quietly. Allegra became aware of the girl still twined against her.

With a slow smile Celina lifted her head and whispered in her ear. 'I knew you wanted to. You loved it, didn't you?'

Allegra stiffened. Suddenly this small, confined room seemed to be the setting for a nightmare. How had this happened? It was only the first day of her new, better life. Trying to untangle herself from the knot of limbs, she became aware of the disgusting wetness on her thighs and the nearness of the girl's immodest, luxurious nakedness.

'Get off me!' she hissed. Celina jumped up, looking pale.

'How dare you?' Allegra continued. 'I do not know what wickedness you have done, but do not say it was I who wanted it.'

Celina opened her mouth to speak, but could not interrupt, now that Allegra was in full flow. 'Deviant! How was I to know you were so unnatural? I took you for a friend; I let you kiss me as a friend. This vileness you have carried out is nothing to do with me. Clearly, you are debased. To say I was compliant, that I wanted such a thing – it's an outrageous lie. I was simply too alarmed to move. Could you not see me struggle? I have no idea what you were doing. If you were to tell anyone, they would never believe you.'

Having caught her breath, Celina pulled the sheet around her, looking sadly down on her new friend. 'My dear Allegra, there is no need to take on so. It is a natural thing. Come along, was it not a delicious pleasure?'

'Get out of my sight!' Allegra screamed. 'You are a liar and a whore and a slut! I will tell the sisters! How dare you say such a thing?'

With many a reproving look and sad gestures, Celina packed together her few things, and taking the only candle, left the room. Alone in the darkness, Allegra pushed all memory of her own pleasure into the farthest, most secret corner of her mind. Guiltily, she rewrote the events of the evening, until she imagined Celina to be a perverse and seducing monster. By the time dawn lightened the walls of stone to palest grey, Allegra was kneeling uncomfortably by her bed, stirring up the courage to complain to the Prioress about her abominable treatment.

Chapter Five

After the cold and dreary service of morning Mass, Allegra hung back from the other girls as they hastily made their way to the refectory to break their fast. From behind a wide pillar, she had watched the Prioress and her retinue pause at the altar and talk in low whispers for a little while. Then they had retreated behind a thick curtain to the rear of the chapel, pulling back a heavy door which scraped noisily shut behind them.

For a few moments Allegra paused. The grey stones of the chapel were quiet now, where before they had echoed to the clattering of dozens of boots. The air at last grew still. Maybe it would be easier for everyone if she simply followed her companions and forgot about the whole thing. But then her heart sank at the prospect of seeing Celina again. That morning the girl had studiously avoided her eyes, seating herself far back from the altar, as far from Allegra as she might be. And Allegra had sensed some idle chatter going on behind her back, where she could not properly look without craning her neck. She guessed that Celina and the others had been laughing at her and mocking her for her outcry. If she were to follow them into the refectory now, she would not know where to look, where to sit or how she could survive such an uncomfortable meal. The food would taste of dust and choke her.

With new resolve, she crossed the stone flags to the curtained door. Cocking her head to one side, she heard low muttering from the sisters, as if they gathered in muted conference. Resolutely, she decided only to slip her head around the door and ask for an audience with the Prioress later that day. With a slightly trembling hand, she knocked at the door.

Sudden silence fell, broken only by the sudden sharp tread of footsteps crossing towards the other side of the door. In a moment she was staring into the fiery face of the dreadful Sister Ino.

'I only wanted – ' she blurted. 'I am sorry, Sister – Sister Ino. I seek permission to speak to the Prioress at her convenience.'

The fierce face glared back into hers for a silently enraged moment. Suddenly it disappeared and Allegra was left to collect her own distracted thoughts. Anxiously, she looked back to the door which led to the corridor and refectory. Perhaps she could still get away? But it was too late. As quickly as she had disappeared, Sister Ino returned. With a brisk nod of her head, she ushered Allegra into the room.

The new novice was surprised to find herself entering a splendid secondary chapel, which was usually hidden from view. Where the main chapel was grey and dismal in the dawn light, created from ancient and rough hewn stones, this one was emblazoned with gold leaf and crowned by a vast fresco across the ceiling depicting spacious blue skies and the gods at their sports in the clouds. It was difficult not to blink at the mass of shining brass screens, jewelled candlesticks and life-like gilded images of saints.

Nervously, Allegra crossed to a dais where the Prioress sat in the midst of the other sisters like a queen amongst her courtiers. The girl was surprised to also see

56

a number of male priests amongst their number, both young and old, as if she had disturbed some particular conference of clerics.

'What is it you want?' The Prioress's voice was firm and cool. Allegra could barely glance at that terrible lined face, cloaked as ever in a cowl of black serge.

'I am so sorry, Prioress. I did not wish to disturb you.'

'You did not wish to? But you have,' came back the rejoinder, as sharp as a knife.

'What I mean is,' Allegra faltered, 'may I beg permission to speak to you alone, later?'

The old woman gazed at her with cold disdain. 'You have already interrupted me, Sister Almoro; you may speak now.'

Allegra looked around her at the unfriendly eyes of the ten or twelve others who also waited to judge her words. Ardently, she wished the building might collapse around her. Again, she tried to defer her announcement. 'It would be a breach of confidence, Prioress, to tell my tale in front of all this company.'

'Let me be judge of that!'

At this, the girl's voice almost failed her. Yet, she had come with a complaint and may as well make it. 'Prioress, I am sorry to say that I have an accusation to make.'

'Against whom?'

'The girl who shares my room, Celina.'

'Who? What name is this?'

'I'm sorry, I forgot. Sister Dorico. She has committed an assault against my person.'

At this, Allegra felt a flicker of renewed attention pass through the collected assembly. It seemed to her that they looked at her more carefully now. Both men and women fixed her with interested fascination.

'What kind of assault?' barked the old woman.

'I am sure I could not say,' Allegra mumbled.

'What do you mean by this foolishness? How did she touch you?'

'Modesty forbids me to describe it.'

'Well, I do not forbid you from describing it. From start to finish, what occurred?'

If Allegra had wished the building to collapse before, she now wished the sun and sky might crash down and smother her in darkness. Where before, her voice had been strong, now she found herself quaking and quavering. 'We were in our room, last night,' she began, taking a large breath, 'when she began to kiss me in a most immodest manner. Before this, she had tried to touch me in various ways – brushing my hair and helping me undress. And then her modesty entirely abandoned her.'

The old woman nodded grimly for her to proceed. The company were now watching her with rapt attention. She could see Sister Ino biting her lip expectantly. The stern but handsome man whom Allegra judged to be the Abbot had even lifted his hooded eyes and fixed them on the young novice greedily.

'She touched my person in the strangest way. She pulled my clothes aside and assaulted me, quite plainly.' As she proceeded, Allegra found herself getting more and more carried away by her own story. Her nervousness disappeared and she now faced the assembled group with a look of fierce indignation. 'As you know, Prioress, I have come here to find a better life. Indeed, I never guessed such a thing could happen here in this holy place. I am appalled to find lewdness rife amongst the novices.'

'Show us then, how this assault took place. Where was it she touched you?'

With some surprise, Allegra pointed feebly to her own bosom, and then less confidently, pointed downwards in the general direction of her stomach.

'And what precisely did she do? What kind of movements did she make?'

Allegra felt herself grow hot in the face, up to the roots of her hair. Gazing down at the floor, she muttered an answer.

58

'We cannot hear that,' the Prioress announced. 'Show us with your hands.'

With arms of lead, the girl raised her hands to her breasts and made a quick, caressing gesture. Then even more slowly, she laid a hand on her skirt at the juncture at the top of her thighs.

'And?'

'She rubbed and kissed me, Prioress.'

'And what state of dress were you in?'

Blushing still, Allegra replied, 'I wore only my shift – that is, until she lifted it.'

The assembly were hanging on every word and now a silence fell that was long and disconcerting. With a darting movement, the Prioress suddenly leant forward, like a snake about to bite. 'And you, Sister Almoro,' hissed the Prioress's voice, 'how was it you could not resist these affectionate advances?'

'I – I,' began Allegra, but was unable to finish.

'I wonder now, if these ministrations had any effect upon you, if you were indeed unable to resist these embraces? The girl is attractive, is she not? You yourself are a healthy young girl who may yet need to conquer the desires of the flesh. What do you say?'

Allegra felt that she might well vomit, so badly was the interview proceeding. Desperately, she tried to extricate herself from the web the old woman had cast about her. 'No, it is not true! I have no words to describe the horror I feel as you describe me thus. I am an innocent newcomer who strives only for the purity of a spiritual life. Let me be free of all this wickedness, then you will see how fine a soul I have. I beg you, Prioress, let me show you I am better by far than such a harlot as Celina.' Throwing herself on her knees, Allegra felt that at last she had succeeded in detaching herself from any blame. With some relief, she heard the Prioress pronounce her judgement.

'Very well, I understand you wish to be judged better than your companion. I will see that justice is done. The punishment will take place this very evening. Be gone, Sister Almoro. You have work with your sisters still to be done.'

With some small sense of satisfaction, Allegra set about finding her companions. However, they had long since left the refectory, and soon she realised that there was no food left to break her fast. Wandering into the kitchen, she found one of the servants, who supplied her with some bread and cheese which she bundled up and carried outside to enjoy in the sunshine. Unable to hear or see any sign of the other novices, she wandered for a while through the gardens, looking for a pleasant, shady spot where she might picnic and also collect her fractured thoughts. At last she set herself down, arranging her skirts beneath a large tree overlooking the small field where the chicken coop and outhouses lay.

With a new appetite, she tore at the crusty bread and salty cheese, feeling glad to be alive on this luxuriously warm day. The other novices must be at work somewhere but it was hard to imagine chasing after them, when the glimmer of sunshine through leaves and the happy trilling of the birds made this such an idyllic spot. Leaning with her back against the trunk of the tree, she let herself doze a little, enjoying at last the new calm which had suffused through her body since the previous night. If only, she allowed herself to think privately, such acts were not a very great wickedness. The girl was so lovely – and so ferociously responsive. Allegra was secretly pleased that just once in her life she had experienced such a passionate coupling. It was a pity, really, that she would never have the experience again. And a pity too, that Celina must suffer for it.

The sound of whistling suddenly disturbed her reverie. Looking about, Allegra noticed for the first time that one of the workmen was hard at work on the small farm. He at least seemed happy at this work, she observed. He was a young, strong-looking youth, with

60

black curling hair and broad shoulders beneath his ragged shirt. He whistled a pretty tune as he threw corn to the poultry and collected eggs from their perches. Next he fed the old donkey and then, seating himself on an old crate, began to comb his hair.

Allegra could not help but laugh to herself to see the youth take such care with his appearance. Maybe he guessed a little about the effect of his manly presence on a community of secluded women. It would not be hard to imagine how a youth such as this could take hold of a woman's desperate daydreams, even though he was clearly of a lower, rougher order. To her secret delight, he next began to fill a tub of water from the pump; in a few seconds he had pulled off his shirt and stood naked from the waist in the sunshine, like a graceful god from the days of the pagans.

She could not help but admire the strong muscles rippling beneath his copper-sheened skin; as he ran a wet rag across his body the sunshine outlined every masculine curve. His shoulders were broad and strong and his torso revealed the powerful effects of good, honest labour. Showing every signs of enjoying his private bath, the young fellow next set to washing his hair. Though lacking the luxury of soap, he set to it like a puppy dog, dousing his head in the tub and then shaking his dark curls until they hung in damp tendrils down his back. Finally, he looked around himself, clearly checking to see if he was being watched. Allegra's heart skipped a beat as he seemed for a second to look directly at her where she sat above him masked by trees. But undoubtedly he could not see her, sitting down low as she was in her dark brown dress.

With a quick, almost furtive movement, he unloosed his breeches. Then, with a rapid sliding movement, they were off and he stood completely naked for her to inspect at her leisure. His legs were as stout and well formed as the rest of him, covered in a fuzz of dark hair. Giggling to herself, Allegra considered the rest of his anatomy. At first he stood with his back to her, and her eye followed the long flank of his back and the paler skin of his neat, curved buttocks. As he turned, her giggles stopped. Indeed, beyond Leon's timid attempt to despoil her, she had never actually seen a male member in all its glory. Now, the youth's long phallus hung swinging down between his thighs, pink and fleshy, with the heavy scrotum bulging behind in a mass of curly hair.

Allegra's mouth fell open; peering between narrowed eyes, she clambered forward on all fours, striving all the time to get a better view of the mysteriously attractive organ. Soon she was crouched on the grass, staring round eyed at the young fellow as he began to douse his stomach with handfuls of refreshing water. Next he grasped his long member and lifted it to scrub its length.

Once again, as she leant on her elbows with her rear end pushed back, she felt a wave of delicious sensation stir in her body. What would it be like to help the young fellow with his ablutions – to touch the very thing he touched? As he washed it, she could see it grow a little wider and ever so slightly stiffer in response to his own touch. So what if a young woman were to touch it, to rub it, to squeeze it?

In response, she felt her own inner muscles squeeze with delight. She thought of playing with it gently, maybe stroking it and watching it rise – as a throng of images rushed into her mind, she found herself squeezing her thighs together in anticipation. If only he knew about her, kneeling here, ready for him – what could she fancy them doing together, what tasks could she find for such a glorious piece of flesh?

It was difficult not to be horribly aware of the growing dampness between her legs, of the tight bonds of her corsets pressing hard against her hanging breasts. Sighing, she wondered idly if there might be any opportunity to befriend the young workman and let events follow the course of nature. But then she recalled his station in life – he was only a rough and lowborn menial. She must not forget herself. She was a member of the nobility, and sworn to be a nun as well.

The next thing Allegra heard was a loud whistling sound very close to her ears. Then she felt a blow, a sharp, agonising blow on her prominent rump. In a moment she struggled to get up. It was Sister Ino, switch in hand, with a face of purple fury.

'I – I am sorry Sister. I was only sitting here. Only watching.'

The terrifying nun stared at her with eyes rolling white in her crimson face. Then with a vicious gesture, she raised her arm.

'How dare you!' Allegra cried, raising her hand to stop her. 'Creeping up on me like that. Why do you people think you can do that? I am only here minding my own business. Now, let me find the others. I have work to do.' At this, Allegra abruptly pushed past the older woman, running at a smart pace back to the convent. Only faintly, she could hear Sister Ino murmur, as if repeating a litany to herself, 'Through discipline is purity. Humility by pain.'

That evening Allegra was surprised to find Celina at her door again. The girl stood meekly outside with her candle, her face a picture of tearful humility.

'What is it?' Allegra asked.

'Allegra, please may I come in? I have nowhere to sleep.'

'You can sleep wherever it was you slept last night, can't you? I will not bother with you again.'

The girl's face twitched, fighting back tears. 'I only need – if nothing else – I beg you, let me get a change of linen. Sister Ino has . . .'

'Has what? Oh, no. Has she punished you?' The realisation that her own complaint might have already led to such a consequence both horrified and excited Allegra. Without comment, she let Celina into the room, watching her with fascination. 'What happened?' Allegra was all ears as she led the girl over to the bed. But on reaching it, Celina winced. It was clear she could not sit comfortably.

'You remember she told me to report to her room. I did so and received fit punishment for taking you wandering in the garden. But it is obviously of no matter to you. Please just let me change my linen.' Suddenly Celina's face grimaced as a sob rose from her heart. 'Oh, Allegra, do take pity on me. I cannot sleep out there on the hard benches in the chapel. Please let me share your room. I will only lie here quietly and not disturb your peace at all.'

Allegra's mind was working fast as the girl spoke. So the punishment she had received from Sister Ino had only been that already threatened on their walk yesterday. It seemed Celina had no idea as yet of her complaint and the second punishment she would inevitably receive that evening. Poor girl. It almost melted Allegra's heart to think of Celina receiving a second, undoubtedly more severe punishment from the sisters later that night.

'Here, let me help you,' she offered. But Celina could not sit, only shuffle on to the bed lying frontwards, so that she might relieve her sore buttocks of any pressure. There was nothing to be done but help her unlace her skirts and petticoat, carefully holding them back so nothing touched the sensitive skin. As her petticoat fell to the ground, Allegra was shocked to see the red weals Sister Ino's switch had left on the girl's peachy flesh. A dozen or so stripes marked the skin of her rounded cheeks, rising in ridges of crimson. The skin was not broken, however, only stinging mercilessly as the girl wriggled this way and that on her stomach, trying to find a position in which the pain would lessen.

Allegra sat on her bed and contemplated the unfortunate girl. It would be a surprise to Celina to be summoned for a second time, but it nevertheless would be most embarrassing to actually warn her. No, she would have to be surprised, for otherwise she might accuse

64

Allegra of betrayal. And indeed, although the two girls had studiously avoided each other all the wearisome day, now they were back in each other's company, it was hard not to feel the glimmers of friendship revive once again.

'Allegra, is there nothing you can do to help me?' Celina moaned, shifting from one side to the other.

'There is nothing I can do, as you well know,' she replied. 'Just tell me, will you, what exactly happened when you went to Sister Ino's room?' For Allegra had cast her mind back to the afternoon, and realised she too might have to face the terrible nun herself at some future date.

'I cannot,' she moaned. 'For it is a terrible secret. I know it is meant to make me pure, but in truth it only heats my humours even more.'

'Celina, you are truly disgusting. I do not wish to know about your perversities.'

At this, a long silence ensued. But Allegra was intrigued. Her friend looked quite fetching now, with her bare bottom raised on a pillow and her thighs a little parted to ease the pain. The series of weals too, looked oddly arousing on the twin spheres of flesh which rose in such a pronounced fashion from the narrow curve of Celina's waist. 'Maybe I could ease your wounds.' Her voice, when it came out, was rather thick and breathless.

'Yes, that would be nice. We have no ointment, only a little oil.'

'Very well.' Like a sleepwalker, Allegra fetched the oil and warmed a little in her palms. Even when she shook herself to recollect her virtue, she reassured her conscience that she owed her friend a little relief from discomfort in readiness for the next assault.

Sitting on the edge of Celina's bed, she let a little oil trickle down on to the reddened flesh. The girl flinched, but sighed when Allegra rubbed it in with the gentlest touch. Allegra's fingers slid sensuously across the soft skin, feeling the flesh give way to her probing caresses.

Soon the whole of Celina's rear was slippery with the oily emollient and still Allegra let her fingers idly wander. Some of the oil had collected in the cleft between Celina's cheeks, and scarcely knowing what she was doing, Allegra began to probe the girl's secret parts. The oil meant there was no resistance as her index finger found an orifice she had not expected to find. Feeling her friend stiffen, Allegra halted.

'No, go on,' Celina gasped.

Ever so gently, Allegra penetrated the little hole, feeling herself grow powerfully excited at this surprising conquest. The effect on Celina was electrifying. Her thighs drifted ever wider and now Allegra could see the reddish hair and swollen lips of her vulva as the girl uncontrollably lifted her rear to get ever more pleasure from that single stiff digit. With her other hand, Allegra reached out to explore the more familiar slit which opened below. It was no surprise that the whole area shuddered and gaped.

Allegra barely knew what it was she wanted to do; just the sight and scent of the girl overwhelmed her senses. Still teasing the little orifice with one finger, she began to probe gently to find another. The lips were hot to the touch and sensitive to the slightest brush of her fingers. A wail of gratification erupted from Celina. At last she found it, and stiffening her fingers, began to thrust them in unison with the other. The girl was in ecstasy now, meeting her thrusts with her grinding hips, soaking her fingers with the unctuous honey released by her body.

'Yes, please don't stop – oh, faster, faster.'

Allegra obeyed, driving her fingers like short, sharp pistons into the girl's twin entrances The result came quickly. With a series of panting breaths, Celina pushed herself down on the two sources of pleasure, faster and faster, until Allegra felt a great muscular grip squeeze her fingers again and again. In her spasm of bliss Celina cried out hoarsely, groaning with the violence of her release.

With a great sigh, the girl relaxed, trembling slightly from the force of her deliverance. 'Please,' she sighed, 'let me kiss your very centre. I want to drive my tongue to your very soul.'

Turning over, she reached up to help Allegra undress. Too dazed by lust, too swollen herself by the blood pounding through her veins, Allegra could no longer resist. She too ardently needed release. She too craved the probings of the girl's sensitive fingers and tongue. Sitting on the bed as the naked girl pulled off her kerchief, Allegra had only one thought in her head: physical satisfaction. Rabidly, the pair both pulled at her unwieldy clothing, dragging at her laces, uncovering her hungry flesh.

So when the knock rapped out loudly on the door, Allegra was too dazed to hear it. It was Celina who whipped on her shift and struggled over to open it. At the door stood Sister Ino. With a shock of recollection, Allegra heard her speak of the time having arrived for punishment. Guiltily, she watched Celina. But Celina crossed back to the bed and took her hand.

'I am sorry,' Allegra whispered to her dear friend, almost choking with regret.

'What do you mean? You must go at once. It is I who am sorry for you.'

'Why?' Allegra felt she might be waking from a dream to find herself living in a nightmare.

'It is you who must go with Sister Ino. She has come to fetch you for your punishment.'

Chapter Six

*A*lmost fainting with fear, Allegra followed Sister Ino down to the convent chapel. At times, she wondered if her legs would carry her any further as she leant against the walls of the corridor for strength. Terror gripped her as fiercely as a fever, leaving her dazed and breathless. She longed to escape, but did not even have the strength to try.

'Get along, now,' the terrifying nun ordered, reaching to grasp her wrist and drag her onwards. Flinching, she struggled to be free of the woman's touch.

'No,' she whispered hoarsely. 'I will walk alone.' As much staggering as walking, she reached the ornate room behind the novice's chapel. At the far end, Sister Ino pulled a second curtain to one side, revealing a steep flight of stone steps leading downwards into the depths of the earth.

'Down there?' breathed Allegra. 'I do not think I can.'

'Stupid girl,' the nun snapped. 'Get down there.'

With a shove to her back, Allegra began the long descent, feeling as if she were dropping down into a dark well. After a few terrified moments, she saw that every score of steps a flame burnt low in a wall sconce, but between these, she had to feel her way down from each step with her toes. With her fingers spread wide along the surface of the cold wall, she did her best to steady herself in the gloom. Behind her, the stout sister grew impatient and jabbed her back and shoulders to make her hurry.

After what seemed almost half the night, Allegra reached the flat solidity of a dead end. With a sudden shove, the stout nun reached past her and pushed a heavy door. Beyond lay the glimmer of candlelight and the sensation of people moving in a large room.

It took some while for Allegra to adjust her eyes. What she saw did not calm her nerves at all. She was in a large and high chamber, painted in the rough, colourful manner of a pagan temple or ancient cave. Where there might have been a figure of Christ on the altar wall there was instead a vast figure of a woman dressed in a thin, revealing toga. In her outstretched hands was what appeared to be a bundle of twigs. Beside her was a life-sized crucifix, oddly striking in that it appeared to be standing upside down. Allegra did not recognise the cold, disdainful gaze of the icon from any book of saints she knew.

The large fresco was illuminated with a mass of waxen candles, so the sharp features and fair hair of the holy woman, if that was what she was, flickered and shifted in an oddly lifelike fashion. Below her sat the Prioress and most of her order, all shrouded in black and obviously expectant of their arrival. With a final harsh shove, Sister Ino propelled her to the centre of the room.

'So, Sister Almoro. We meet again.' There was the slightest lilt of laughter in the old woman's voice. The rest of her company appeared also to watch her with a measure of amused detachment. There were males as well as females in the group, of various ages and ranks. The handsome Abbot could also be seen, observing her wryly, among younger, fresh-faced priests.

'Let me recall,' the Prioress announced exultantly. 'Was it not you, our new Sister, who begged to be judged? Who claimed she was better than her companions? Who wished to be tested? Well,' and here the old crone's eyes shone with twinkling venom, 'tonight we will test your resolve.'

The flesh around Allegra's heart constricted so tightly, she felt she could hardly breathe. She spun around to escape, but the formidable Sister Ino stood guard by the only door.

'Come forward. Let us see you.'

Quaking, Allegra shuffled forward.

'Your dress is in some disarray, is it not? Now why, pray, is that?'

It was true, for half of Allegra's laces hung open and her shoulders and chest were bare where the kerchief had gone astray.

'I was preparing for bed,' Allegra mumbled.

'I cannot hear. You must indulge an old woman. We have an aid to make you speak a little clearer. Step on to the birching block if you please.'

Wild-eyed, the girl looked about her. Between herself and the gathered assembly stood a carved block of solid wood. In the centre of the surface was a pointed promontory, like the sloping back of a settle. She had no idea what it was.

'I don't understand,' she whimpered.

With a loud sigh, the Prioress turned to a figure waiting quietly at the side of the room. 'Domica, help the girl.'

At this, the figure approached Allegra. Although dressed in the dark habit of the order, the figure wore a mask of black velvet, such as the Venetians wear at carnival time. This made Allegra yet more fearful. Suddenly, she realised what it was that the block of wood reminded her of – the grim blood-blackened wood of an executioner's block. And this figure, although garbed like a sanctified nun, also wore a mask like one of the State's official executioners. As the figure grasped her arm, Allegra screamed.

70

'Do not fear,' the figure whispered secretly into her ear. 'You will bear it.'

Only slightly less alarmed, Allegra allowed herself to be led to the block. Flinching, she noticed a pail of liquid by the side of the block wherein stood several bundles of birch twigs. Terror of the pain to come gripped her. It was only with the mysterious Domica's help that she was placed in a kneeling posture, with her upper body bent over the promontory of wood.

'Now that you are a little more comfortable, perhaps you can tell your sisters how your dress came to be disarrayed?'

Allegra was closer to the Prioress now, and recognised from her easy tone that this was to be some kind of preamble to an habitual, ritual punishment. Desperately, she wondered for how long she might be able to spin out the time. 'I was preparing for bed,' she announced in a stronger voice.

'For whose bed?' At this, there was the sound of gentle tittering from the rest of the group.

'For my own,' Allegra asserted.

'You lie. Domica, inspect the subject.'

At this, the girl felt the masked figure reach behind her and try to lift her skirts. Twisting around, Allegra struggled to shake her off.

'Domica. Brother Guillam. The restraints.'

The next moment Allegra found herself held in two sets of strong arms and pushed forward across the little hill of wood. First her wrists and then her ankles were seized, and bound in leather straps which neatly slid through metal rings attached to the birching block for that purpose. Frantically, Allegra pulled on the restraints, but they held her as tightly as a dog in harness. She was kneeling on the block, with her upper half held bent across the stepped back of the block. Her head hung down, facing the company of clerics, with her wrists closest to them in the bands of leathers. Her ankles were held slightly apart in similar straps. She was

71

completely helpless, at the mercy of this strange sister-hood whose violent rites of gratification she could barely imagine. The two figures moved back behind her as she stared at the Prioress with heartfelt fury.

'I ask again, inspect the subject.'

This time, as her skirts were lifted, Allegra could do nothing but pull despondently on the restraints and look with eyes like daggers at the loathsome perpetrator of this indignity. She could feel the woman Domica care-fully pin her skirts up above her waist. The effect upon the victim was to produce a burning paroxysm of shame.

'What do you find?'

In a gesture of supreme humiliation, Allegra felt the nun known as Domica slide her fingers between Alle-gra's bare cheeks. With a rapid gesture she found the girl's secret entrance and slipped a finger in and out. 'She is damp.'

'And what is your opinion, Brother Guillam?'

Allegra almost exploded with anger as the young priest now pried into her flesh as well. 'How dare you!' she screamed. 'This is defilement; may you all be witness to my violation!'

But again, it was no use. The restraints allowed her virtually no movement. Although they did not hurt at all, they were effective in keeping her tightly bound in only one undignified position. As the priest's more stubby hand slipped into the warm liquid at her centre, she felt him spread his fingers in seeming delight, probing her sex with a sensuous, caressing touch.

'She is indeed damp and ready,' the priest reported in a surprisingly cool, detached voice.

'Very well,' the Prioress continued. 'Let the charges be stated.'

It was Sister Ino who read the charges, and read them with delight.

'The sister known as Almoro is charged with the following offences. That she did, on her first night in this institution, take carnal pleasure with the sister known as

Celina or rightly as Dorico. That she was herself lewd and lascivious is proved against her. On the second day of her habitation here, she was found, by myself, to be spying upon the youth Luca as he stripped to a state of complete undress. That her intentions were again of a lewd nature was made clear by the abandoned posture I discovered her in. Later that night she did again inflict carnal pleasure of a most unrefined manner upon the novice Celina known as Dorico. Only my own interruption at their room prevented her from further indulging in her craving for lustful satisfaction.

'Finally, the above offences are greatly magnified by one single fact. She does not accept her own nature. She is in a state of rebellion against every instinct of her body. So, to the charge of lewdness, I add the far greater offence of hypocrisy. In complaining to us of the wickedness of Sister Dorico, she intentionally acted as a hypocrite and liar. In accusing others she tries to make herself appear good. Her soul is at war with her flesh. This is the charge I make.'

Throughout this speech Allegra's jaw dropped with astonishment. How did they know these things? Furious as she was, a glimmer of recognition twinkled in her mind as she listened to Sister Ino's description of herself. And yet, and yet – she tried so hard to be good. There was still within her the capacity to withstand all of this, she knew it.

'What do you say to the charges?' The Prioress eyed her with disdain.

'I deny them,' she shouted.

'You what?' The Prioress was truly enraged. 'It will be the worse for you if you do not confess.'

'I do not care,' Allegra spluttered. 'You are all wicked, too. I have tried to be good, I know in my heart. If you punish me, it is you who do wrong.'

The company appeared to mutter reproachfully. Clutching the arms of her chair, the old woman leant

73

forward, with eyes blazing like live coals. 'So, you deny your offences? I warn you, it will be the worse for you.'

'I do,' Allegra cried, holding on to the last vestige of her pride.

'Domica. Prepare.'

For some time, Allegra lay across the block, panting with extreme fear and anger. For a while she closed her eyes, wishing with all her heart she might wake up in her narrow bed, or even back in the green luxury of her chamber in the Palazzo di Rivero. But when she opened her eyes again, she was still in the gloomy, underground chamber with the vast fresco of the enigmatic woman staring down upon her. In time, a hush fell on the room.

'Aphrodite Philomastrix, Our Lady of the Scourge,' intoned the Prioress, 'we bring before you our rebellious sister, Almoro. She has lost her way in the byways and labyrinths of untruth and hypocrisy. She is misled by pride and self glorification. We ask that you help her to find her true nature.'

It seemed to Allegra from her position on the block that the great painted image of the Aphrodite nodded benignly.

'Sister Almoro. Do you repent?'

Again, it was anger rather than fear which flooded through her veins. She would show them her strength, for sure. 'I do not.'

'Sister Almoro. You know why you are here. I warn you, take this opportunity to repent.'

'No!'

'This is your final chance. In a moment I will instruct Domica to thrash you with the birch upon your naked flesh. I have calculated the punishment to represent each of your offences, multiplied by the further offences of mutiny and pride. The total number of lashes you will receive is twelve.'

The company around the Prioress muttered at this. The victim herself could hear Domica gasp at the decreed

74

total of lashes. Suddenly fear raised its worm-like head again, but Allegra swore to herself she would prevail.

'Do you, for the very last time, repent of your offences? Do you beg Our Lady of the Scourge to be spared the gift of chastisement?'

'No!'

'Very well. It will be the worse for you. You will receive twelve good lashes on your bare buttocks. They will leave a mark by which you may remember this foolhardy act of pride. Head down! Lie still! Domica, the birch!'

In a frenzy of fearful expectation, Allegra did as she was bid. Holding her breath, she waited. A loud swish filled the air, and she tensed her muscles for the impact. Then a loud crack split the air. Pain engulfed her, almost forcing a howl from her throat. But she withstood it. Again, the high pitched hiss rose in the air. Again, there was the burning agony of contact. By the third stroke, her eyes were running with water, her face screwed up against the hard wood. How could she bear any more? Now she could feel the stripes rising in ridges on her flesh. The thought entered her mind that she might do anything to save herself from more pain. Then she gritted her teeth with hatred for the Prioress and told herself to be stronger.

The fourth and fifth strokes fell like molten rods. At the sixth, a cry mixed of pain and affront rose to her lips which only the greatest self-control succeeded in stifling. At last there was a pause. To her surprise, Allegra found that once the birch ceased, much of the pain ceased too. It smarted well enough, but in a more diffused, tingling fashion.

'Well,' said the old woman. 'Now you have tasted the pleasures of the birch, do you repent?'

Could she take any more? After half the allotted strokes she had been close to begging for mercy. And yet – only half were now left. Perhaps she could leave the chamber still with her head held high.

'Very well. I interpret your silence as continued mutiny. Brother Guillam. Administer six lashes at once.'

This time as Allegra tensed, it was not the thrash of the birch she felt first. Instead, the young priest reached forward and gently centred her buttocks to achieve a better aim. There was something about his caressing manner which again reminded her of his indelicate exploration of her sex. She judged the young priest was not averse to his role – indeed, quite the opposite. He had not hurt her, only brushed across the reddened surface of her flesh like a harmless flame.

When his first blow fell, Allegra realised that the woman Domica had indeed spared her the worst. With a crash the bundles of birch twigs fell and this time only the leather restraints held her in place. Without them, Allegra would have instinctively fled like a scalded cat. But again those softly intrusive fingers guided her throbbing rear back into place. Only this time, as he departed, he could not resist a sensual flicker downwards to the readily parted lips below.

In spite of the pain, Allegra flushed yet more at this casual transgression. The thrashing by the woman Domica had been light and oddly neutral. Now, as Brother Guillam lifted his arm to chastise her, he heard a deep groan emerge from his chest. Secretly, she knew it was not a response to physical effort, but to deep, choking lust. Almost playfully, she wriggled her bottom, so he had to break off his duty and grasp her flesh between his hands. His breath was fast and uneven; he seemed to knead her cheeks as he pushed them down into place. Again, as the birch fell, a tortured groan escaped from his lungs.

Three strokes remained. Her skin burnt now, like molten flame. But the worst of the agony was countered by her overwhelming awareness of the young priest's appetite. Now she wanted him to want her, indeed wished she could command him to kiss and lick the painful results of his labours. Secretly, she guessed he must be wildly throbbing beneath his robe, struggling in a private agony of violent lust. Again, she wiggled the fleshy target of his rod, feeling the power of her sex smiting him down.

Unnerved, he put the rod down and reached out with both his hands to hold her still. She could hear him panting as he grasped her thighs, pushing his thumbs into the warm flesh, leaning against her as if he desperately wanted to throw himself on to the block too and summarily mount her fiery rump.

'What is it?' the Prioress barked impatiently. 'Why do you delay?'

'She will not stay still,' Brother Guillam protested, his voice cracked and hoarse. 'I believe she is playing the wanton.'

'Ah,' the old woman cried. 'Then finish your task, for I have another idea for our spirited Sister Almoro. Get along now, administer the twelve.'

With some trouble still, the young priest administered a further lash. As the last one was about to fall, again Allegra moved, jutting her rear towards him, so she guessed he might be once again smitten by desire. Unable to control himself this last time, he grasped her by the parting at her thighs and pushed her back towards the block. In doing so, unseen by the others, his broad fingers pushed hard inside her, penetrating her most secret entrance. So it was with a shiver of excitement that she felt the last blow fall and the pain seemed to mingle with her pleasure in a seething cauldron of arousal.

'Now, let her kiss the rod,' the old woman commanded.

As she still knelt in bondage, the young priest stood before her, with the harsh birch rod in his hands. 'Kiss it,' he murmured.

Stretching forward, Allegra raised her heavy, lust-filled eyes. 'I should rather it was your rod I kissed,' she whispered. And as her lips met the brittle collection of birch twigs, she looked at his face and saw there, too, the flush of stifled carnality and eagerly parted, gasping lips.

'Brother Guilllam, stand before us now.' Reluctantly, it seemed, the young priest left his victim's side and presented himself to the gathered company. 'I have a fancy,' the voice continued, 'that you are not of such a continent nature as your priesthood would suggest.' Again, there seemed to be the suggestion of a snigger from some of those who listened. 'Would I be correct in saying you took pleasure in this grave duty?'

The young man shook his head, but did not speak.

'It is proved easily enough. Lift your robe.'

Shaking his head again, the young priest backed away, horrified at the Prioress's command.

'In the name of Our Lady Philomastrix, lift your robe.'

Slowly and with great reluctance, Brother Guillam raised the hem of his robe. Straining her neck, Allegra tried to watch the scene. Unmistakably, she saw the silhouette of a stiff and ready phallus rising from the pit of Brother Guillam's stomach. A collective murmur of reproach and excitement spread through the watching group. The young priest emitted a sigh of despair.

'Do not be dejected, our beloved Brother. For Our Lady has suggested to me a test, by which we might examine your control of the flesh. Do you beg to be forgiven?'

Throwing himself on his knees, Brother Guillam groaned that he would do anything to prove himself worthy again.

'Very well. Domica. In a few moments I will ask you to administer twelve loving strokes to the buttocks of this, our beloved brother. Guillam, meanwhile you must prove your mastery of the lust which this young girl has aroused within you. For the duration of the beating, you must copulate with this girl, but at all times demonstrate your complete control. At the end of the beating, you must not have spilt a drop of semen. Do you understand?'

78

'Yes, I do.'

'Only if you can exhibit such complete self-denial will I allow you to wear again your priestly garb. If you should spill yourself, you will be defrocked this night.'

'Thank you. I will not fail.'

'Very well. You may prepare.'

As Allegra listened, she could scarcely believe the words she heard. Again, anger fuelled her to struggle against her bonds. This was outrageous; she was being used as no more than a receptacle to test the youth's self-mastery. It was the ultimate height of mortification.

'How dare you,' she began, but before her haranguing could continue, the Prioress had interrupted her.

'Domica, the gag.'

Before she could do any more than wail in indignation, a thick leather strap had been wound about her mouth and quickly fastened at the back. Not a sound could emerge from her stifled mouth. The feeling of helpless vulnerability was complete. As the priest moved behind her, she felt like a trussed animal, held rigid on the block. The indignity of her position, with her rear exposed by the pinned-up petticoat seemed to her complete.

But next she found that the priest and nun were adjusting the straps which held her ankles. With two sharp movements her legs were pulled wider apart, exposing the soft, vulnerable inside of her lips. Unable to protest, Allegra could only whimper at the shame of it, knowing the priest must be eyeing her stretched labia with lust-engorged senses. At last it seemed all was ready. Domica lifted the birch and behind her Brother Guillam swung on to the block, kneeling behind her.

With a sudden tender gesture, he stroked Allegra's hair. 'Forgive me,' he murmured. 'For I would not choose to despoil you.' Then, turning to the Prioress, he asked, 'Is she not virgin?'

'In flesh she may be, but not in spirit.' The old woman sounded bored. 'And for certain if you do not climax, she will still be untainted. But if you cannot restrain yourself, then you must bear that as well on your conscience.'

'I understand.'

Allegra was aware of the heat of his body pressing against her. With a sudden movement he lifted his arms and pulled off the priestly robe. Now she could feel his firm flesh, warm and sensual against her burning skin. Gasping for breath now, he edged forward.

'I shall try not to hurt you,' he whispered. At this she felt for the first time the rounded head of his cock nudge against her gaping thigh. It felt large and heavy and stickily damp. Uncontrollably, she rolled her head to one side, gasping with delight. It was bumping against the soft skin of her thigh, teasing her with its promise of complete gratification. With a suppressed moan, he grasped his own pendulous flesh in his hand and aimed it at the girl's entrance. He pushed as gently as he could; the sweet wetness of her cleft guided him until he found what he sought. Meanwhile Allegra felt her heartbeat race as if she were reaching the end of a long and arduous race. Instinctively, she tilted herself backwards to receive him, but still his girth held him back from an easy entrance. The sensation of the smooth, round end of his flesh pressing only a finger's breadth inside her made her swoon with pleasure.

'To enter, I must anoint myself at your fountain,' he murmured, and began to rock slightly back and forth, so the swollen head became wet and slippery. Gagged as she was, and held helpless, Allegra could barely tolerate the waves of rapture engulfing her sex. If he had set out to tease her to the edges of ecstasy, he could not have done better. The head of his weapon was slowly working across her swollen lips, her throbbing bead of pleasure, and back again to the rim of her entrance. Very, very slowly, he eased the blood-engorged member deeper inside her, stretching her passage around it in a deliciously satisfying manner. Soon she could feel the swollen head inching its way inside her, nudging and tormenting her until she whimpered into the leather gag with frustration.

'Are you not ready yet?' the Prioress barked impatiently.

'Almost,' the priest grunted. 'She is unused to penetration.'

'Then push and be done with it.'

Gasping for breath, that was all the priest could do. Getting a firm hold of Allegra's waist, he leant forward and thrust the wide swelling of his phallus hard inside her. The effect was like spark to tinder. Suddenly Allegra felt herself pushed hard against the immovable force of the birching block. Then she could travel no further. The stiff rod drove its bulky way hard into her being, further and faster than she had ever imagined anything ever could. Closing her eyes, she felt herself hang there, with her sex upended, almost lifted aloft by the length of the priest's stiffened member.

'Domica. Begin.'

As she heard the first of Domica's harsh lashes against the priest's bare buttocks, he began to ride her with cool assurance. As his long rod thrust back and forth, Allegra tumbled into a fiery dreamworld behind her closed eyes. She could feel the full engorged girth of the thing, rubbing back and forth, torturing her senses to the limit. One second she could feel the bulky head ramming against the very depths of her stomach, the next it silkily withdrew, almost to the tip, before see-sawing back, again and again. She was only vaguely aware of the sound of the birch, although on its impact each time he dug deeper and deeper into her rapidly pliant flesh. Now, as he filled her, she became aware of the complete length of his flesh, titillating the very gates to her womb with the hard pressure of his tip. Each time this happened, she heard him stifle his breath, desperate not to climax inside her.

Now that her entire passage was slippery and yielding,

Allegra felt the urgency spread through her loins to climax. The thing inside her was turning her most delicate nerves to fire, stoking her muscles to squeeze every drop of satisfaction from his bulging rod. With an instinctive loss of control, she began to thrust backwards on to it, driving herself back and forth onto his cock like a wild harlot.

'No,' he whispered wretchedly, 'keep still! You make me wild. Any second I'll shoot my seed.'

Hardly able to control herself, Allegra froze. She was shivering on the edge of climax, her nerves tormented by his ceaseless pounding, back and forth. Like a raging poker, he stoked on and on, slapping into her dripping entrance. Suddenly it was too late – she felt her inner muscles begin to tighten, gripping the vein-ribbed length of his member. With a desperate gasp of abandonment, her pelvis began to spasm around him. But it was too late. At that moment the last blow from the birch fell and with heartfelt relief he pulled his agonised member out of its honeyed nest.

Allegra wanted to scream. She had been only a second away from full womanly satisfaction. If they had been alone, she knew that he too would have been unable to resist the powerful spasm and would have emptied his flood inside her aching womb. If they had been alone, she would have thrown herself at him, licking and rubbing him until he begged her on his knees to let him continue. Miserably, she buried her head against the hard wood and cursed.

Around her, she was aware of Brother Guillam's feat being applauded. Glancing up, she could see through tear-filled eyes his crimson posterior and the even redder bulge of his stiffened wand, dancing above his hairy stomach. In time, he was allowed to dress once more in his priest's garb and slowly it seemed that the throng dispersed.

Soon, only Domica remained, and she set to unloosing Allegra's bonds.

'You poor creature,' she soothed. As Allegra stiffly rose from the block, she felt her body ache with both ill treatment and unsatisfied passion. 'Would you like me to soothe you?' the masked nun asked, holding out her arms. 'I will soon help you feel better.'

Allegra guessed what she meant. No. She had experienced enough of their games and their violent rites of satisfaction. She felt weak and very tired. 'If you please,' she said humbly, 'I only wish to be shown to my bed.'

Chapter Seven

The next day, Allegra dutifully followed the other novices as they carried out their tasks. In the morning they sewed for the poor, sitting in a high, airy room next to the chapel. Allegra listened to the other girls' idle chatter and found it soothing, so ragged and fretful were her own innermost thoughts. The lofty walls of simple, white plaster soothed her mind, as the girls gathered beneath a modest image of the Virgin, so different in character from the strange figure of the Aphrodite she had puzzled over the previous night.

After a simple lunch of barley broth and sweet bread, the novices were given leave to go outside to harvest the lavender from the fields by the shore. Each girl was issued with a large straw hat to save her complexion and, with cotton gloves to protect their hands, they ventured out into the summer heat.

'Are you no longer speaking to me?' It was Celina, who had kept back from her all day, only giving her occasional sorrowful looks as their eyes met across the sewing room.

'Of course I am. I am distracted, that's all.'

They walked together down the path, falling back a little from the others.

'I wanted to ask how you are. After last night.'

At first, Allegra could not answer. Indeed, when she recalled the bizarre events in the underground chamber, she could barely credit their really having happened. 'It was strange,' was all she said, after a long pause. 'Very strange. Listen, why did you not tell me more about this strange cult of Aphrodite the sisters follow?'

'Shh! It must not be spoken of. I told you there was a secret.' Celina lowered her voice confidentially. 'The Philomastrix is only another name for their Santa Agnetha, but they do take her worship very seriously. If I had told you, you would never have believed me.'

'That's true. It is certainly a strange set of beliefs.'

Celina took her friend's arm companionably. They were entering the cool, speckled greenness of the woods. 'Allegra, it may be a harsh way, but their hearts are well intentioned. They truly believe it is a hard road to achieve goodness. It may not be our way, but their tests are honestly designed to scrutinise the innermost workings of our spirits.'

Allegra looked at the calm and placid face of her friend. For her, it seemed life truly was so simple. 'But what about you, Celina? You and I have enjoyed ... pleasures together. How can you bear your shame?'

'What shame? I do not aspire to be a nun, or even a respectable woman. Why die a respectable woman and never have experienced any real fun? I am here by way of circumstance. It is you who have all these high ideals.'

They were silent for a while, as they followed the path through the woods. Celina stooped to pick some wild flowers and then wound them with grasses to form little posies of pink and blue and violet flowers. Laughing, she caught up with Allegra to pin a posy to her dull brown costume. 'Let me rather be a vain little starflower, who enjoys the sun and then fails, than one of your stiff and prickly thistles who lives on and on and on. I should die of boredom.'

'Is that what you think of me? A thistle?'

'Well, you are rather prickly,' Celina laughed. 'Do you never just want to give in and be happy and carefree?'

Allegra stroked the little nosegay pinned at her breast. The petals were exquisite shades, as lovely as any jewel. 'I do not know,' she answered. 'I have never really thought.'

Eventually, they found the others in one of the large fields by the shore. Already some of the novices had begun their work, stooping to slice away branches of tall lavender spikes. Later, these would be spread in the ovens to dry, in readiness for hanging inside the convent through the long, stale winter months. The girls, in their broad-brimmed hats moved gracefully at their work, and soon the air was sweet and heavy with the balmy fragrance of the herbs. Again, as she immersed herself in the simple work of cutting the boughs and loading the scented spikes on an old cart, Allegra felt herself regain some of her former peace.

The afternoon seemed to last forever; the air grew softer and wore a hazy burnish of gold. Conversation ceased; the only sounds were the snap and rustle of the herbs and the buzzing complaints of droning bees who puzzled at the disturbance of their familiar crop. After some hours, Allegra found an area of soft ground next to Celina, and together they stretched their tired limbs in the last of the golden sunshine.

'Would it not be bliss to go bathing tonight? The water will still be deliciously warm.' Celina kept her eyes dreamily to the front of her, as if she were addressing no one in particular.

'Where?'

'Out by the shore is the most perfect little island. Tonight there will be a full moon. Shall we go together?'

'I don't know,' began her friend. 'I cannot say, I seem to have broken so many rules already. What would happen if we were caught?'

'How do I know? Very well, we may be punished, but

it would be worth it. What is a punishment in return for a lovely moonlight dip. Especially after such a warm day. Are you not dry and dusty?'

Indeed she was, and the prospect of a dip was certainly enticing. Only there was the other view all the time – would she be letting her better nature down? And what if the sisters were to find out – surely she would deserve yet more punishment again?

'I am, but that does not mean I will go with you,' Allegra said carefully. For a while she watched her friend as she stretched out languorously on her stomach. Celina really was as much of a temptation as one of those little demons who tormented the saints in the paintings displayed in the churches on saints' days. Though she certainly was not ugly – quite the opposite indeed, with her soft creamy skin and plump little lips. Quite artfully, Celina kicked up her legs in the air, showing a long length of knitted stocking and an inch or two of bare flesh above the knee. She really is scandalous, Allegra decided.

'I am going back in,' Allegra announced. 'No, no need for you to stir yourself. I need a little time alone in the chapel.' Seeing the beginning of a sulk form at Celina's mouth, she added, 'There is no need to be upset. You forget, I still want to be a nun, or at least try to be one. If you are truly my friend, you will not oppose me, will you?'

Celina shook her head smiling. 'Get along then,' she teased, laying back in the grass. 'And I will stay here, as idle as the lilies of the field.'

'I'll see you here later?'

Celina nodded as her friend quickly squeezed her hand. But before Allegra even reached the main building one of the other novices came rushing up to her.

'There is a letter for you, Sister Almoro. It arrived just now with the boatman.'

She could not imagine who might wish to write to her here. Her immediate family were no longer on this earth, and her guardian and his son had seemed to find her departure little enough of a trial. Curious, rather than concerned, she made her way to the little grille at the convent parlour. The letter waited there for her, in the care of one of the older sisters. Allegra stared at the ivory parchment and scarlet seal. She could not think who might write to her with such pomp.

Noticing the prying looks of the nun, she decided to take it back to her room. Only once she was sitting sedately on her bed, well away from the inquisitive eyes of others, did she carefully inspect the missive.

Her first observation, on inspecting the seal, was that it was loose. Closer scrutiny showed that the seal had already been broken and then hastily sealed again to disguise the breach. What was this? Did they really believe it was right to interfere with her private things? Her fingers shook as she pulled the letter open.

It was from a Signor Bartolemeo, a notary of the Castille district of Venice. Within a few eloquent lines he had explained to Allegra that her guardian had recently died of a low fever; for reasons of public health the funeral arrangements had been speedy and he had only this week succeeded in locating her whereabouts. Now, Signor Bartolemeo wished to explain the terms of her guardian's will.

In summary, the Palazzo di Rivero and almost all of its contents, the estates in the country and the title of Senator were all to pass to Leon. The only mention of herself in the will was the acknowledgement of her dowry, which the notary understood was now signed over to the Prioress of the convent of Santa Agnetha, and one small bequest. The personal bequest, which was described as a sentimental gift, amounted to the contents of her guardian's private study at the Palazzo di Rivero. He understood it to contain a number of rare and unusual books and paintings. He now awaited her further instructions.

'I cannot believe it,' Allegra muttered to herself again

and again as she read and re-read the paper. Her dutiful sympathies of course went out to her guardian, who had always appeared to be a strong and vigorous man – but the indignity of his bequest! He must have written such a thing only to vex her; there could be no other reason. Was it not enough that he had shut her away in this strange, unholy place, without continuing to laugh at her like this, from the very grave?

Allegra felt the blood in her veins boil. All the heat of the day, the close air and beating sun seemed at that moment to oppress her. Her skin flushed red with fury; she could barely breathe. No, there had to be some way to strike back. He would not badger her in this way.

The question was what instructions she could possibly give to the earnest Signor Bartolemeo. For a while she frowned, then collected some writing implements and began. Back in the privacy of her room she carefully described in writing exactly what course of action the notary was to take. With a sense of satisfaction, Allegra delivered the missive to the nun at the convent grille that same evening and asked that it be conveyed with direct haste to the city.

Her immediate duty done, Allegra wandered back through the gardens in search of Celina. It was indeed an enchanted evening; the sun was sinking like molten gold among pillows of violet and amber clouds. The air was still warm and heavy, though purple shadows now lengthened beneath the black towers of cedars. All of nature seemed sleepy and contented: the insects droning happily over the water, the wild flowers drooping like nodding children. And there, amid all this loveliness, lay Celina, contentedly sleeping in a bower of summer grasses.

Allegra sank down beside her, watching her smooth face for signs of waking. Indeed, she looked like a woodland dryad, slumbering after a wild hunt with Pan through the forest. Her hair had become tousled in the sunshine and tangles of grass and seeds stuck to her dress. It was a face and form that would suit an archer's bow at her waist, an ancient linen toga and garlands of flowers across her brow. Smiling, Allegra chastely kissed her nose.

'Do I now wake to find a hundred years have passed?' Celina murmured, her eyes blinking open.

'Why, do you feel an enchantment wearing off?'

'No. I swear I feel one beginning. I am glad you are here at last. Let us be off.'

With this she was up and away, dragging Allegra after her, pelting down to the ocean's edge. Halting by the tumbling waves, Celina pointed up to the huge harvest moon. Although the sun had barely set across the sea, already the moon cast a baleful silver light across the waves. In the endless violet of the sky, the first stars were blinking, like diamonds scattered across the dusk.

'Does it not make your heart ache? If only we could swim out far, far away to some magical other world.'

'The only magical world we might find out there is that one.' Allegra pointed back to the mainland. In the far distance, at the very edge of sight, there was a misty glow reflected in the blackness of the water. 'Is that really the city, shining at night?'

Celina turned from the glowing disc of the moon and peered into the darkness. 'It is indeed, for at night when the city wakes, all the ships are guided into port by torches burning on the quay. And all around the Doge's palace flambeaux are kept alight to defend his grace from assassins. Maybe we could swim out to see it.' At this she began to pull off her dusty gown, letting the skirts and petticoats drop on the sand. In nothing but her corset and shift, she waded through the edges of the water, splashing the spray up to her knees. 'Come on, it's so wonderfully cool. Get your boots off and feel the sea run through your toes.'

Enviously, Allegra watched Celina wade deeper and deeper, lifting her shift up in bunches around her thighs. The leather corset pinched Celina's waist in tightly, so the voluptuous spheres of her buttocks curved roundly below, moving gracefully as she waded. Watching the shift grow damp and transparent, Allegra felt a sharp flame of tenderness ignite in her breast.

'What about your clothes?' she shouted nervously.

'Very well,' Celina pronounced and, running back to the shore in a great splash of spray, grasped her friend's hands like an over-excited puppy. 'Come on, help me.' As she proffered the cords on her corset for her friend to unlace, Allegra slowly set to helping her. With a welcome creak, the heavy stays unloosed, and the compressed flesh below was released. Standing only in her wet shift, for a moment Celina hesitated, looking back at the sombre shadow of the convent buildings. But next moment, with the moonlight reflecting on every curve, she stood naked on the sand, looking soft and vulnerable, like a smooth pink sea creature freed from its shell.

'You thought I wouldn't dare,' she taunted, slipping back into the water. Slowly the dark water lapped over her calves and knees. For a while she stood dreamily beckoning to Allegra as the waves lapped and sucked about her thighs. Against the blackness her body looked palely translucent, accentuating the curve of her stomach and pointed breasts and the waves of pale hair covering the narrow shoulders. 'Come join me,' she called, like a siren.

Again, Allegra remembered the sisters and their harsh ways, the impossible standards of goodness she never seemed to be able to attain. Suddenly a cool rivulet of water splashed against her thick boot. The barest coolness of spray soaked against her bare leg. She could see Celina's head bobbing up and down now, like a porpoise immersed in its own salty element. The waves rose and fell beneath the moonlight. To turn and leave Celina alone: it would deny some fierce and greedy part of herself that should never be suppressed.

Tearing at the laces and fastenings of her costume, Allegra threw the dull, dusty clothes on to the smooth sand and waded into the sea. The air was still warm about her skin; she was surprised by how natural it felt to be naked out of doors.

At first the water was cool, easing her swollen feet and refreshing her legs. Then it grew warmer, as mild as a bath, as the water lapped at the juncture of her thighs and body. With a small leap, she threw herself forward, sliding into the water like a gull into the air. Far ahead now, she could see the silvery back of the other girl, always skimming just out of reach.

'Celina! Just wait until I catch you.'

With a little scream, Celina sped ahead, splashing and panting like a dog in a pond. But with the long easy strokes of a natural swimmer, Allegra bound up behind her until the girl's silky foot paddled a few tantalising inches in front of her. With another laughing scream, Celina tried to struggle away but it was too late; with a hard grip Allegra grasped her friend's silky calf. In a second Celina had kicked herself free, but in the struggle that ensued Allegra once more gained a hold of her legs and this time Celina gradually lost her momentum and succumbed.

For a long moment they found themselves flung together by the tide, rising and falling on the high waves which rolled at this depth. Tenderly, Allegra held her friend safe above the surging breakers, holding her very close. Beneath the water she felt as slippery as an eel as she still tried to struggle and continue the chase.

'Stop it,' Allegra whispered. 'Let us roll on the waves.'

Relaxing beneath Allegra's grip, Celina nestled warmly against her friend's body, their arms folding around each other and their limbs cradling around each other's legs. Side by side, they floated a while on the rolling brine, swinging up and down, until Allegra could bear it no longer and kissed the girl long and deeply on the lips. In response Celina pressed harder against her, rubbing her breasts against those of her friend and pushing against her so that more and more of their skin

92

was in smooth contact. A primitive passion arose in Allegra's loins, to possess the girl, but she did not fully know how. Reading her desire, Celina suddenly struggled away, out of her grip.

'I am off to the island. Catch me if you can.'

With a sudden plunge head first into the water, Celina disappeared. For a few anxious moments Allegra watched the dark seas rolling around her, searching for a glimpse of the fair-haired girl. Then, some dozen yards away, she saw her break the surface and, gasping for air, begin to thrash out again into the ever deeper sea. With a series of fast, gliding strokes Allegra followed her, delighting in the gliding passage of the water over her naked skin.

Again, Celina's foot danced teasingly ahead of her. But this time Allegra decided to outflank her. Moving out to the left, she pushed her muscles to their limit, speeding around Celina's splashing motion. With a swoop, she reached for her shoulders but, like a slippery eel, Celina evaded her grasp, laughing and shrieking as she swam onwards. Feeling the passionate heat of pursuit burning ever stronger, Allegra sallied forth again, driving her legs in powerful kicks and her arms circling in ever stronger and faster strokes. This time, when she reached the narrow, bobbing back of the girl, she threw herself on to her slippery back.

Barely knowing what it was she wanted to do but possess her, she buried her mouth in the soft nape of the girl's neck, clutching her waist and squeezing her open legs against her plump rear. Surrendering, Celina let her friend fondle her breasts. The nipples were hard and stiff to the touch, driving her assailant to distraction. With a furtive movement she probed downwards over the soft swelling of her stomach to the wet fur below. Groaning with satisfaction she found the small cleft, hot and smoothly slippery, offering no resistance to her gentle fingers. Desperately, she wished they were natural sea creatures, even that nature had equipped them with contrasting organs of sex. Then she might take Celina fiercely as she was now and be done in a few seconds of violent attack.

'The island,' Celina breathed, her voice choked with playful excitement. 'Come on, I will show you.'

There on the horizon, like the dark shape of a slumbering whale, lay a solitary block of stone rising out of the water. Hurrying through the water, hand in hand, the two girls glided towards the hard rock. At the furthest side was a ledge, which with some effort they could reach from the water and thenceforth clamber on to the barren rock. It was still warm from the sun's long beating, but decorated only with a few fronds of seaweed and a colony of clams clinging to the niches in the rocks.

Following Celina up on to the dark island stone, Allegra could not resist catching her once more into her arms. The chase had roused her appetite which had been left so cruelly unsatisfied the night before. But now Celina seemed oddly diffident. Crossing the rock away from her companion, she turned and stared once more at the moon. 'I would love to have been born a mermaid,' she said, 'and sit in such a lovely place with my mirror and comb.'

'That would suit you,' Allegra replied, admiring the long curve of her friend's wet hair clinging around the stiffly pointed breasts. Taking Celina's hands, she pulled her down to sit beside her on the rock. 'And many sailors, I am sure, would be enticed by you.'

Celina dropped beside her, and the moonlight glinted in her eyes so she did indeed seem a mysterious, otherworldly creature. 'But why should we bother with them?' Celina suddenly whispered, cupping her friend's face in her hands and laughing sweetly. Their kiss was long and deep and tasted of the salt of the ocean as well as their own sweet mouths. Again Allegra felt the burning need to possess the girl, and pushed her tongue in deeply to lick and probe the sensitive recesses of her mouth. She could feel her own breasts jar and jut against the girl's spiky nipples, making the blood course faster through her veins. In a sudden surge of abandonment, she reached down and cupped her own swollen breasts, rubbing them against the girl's stiff and darkened nipples. The effect was like flame to a taper; Celina seemed all at once to surrender, laying back with her hips arched high as Allegra straddled her jutting pubis.

Greedily, Allegra eyed the delights of her friend's craving body – the straining back which pushed up the twin tips of her tender breasts, the opening rift where the reddish hair parted to reveal aching, hungry lips. With trembling fingers she caressed these delights, squeezing the hard buds of Celina's breasts until she moaned with pleasure, massaging the sensitive pit of her stomach and finally exploring the delicious open seam of scorching flesh at her very centre.

As sensitive as a hair-trigger, the girl responded to Allegra's soft fingertips with a downward bearing movement, so ardently did she crave the full impact of satisfying touch. With a whimper of frustration, she at first clutched Allegra's hand, and then her neck, in desperation.

'Please kiss me,' she whispered, but the tug on Allegra's neck revealed she did not merely want the same ardent kissing on the mouth as she had experienced before. Instead, Allegra began to move very slowly downwards. Firstly she kissed the girl's soft and sensitive throat until she thrashed about in the grip of desire. Then each breast was slowly kissed and teased, the elongated nipples sucked until they stiffened as hard as wooden beads. Next, Allegra wriggled down to kiss Celina's stomach, her thighs and the reddish hairy pubis which now tasted of sharp salt.

In her eagerness, Celina had parted her legs as widely as she could, and for a few seconds Allegra lingered, transported by the beauty of the unfolding flower at the girl's centre – the series of shiny lips, the arched bow of pleasure and the mysterious entrance to her dark, salty

95

chamber. As her lips dropped on to the shiny skin, her friend gasped, pushing her thighs about her head. In a delirium of pleasure, Allegra worked her tongue and lips from the swelling bud of pleasure at the front of her lips to the darkening opening behind. When she flicked her stiffened tongue towards that aching chamber, she felt the girl's thighs tremble with excitement and a series of moans escape into the empty air.

Suddenly in a hoarse voice, Celina cried, 'Quick, kneel over me.' With a few struggling movements, the girl had pulled Allegra backwards so she now straddled Celina's face. Like a flame shooting into her bowels, she felt the girl ram her tongue into her own being, teasing and tormenting her with its silky surface. Rocking and groaning, she mimicked the same actions on the girl's twitching cavity, probing and jerking in unison with her tongue. It could only continue for a few more moments. Not only the bliss of probing the wonderfully sensitive gorge she was working on, but the heady delight of the girl's miraculous mouth nipping and flicking and sucking her most sensitive parts – both of these were driving Allegra towards a violent climax.

Then, all at once, she felt the girl beneath her buck and ride, pushing herself upwards on to the erect tongue, so her very sex seemed to clutch and snatch at those few inches of exquisite pleasure. As her peak ebbed away, in ever slower spasms, so did this bring Allegra to the brink of hers. As if knowing this, the tormenting tongue at her centre slowed down to a maddening, excruciating pace. Moving to her swollen bud of delight, it idly slapped against that most sensitive spot. Then, as Allegra cried out that she could bear it no longer, a pair of long fingers suddenly shot into her innermost chamber which clenched like a fist around their thrusting rhythms. With a hoarse cry she felt her body convulse in ecstasy as she thrust herself down on the deliciously spiky fingers. Then, with a sigh of relief she crept down beside Celina and they lay for a while entwined and at peace.

For a long time they lay, watching the twinkle of the stars far, far away in the heavens. Still the air was mild and pleasant, ruffling them occasionally with a mild refreshing breeze. Only as she slipped across the edge of sleep did Celina wake her. Then, like two strange mermaids thrown up from the ancient deeps, they set out into the oily blackness, their hair flowing behind them like cloaks and their fingers interlocked. By the time they scrambled up to the shore the stars had begun to fade and the moon was turning paler. Picking up the bundles of discarded, sandy clothes, they turned to the woods and the shrouded building beyond, their bodies clean and spotless and both of their hearts strangely innocent and light.

Chapter Eight

To Allegra's surprise the Prioress held the letter she had written to Signor Bartolomeo in her scrawny hand. She had been called out of the peaceful retreat of the sewing room by Sister Ino. Fearfully, she had followed the robed back of the nun down the labyrinth of corridors to the familiar doorway where the Prioress resided. Inside, candlelight glittered across the gold and jewels set around the chamber; dark faced images of saints frowned down disapprovingly upon her. Flinching, she stood before the Prioress, feeling the power of her baleful stare, as steady as Medusa turning her victim to stone. For a long time she waited, the silence chilling her to the quick of her bones.

'And what,' the aged nun finally enunciated, 'is this?'

Lost for words, Allegra's mind raced over the contents of the letter. It had been a plain and sincere response to the notary's question. With some trepidation, she tried to explain. 'The notary – sorry, Signor Bartolomeo – he wrote to me about my guardian's death. There was a bequest, you see.'

With a sharp movement of her wrist the old woman cut her short, revealing the notary's letter lying open beneath her reply.

'I see you know the situation. I am sorry then, if I have offended.' Her words trailed away to a mumble. So they intercepted her letters. Was there nothing these people left sacred to her? But any anger she felt was powerfully distilled with a strong dose of concern at what might be the consequence of yet a further misdemeanour.

'Sister Almoro,' the Prioress began, leaning back in her carved oak chair in the style of a bored teacher lecturing a recalcitrant pupil, 'whose property have you just ordered to be destroyed?'

'Why, it is mine by right,' she asserted boldly. 'The goods were left me by my guardian. They are mine by law.'

'Think again.'

With a quick motion, the Prioress cast both of the letters into the fireplace. In a sudden flare of red and yellow flame the papers ignited. Soon there were only blackened ashes fluttering on the grate.

The ensuing silence made Allegra's skin crawl. She did not want to look into the crone's gaunt face, where the two eyes burnt with zeal like those of a grand inquisitor. Her mind froze to solid ice.

'Are you stupid then, as well as proud?'

The words were like a slap in the face. Allegra felt her heart race and without time for caution, she spoke. 'I am not stupid at all, Holy Mother. I may be ignorant of your ways, but that is no crime. The gift my guardian left me was impure. To have accepted it would have been an offence to my own nature. These pictures and books – they are filth. I want nothing more to do with them.'

The old woman propped her wrinkled chin in her bony hand. Her face expressed spite compounded with amusement, even entertainment. 'But they are not yours to destroy.'

'What do you mean?'

'Only eight days ago you signed all of your worldly possessions over to my care. Undoubtedly you choose to forget. Your pride in your position certainly did not

99

leave you when your fine dress fell to the floor. This unassailable rectitude is as hard as armour, is it not, signorina? Well,' and here the Prioress smiled with loose and twisted lips, 'it is time to see what truly lies beneath.'

'What do you mean?' Allegra stuttered. 'Surely you don't want those depraved things?'

'Our sacred house,' replied the Prioress in a tone of great solemnity, 'is in need of any charitable gift, however small. It is no longer yours to destroy. I believe Santa Agnetha would cherish such largesse.'

At this, the girl lost her temper. At best there was a wilful ignorance at work here; at worst a kind of greedy duplicity. 'But it is not suitable. You do not understand.' Her voice rose to a furious shrillness. 'I will not have those things here!'

'Kneel!' the Prioress commanded, raising her palm.

Grudgingly Allegra dropped to her knees, staring at the hem of the old woman's robe with thoughts of wilful violence.

'You will never again speak to myself or any other member of this order in such a manner. You are a proud and vainglorious creature,' the voice continued above her. 'And indeed you have been sent to me to learn a harsh lesson. Almost every rule has been broken by you – humility, chastity, honesty, charity. I must indeed devise the means to correct your wayward nature. For the start, however, we must rid you of this pride.'

Glancing up with eyes narrowed with rage, Allegra listened to hear what diabolical punishment would be meted out next.

'Ah,' the woman laughed softly at her own thoughts, 'I have a wise idea. In this house there is a strict hierarchy of personages. It is obvious to all that the order of sisters is at the head of that hierarchy. By nature of your company with us, the novices have, by affinity, the next place in our little state. I would then count my personal servants, the servants of the sisters and those who keep the boats. At the very last I should place those men who do the menial work about the place. They are mere peasants from the islands, whose speech is coarse and whose manners bear little examination. They are the lowest members of our community.

'Your lesson must be to serve them – to place yourself beneath even the lowest of the low. Maybe then you will learn some humility.'

'What do you mean, to serve them?' she asked, as much curious as startled by the old nun's strange command.

'In every way. Feed them, work for them, do as they command. You can wear the outfit of a common maidservant. For one day and one night, beginning directly. Now go.'

Still puzzled, Allegra rose from the floor and with sullen grace, kissed the ring on the finger of her spiritual mistress, though in her heart she would as soon have spat upon the heavy yellow gold.

Shortly afterwards, Allegra found herself preparing the men's midday meal in their wooden hut by the fields. Inside, it was rough hewn but comfortable. Set about with wooden benches around a central table, Allegra could just see neatly covered sleeping couches set behind red chequered curtains. Against the wall a small fire burnt on a slab of stone and over this was simple cooking gear; a boiling pot and tongs and spoons. Above, a metal pipe led away the smoke, but besides this the smoke escaped through curtained windows and beyond the door to a raised veranda at the front where the men could take their ease with a view of the ocean.

She had no idea how her role had been communicated, but the two men appeared to accept her presence without any perceptible interest. As she poured them bowls of milk and cut slices from a lump of brown, ill-favoured bread, she did indeed feel a savage pricking of her pride. The situation was made worse as a result of the unflattering costume the servant Silva had fitted her with.

Unlike even the simple outfit of a novice, this dress had no dignity at all. The skirt was of a tattered red hessian that stopped high above her ankles with an apron of faded white linen. The bodice fitted her badly, pulling tight at the sleeves and low at the front, so that she looked like some kind of cheap tavern maid. The white puffed sleeves of her shift were embroidered with flowered woollen braid. Lacking even a cap, around her hair she had placed a triangle of cloth and tied it at the nape of her neck. She felt like one of the gypsy hawkers who hang about the arcades of San Marco with fortunes for sale to dupe the credulous travellers.

Nevertheless, the two men ignored her as they ate. The secret part of her wondered at this, as she brushed past them to serve at table. The one she had watched as he washed she learnt was named Luca. Close by, she could see that he was not quite the Adonis she had pictured when she had spied on him from the trees. His face was handsomely regular but unintelligent and his hands were roughly chafed by steady hard work. His companion was nicknamed Nico; he was a broad and stocky fellow with fine eyes and a head of curls like an Emperor from the old times. Occasionally, the latter pointed to articles he wanted at table and Allegra did her best to serve him with some small grace. Beyond the odd word, or the repetition of their respective names, Allegra had difficulty understanding the guttural island dialect in which they spoke.

With a haphazard signal Luca called her over. Still chewing his bread, he pointed to a jug on the trestle table by the door. But however much he pointed to the jug and uttered strange, inarticulate phrases, she could not understand what it was he wanted. To her annoyance, the two men began to laugh.

'It is not me, it is you who cannot speak properly,' she muttered.

The youth raised an eyebrow, no doubt understanding well enough the gist of what she said. With a sudden incomprehensible phrase he had the other man hooting with laughter. Red faced, Allegra glared back at them indignantly. There was no doubt she was the butt of their joke, and at last it seemed they saw her before them, eyeing her in the ludicrous, undignified costume with amused expressions. She wished she could pull a cloak on over that horribly tight bodice which left her shoulders and breasts so plumply exposed. Hotly, she felt the blush move downwards, heating her white skin like a breath of fire.

With a shrug and a few words which must have expressed his reluctant prompting to action, Luca rose and roughly seized her arm.

'Get off!' She shrugged him off and stared at him furiously.

But another quick retort to his friend reduced them once more to howling laughter. With a broad smile he bowed ironically and ushered her in front of him, suggesting she walk ahead of him outside. Still clutching the jug, she let him take her to one of the low barns where at last she saw the purpose of their expedition. Inside the low and gloomy building was a store of liquor. Expertly, he opened the tap on a large wooden cask and motioned her to fill the jug with beer.

Slowly the jug filled with frothing, splashing ale. Rising from her task, she found the youth once more watching her, this time with an eager, predatory look. Murmuring softly, he reached out and took the jug from her hand and stood before her, his face alive with attention. Suddenly Allegra wished she had never looked on him with foolish interest before. It truly made her feel ashamed to think she had ever wanted him in such an appalling manner. Towering so close above her, she was repulsed by the roughness of his skin and even the salty smell of his flesh. He seemed strange, like an untamed animal, with dusky skin and dark hairs on his powerful arms. As he reached out to touch her shoulders every particle of her flesh rejected him. With her free hand she slapped him hard on the face, so hard that her palm stung.

Shaking his head, he laughed, showing his perfect white teeth. Then rubbing his face, he looked into her eyes, making a little grimacing smile at the pain.

'Oh, I'm sorry, she murmured involuntarily. Raising his eyebrows he again looked into her eyes with a wounded, appealing expression.

'I cannot believe I have truly hurt you,' she muttered, but he in his turn, reached out to her hand and gently placed it against his warm face. It was impossible to pull away, for it was only a forgiving caress. And so she stood before him as before, as he rubbed her hand against the rough texture of his face. Then, subtly, he began to kiss her hand, turning it around so he could press his mouth to the sensitive skin at the inside of her wrist. Struggling at the new sensuality of his touch, she tried to wrest it away, but he held it firm. The worst of it was, the sensation of his lips against her skin was curiously enticing, but no more than if a dog might lick her bleeding hand. With a sudden wrench she freed herself and picked up the jug, motioning him to lead her back to the hut.

But still he was not to be deterred. As they reached the door he idly swung his arm against the door and barred her exit.

'I am getting tired of your games. Would you please let me pass?'

Playfully, he pretended to drop his arm, but as she passed he reached out for her waist. In his struggle to kiss her, she struck out desperately, losing her balance for a moment. Too late, she steadied herself and the jug of ale fell to the floor.

Still he barred the door, and pointing back to the cask, motioned her to refill the jug. Only with many loud sighs and the greatest reluctance did she once more pace over, and feeling his eyes bore into her back, lean over and open the tap once more. This time, as she bent over, she suddenly felt him come up behind her and again clasp her waist. Leaving the foaming jug once more on the floor, she struggled to get free, but this time he had her tightly around the middle and all her kicking and hitting out could not deter him. Laughing once more into her ear, he began to rub one hand across her body, feeling the shape of her narrow waist and sudden flaring ripeness of her breasts. Redoubling her struggles, Allegra twisted and turned, grappling with his exploring fingers. But with the ardour of youth he had found her breasts and with a quick shove had pulled back the braided shift, to reveal one crimson nipple overhanging the stiff cloth of her makeshift bodice. Panting a little, he began to rub this, cupping her breast and trying to kiss the exposed back of her neck.

Outraged, Allegra cried out at him to leave her alone but his ardour was raised and he seemed to be set on an irrevocable course. Fighting his every move, she tried to free herself from his intrusive lips and his fingers which kneaded her breast unmercifully. Did he really think she was just some peasant girl, to be bent over in a barn and pleasured? Well, he would have to learn the truth. Sensing an opportunity, she slowly relaxed into his arms, letting him slowly loose her other breast, so he was pinning her against the cask, massaging both her over-hanging breasts in a state of breathless excitement. Indeed, she could feel the extent of his pleasure as he pressed against her back; his manhood was a massive solid bulk pressed hard against her skirts like a ready rod of iron.

Counterfeiting a sigh of pleasure, she leant forward, suggesting by her posture he might take her there and then. Pretending to unlace her bodice, she felt him also reach down and around her to help her undress all the faster. Waiting for the right moment, she sensed his head hanging just above her own. She was ready with the jug; it was but a second's movement to swing the jug up and over her own head and on to his unprotected scalp. His yowl of pain brought Allegra only pleasure. The drenching too, amused her just as much as her struggles had entertained him. Laughing over him now, she quickly refilled the jug. Then, escaping to the open door, she watched him as he tried to wipe the beer off his soaking clothes, cursing her all the time. With a smile of satisfaction, she turned on her heels and sauntered back to the little wooden house, adjusting her clothing so that as she walked in the door, Nico might never guess they had been disarrayed.

The afternoon brought more work, for when the men returned to the fields she had the little house to clean and some vegetables to pick for the evening. Soon the elation of her victory over Luca faded as she set about her tasks. Sullenly sweeping the bare boards of the ramshackle hut, she found herself watching the youth as he tended the animals out in the fields. Occasionally he looked back at the house with an expression of hurt pride. Certainly his companion had found the sight of him soaked in beer even more amusing than the jokes he had made about her earlier. His harsh belly laughs had clearly mortified the younger man, who had no doubt boasted of his womanising skills before he had taken her to the barn.

Later, once her chores were done, she leant awhile on the rickety veranda and watched Luca carrying sacks of grain to the animals. Certainly from a distance, she was again struck by his manly beauty as his silhouette was framed by the golden sun of late afternoon. In his slow, rhythmic movements as he lifted the sacks on his back and then dropped them to the dusty red ground, she could see the rippling of his muscles beneath the bronze skin, like a living statue from the Greeks. Oddly, now, when she remembered his touch, it was not the revulsion she remembered but the frisson she had worked so hard to stifle. Why then, she puzzled, do I find him so attractive now?

In her musings, she suddenly remembered a fearsome stallion named Drusus she had known back at her family's estates in Torrinocella. As a little girl, she had hated that horse, with his rolling eyes and great stamping hooves. So great had been her fear that he had visited her nightmares, appearing as a vast, red-eyed steed from Hell, kicking her to the ground and biting her with long, sharp teeth. Then, many years later, a kind groom who had taught her to ride her own gentle mare encouraged her to take him for a gallop. With trembling legs she had waited at the mounting block, dressed in her new blue velvet riding dress and cloak.

As the massive animal trotted before her, it had taken all her courage not to jump back down and run into the house. But he had stood still enough as she waited, and finally she had grasped the pommel to mount the fine leather saddle across his back. Even as she led him at a slow trot through the archway of the park, the great nodding black head with stiff pointed ears had frightened her. It had felt like balancing on an unruly ship at sea, rushing on the storm waves rolling beneath her. But then they had reached the open grassland and she had pricked him with her heels. Oh, the joy of it! The wind had sailed through her hair, the green park had flashed by them and beneath her she had felt his powerful frame surging on and on like a bird skimming over the rolling ocean. She had loved Drusus to his death, loved his strength and speed and power. But now she remembered from what it was that devotion had sprung; it had been born in quivering fear.

Was it fear then, that had kept her back from the youth this afternoon? He had seemed strange and other worldly, like another species of creature altogether. His masculinity both excited and repelled her. If she could but surmount her fear, what then?

Leaning against the wooden veranda, she contemplated both the distant figures, for neither man was unattractive – at least from this safe distance. Nico was

107

watering the crops, stripped to his shirt and breeches, showing strong arms in the sunlight. Certainly his aloofness had been intriguing; his sardonic looks suggesting a manly pride of his own. What had the Prioress meant when she had said that Allegra must serve them in every way? The sun was dropping now towards the smoothness of the ocean. The ghost of a silver moon had appeared in the evening sky above the glimmer of the distant Alps, far away on the mainland. With a growing feeling of both apprehension and excitement, she pondered what the night would bring.

It was therefore with some disappointment that Allegra served their evening meal of boiled chicken and tomatoes from the vine. Luca would barely meet her eye; he was clearly tired and out of sorts, moodily poking his food about his plate. Nico was more cheerful, and it was he who motioned her to fill the jug with beer. Taking a lighted tallow she set off to the barn with a slow backwards glance to the youth but he, having learnt his lesson, stayed resolutely fixed at the table.

Outside, the night was warm, and Allegra lingered beneath a black shadowed tree, watching the moon shimmer across the silver ocean. Like the ceaseless waves, something stirred within her. Her memories of Celina's lovely softness mingled with this new desire for the strangeness of a man, with his different scents and shape and manner. Lost in a daydream, she did not notice soft footfalls until a dark shadow beneath the tree announced that Nico had followed her. In the dim light, she recognised the broad vigour of his frame and the dark curls trailing down to his shoulders. Reaching out to her, he took the jug, and without a word, drank deeply.

In the trembling light of the tallow, she watched the older man wipe the rim of the jug and offer her the clean edge. Hesitating for a moment, she wondered why he now offered her the drink. Then, realising that this was somehow the starting point to some age old ritual, she grasped the jug and drank deeply. The ale was sharp and strong, burning her throat as she swallowed. With a nod of satisfaction, he took it back and set the jug down firmly on the ground.

When he came to her, she was not surprised. Maybe it was the quick action of the liquor on her senses, or maybe she had glimpsed the inevitable when he laughed so heartily at the youth's bungled attempt. With supreme assurance he reached out to her and wrapped her in his warm arms. His mouth found hers and, almost insensible with suppressed excitement, she surrendered completely. Everything about him was hard and confident: his broad arms which held her carefully but tightly, his searching fingers which teased her neck and shoulders, even his tongue, which probed stiffly, tasting of salt and alcohol. So unlike Celina, he remained in control, eyeing her somewhat dispassionately, while she found herself clinging to him, pressing her hips to his, ravenous for this new experience of giving herself fully to a man.

Breaking loose from her, he again lifted the jug and offered her the contents. Feeling as abandoned as any harlot, Allegra drank deeply, feeling her head swim a little as the cool liquor drowned her senses. This time it was she who moved to him, offering her lips to his, melding her body into the hard hollow of his chest and shoulders. With skilful art, he teased her tongue with his, then kissed her ears and throat, so gently and so expertly, nothing could have been more different from the naive thrashings of the inexpert youth. Kissing her breasts where they arched up above the tiny bodice, he looked up and slowly smiled. She was dizzy with desire, wishing he would only move faster and take her there and then by the tree. But no, he was not a boy, and his method was slow and stately, keeping her hot and waiting while he took his leisure with her rich store of delights.

To her surprise, he grasped her hand. Not knowing

what he wanted, she let him lead her hand downwards to the swelling in his breeches. There, he rubbed her hand gently against the warm hummock until, with a will of her own, she began to explore the swollen flesh, discerning its ample length and the swinging softness of the mass below. Here at last, it seemed, was the answer to her needs; inside she felt empty, aching and feverish, wanting above all to let this man take her any way he pleased. Ever more wantonly, she pressed against the stiff tool, trying to ease it from his clothing, so that she might at last touch and taste that secret pleasure. But now he appeared reluctant. Grasping her wrist, he pushed her away, and with a last kiss on her lips whispered, 'Let us go inside.'

'Why?' she whispered back. But he only answered with a tug to her sleeve and soon she was following him, stumbling into the house in a state of confusion. Luca at first seemed to have disappeared, but then Allegra noticed that the curtain around his bed was drawn. Matters became no clearer when Nico left her at the doorway and began to snuff out a number of candles, lighting an oil lantern from the tallow but turning it down low so it cast a warm amber glow across the walls. All she could think of was how much she wanted him – her body suffered with desire, every particle needing to be touched and caressed so she could somehow be released. And now they were inside the house the difficulty of the situation struck her more forcibly – with Luca in the same room, only lying behind the curtain, how could they possibly satisfy themselves without disturbing him? If only they had stayed outside, they might have pleasured themselves by the tree or even slept on the warm sand by the ceaseless music of the ocean.

At last Nico returned to her, carrying the oil lamp in one hand and reaching out to caress her shoulder with the other. Slowly he led her to Luca's curtain, and to her astonishment, pulled it aside. The youth was lying

110

miserably on his cot, his boots kicked off and his clothes in disarray. Both he and Allegra looked at each other in astonishment, but behind her, Nico smiled and nodded encouragingly. Through the fog of lust and liquor Allegra's mind stumbled to a conclusion. Surely he was not giving her to Luca after all? For now she wanted Nico and his strong caresses and slow tormenting manner. But when she looked at Luca he was so beautiful and appealing, his boyish face surrounded by tousled curls and his desire so manifest he might devour her there and then. For guidance, she looked back to Nico, sensing he might leave her now, having safely delivered her to his young friend. But nothing could have been further from the truth.

Taking her arm, he led her to sit on the edge of Luca's bed where he once more began to kiss her lips. At the same time he took Luca's hand and placed it on her bare shoulder. Startled, Allegra looked at the older man, but he simply nodded quietly in encouragement. The youth needed no urging, in a moment he was kneeling behind her, kissing her shoulder, seeking her breasts. Alarmed, Allegra suddenly realised what it was the older man planned. It was not that he was giving her to Luca – he was sharing her with him. Instead of one, she might enjoy the both.

Whatever reluctance and shame rose in her conscience at the prospect of sharing a bed with both men, the giddy excitement which filled her damped down any misgivings. Reeling with pleasure, she submitted to Nico's mouth while Luca hastily began to pull at her bodice. Already she could sense the youth's clamorous arousal as he freed her breasts and moaned with pleasure, kneeling against her with his cock already hard and ready against her back. Nico too was losing a little of his control, as he grasped one of her freed breasts and eagerly sought the stiff nipple with his mouth.

For a glorious minute Allegra sat with her head flung back as both men fondled and caressed a breast each, driving her into a state of rapture as her nipples were sucked and squeezed at the same time. Looking down, she could see Luca in a state of frantic arousal, moaning as he buried his face in her breast, squeezing her ample flesh. Unable to control himself, he began to explore the folds of her skirt, eventually finding her thigh where the coarse white stockings ended with a garter. With long, needy caresses, he stroked her thigh, making Allegra quiver with anticipation as she leant back, letting her senses fill with this paradise of eager manhood.

Taking the lead once more, Nico dislodged himself and helped her to pull off the tawdry dress. In a few moments she was sitting on the bed, naked but for the leather corset as the two men began to undress as well. For a moment Allegra regained the full capacity of her mind and wondered what it was she was doing here. Surely this was an act of utter depravity, to give herself so fully to the lust of these two men. But it only needed Nico to touch her shoulder once more and guide her, and she was again under a spell, desperate to surrender herself to this wondrous opportunity to fully and totally be overwhelmed by both of these men's lust.

In the golden lamplight, both Luca and Nico's skin shone like brass, their dark hair falling on naked shoulders. Allegra drank in the sight of their broad chests and long, hair speckled stomachs. Both men were eagerly ready too, their members crimson in the soft light, rising and jutting stiffly with faintly damp ends. She had no idea what to do, or what would happen next, but whenever fear slipped into her mind, she remembered Drusus and closed her eyes, enjoying only the sensation of wild and passionate lovemaking.

Like a supplicant, Luca slipped down and kneeled before her, kissing her legs and slowly parting her thighs. From his breathless abandonment, she guessed he knew little of women, but his curiosity more than made up for any inexperience. Entranced, he bowed his head before her, kissing her trembling thighs until he reached the parting of her lips. Then, with a groan, he buried his head there, kissing and licking her sex, sucking and flicking with his tongue. Unable to stop her panting excitement, she found Nico standing watching by her side. As he reached down to squeeze her breasts, she grasped him, taking the solid muscle of his penis into her small fingers. Sighing, she found it large and pleasurable to hold but in her inexperience she looked up to the older man for direction.

Very gently, so as not to startle her, he took her head into his hands and led her lips to its bulbous end. Ignoring her fear, she let the salty swelling slip inside her lips, experiencing an uncontrollable swooning as her mouth closed around it and Nico very gently nudged it back against her tongue. The taste was sweet and briny; without guidance she rolled her tongue around the head, feeling breathless rapture, as if she were drowning in physical bliss. Still Luca kneeled below her, his tongue probing deeper like a snake, his dark head lost between her white thighs. From nowhere, it seemed, a titanic wave of release rose within her. Instinctively, she sucked on the older man's sticky phallus, as if she might milk it there and then.

But as she did so, her legs trembled uncontrollably, and it seemed that as she glanced down at Luca's dark head he touched a maddening spot deep within her. Again and again, his tongue tormented her. Crying out breathlessly, her hands flew to Nico's penis and in a vain attempt to possess him she squeezed the shaft so that her mouth was full of him, desperate to drag him along on her violent climax. All the time, Luca's mouth continued sucking the tiny bead of pleasure until, with a spasm almost as fierce as pain, her senses erupted, squeezing her muscles again and again as Luca pushed his mouth as deep as he could into her hungry chasm. Then, as her crisis subsided, they let her lie back, stretched senseless on the bed. It seemed every nerve in her body had been wakened, from her deepest centre to

113

the hairs on her skin, all of her body thrilling and tingling with pleasure.

In only a few moments she found Luca lying beside her, his handsome face smiling into hers in the lamplight. Eager as ever, he reached out to stroke her, fondling her breasts and stomach and murmuring encouragement in his strange speech. If she had believed for a moment she was satisfied, he wished to prove her wrong. As he placed his heavy cock against her sticky thigh, her senses fluttered back to life. True, she had begun to explore Nico's manhood, but here was another interesting object for her to delight herself with. For a few moments she stroked it, feeling it quiver beneath her fingertips, the skin so hot and taut she longed to cram it inside her. Then she explored the soft but heavy balls covered in fine hair and felt a new sensation of mastery as she saw his eyes momentarily close and his lips murmur desperate encouragement.

Meanwhile, she felt Nico climb on to the bed behind her and again experienced complete contentment as she lay between the two men, feeling both of their phalluses stiff against her naked skin. While the youth caressed her nipples, soon driving her back into that wild heat of excitement, Nico grasped her buttocks from behind and began to explore the wetness left by his companion, probing and stroking with determined, experienced fingers. He filled first one then the other orifice with his fingers, so she was soon moaning again and thrashing, driven frantic by the friction at her breasts as well as the regular thrusts of Nico's blunt fingers. Unable to stop yet another convulsion beginning in her loins, she began to whisper to them both. 'Please,' she moaned, 'this time, please take me.'

Impulsively, she looked down at the thick and ready flesh rising from the youth's stomach; greedily, she bent down to take her pleasure. But this time as her lips reached the round knob of flesh, she felt the older man quickly and neatly lift her by the hips and swing her

114

around on the bed. Scarcely able to think any more, Allegra attacked the youth's cock with her tongue and lips, gorging herself on his swollen genitalia. Again, she felt the delightful rushing of her senses as her mouth was filled to overflowing. Above her, she could see the youth's face, dazed with lust, his eyes glazed at the sight of her eagerness.

Just as she felt that her pleasure could not possibly increase, Nico pulled her up on to all fours and with a gasp of pleasure she felt Nico's stiff rod brushing against the hot cleft at her centre. Almost fainting, she felt the head of his penis slide along her lips as Nico grasped her waist, ready to enter her. Glancing down between her swinging breasts she could see the hot, red tip seeking entry to her passage. She felt the wide head of his member press against her entrance with a delicious pressure. With a moan, she held still and let him slide inside, feeling the shaft like a spear, so far did it reach into her body. Seeming to hold her aloft, he began riding her, giving her long, luxurious strokes which slipped back and forth in her aching wetness.

In a fever of lust, she let Nico set the rhythm then, as he worked her, she followed, slipping her mouth back and forth over Luca's throbbing rod. With expert timing, Nico let her take his full extent, pulling out to the tip and then cramming her full so that she could barely stand the mounting force inside her. With each forward thrust she bore down on Luca who was almost swooning with lust. Dazed by the torment his sensitive flesh was receiving, he reached out every so often to catch her breasts as they swung back and forth under the accelerating rhythm she was receiving from Nico. Suddenly Luca's face contorted into a grimace, his slender hips rose and Allegra felt a frantic spasm beginning to work within his rigid member.

'No,' groaned Nico throatily, seeing this from his position above; Allegra was pleased to hear that at last lust was getting the better of this assured lover too. With

115

an almost painful shudder he withdrew. Aghast, Allegra looked about her – she had been close once more to climax and was desperate not to be left without satisfaction. But that was not Nico's intent. With a few murmured commands he set Allegra to lie on the edge of the bed and called Luca over to take her. By now she no longer cared how it happened, or which man's cock it was that rode her. As the youth knelt before her and slipped his reddened penis between her lips, she only rejoiced to feel that ecstatic rhythm once more. Reaching downwards between her legs, she delighted in the sensation of his thick shaft slipping back and forth between her fingers and the regular thud of his testicles thudding against her buttocks.

Like a man possessed, Nico stood watching over them. Now she could see that he had lost his previous control. His reddened face watched them like a man possessed; like Luca's, his eyes were fixed and brimming with lust. Without any shame, he stared at the young pair coupling frantically in front of him, his hand reaching down to work at his own stiff phallus, jiggling it up and down like a man past caring.

'Please,' she whispered up to him, as Luca worked within her, beating her slippery passage with his heavy shaft. Nico stared at her like a man drowning, watching her breasts rise and fall, panting at the way she lifted her thighs high on to Luca's shoulders to gain every inch of him into her greedy body. Then he understood.

As her body was driven ever closer to another, almost unendurable spasm by Luca's endless thrusting, the older man came to her and, straddling her waist, let her do as she pleased. It was more than she could bear. As she took Nico's weighty shaft as deeply as she could into her mouth, her muscles instantly began to cramp and grip around the other cock driving within her body. Again, like a blinding light, her body filled with the anticipation of pleasure and she reached forward like a starving woman to take even more of Nico's delicious

116

flesh into her aching mouth. A groan from the youth between her legs told her that he, too, had taken all he could bear. With a muffled scream she felt a strange hotness fill her mouth as Nico delivered into her, making her senses reel with heady delight. At the same time her muscles exploded, almost pushing Nico from his mount as her back arched and her rippling muscles grabbed at the youth's throbbing member. Unashamed, she felt heat at both ends, matching their pent-up desire. In ecstasy, she felt them jerk and groan, opening herself wide.

As they finally pulled away from her to let her rest, she felt she had never before experienced life so completely. Her body was sore from its hard usage but was deeply calmed, her muscles soothed as they had never been soothed before. She curled up like a child in Luca's bed; the two men let her be and she slept soundly all night to the lilting lullaby of the ocean, which rocked back and forth at their door.

Chapter Nine

Within the cool, clean walls of the sewing room, the two girls quietly stitched at the white Madonna lilies covering the great blue altar cloth. There was a deep tranquillity here, Allegra reflected, in the steady rise and fall of silver needles across the wide expanse of embroidered cloth. Looking up at Celina's serene face as she puzzled over a broken thread, Allegra wondered again at her own actions. She had not told her friend about the way she had behaved with the two men, only complained a little at her exhaustion after the hard work. It was difficult to believe what she had done the previous night – and yet still the memory secretly thrilled her.

'Do you think we will ever have it ready for Easter?' Celina grumbled as she knotted a length of yarn impatiently, gazing askance at the vast quantity of cloth as yet unpatterned.

'I should think so. Just think of all the empty winter days. But I suppose the light will be poor, so we must make haste now.'

'And everyone in the city will be celebrating carnival all winter, from Christmas through to Lent. All the costumes and the dancing, all the balls and the parties! And we are stuck here in this old tomb. If only we could

118

escape! Why, I'd do anything to go there at carnival time. There is so much I have never seen: the acrobats, the bull races, all the operas and circuses. All we would need are a couple of masks and we could pass as anyone. With everyone disguised in their carnival clothes we could soon get lost in the crowds. And to wear masks – how romantic! We could pretend to be only disguised as nuns so as to seduce the kind of men who secretly like that sort of thing.'

'Shh,' said Allegra, laughing. 'Someone will hear you.' Shaking her head, she glanced over to the high, gothic window but the city was nowhere in sight from this side of the island. It was always a presence to them, casting a siren spell across the water. 'Maybe you are right,' she conceded. 'It must be wonderful to see the city then. But now I never shall.'

After looking furtively around, Celina bent her head low to her friend's ear. 'It is not so difficult as you believe. The boatman is always open to a little bribe. I know girls, and even one of the sisters who have made the crossing.'

'And when the Prioress found out?'

'She never has.' Celina nodded earnestly. 'What do you say?'

'Celina, I cannot believe you mean it. Besides, I am not sure about the Carnival. As a child I was always kept away from the annual excesses, and then when I grew older, I suppose I disapproved.'

'Disapproved? Of what?'

'Oh, it may appear foolish to you. All the depravity, the gambling, the loose behaviour.'

'You mean the fun?'

Allegra smiled reproachfully, bowing her head over the complex design. 'That is a matter of opinion, as you well know.'

Later, as they folded the altar cloth into a casket, in readiness for the next day's work, Allegra found it impossible to hold back her questions. 'The boatman – is he a trustworthy man? He wouldn't tell the sisters?'

'Allegra. I cannot believe it. Are you of all people sneaking back to the city for some excitement?'

Frostily, Allegra looked about her to make sure that the others had left, then took Celina's sleeve rather harshly. 'No, Celina. Of course not. There is some business I must attend to which the Prioress does not like.' Even as she whispered, she checked over her shoulder. 'If I could only get to the city for one day, the task would be done and I could have a clear conscience. So I ask you, is he to be trusted?'

'I think so. Well, I know so. For no one has ever been caught.' Then with a sulky pout at her lips, she continued, 'I could come along too, you know. I should try not to be a burden. We could both go together.'

'No,' she hissed. 'There is risk enough in my going. I need you to stay here and pretend I am ill. Can you do that? My business will take only one day.'

She could see Celina about to wail in protest, and hushed her quickly as they heard footsteps in the corridor outside. The footfalls died away.

'Will you help me then?'

The girl's face was an absolute picture of misery. 'I wish now I had never told you,' she whimpered. 'But of course I will do it for you.'

'And not tell?'

'Now, you do more than injure me. You insult me.'

'Very well, then. Thank you.'

With little trouble the journey was arranged for a week's hence, once a clandestine communication had been despatched to the notary by way of the trusty boatman. Complaining of a stomach ague, Allegra excused herself after lunch. On reaching her chamber, she slipped out of the window and quickly passed around the building through the mass of heavy bushes. Exactly to plan, the

120

boatman was waiting for her, hidden beneath the prow of his boat.

'My thanks, signor,' she said, lowering herself into the gloomy depths. With some relief, she quickly felt the boat judder and bob as it left the security of the quay for the open water. Settling back into the deep leather seat, Allegra watched the convent slip away further and further behind her until at last it was only a black speck on the horizon. Then there was only open water around them, punctuated by small banks of reeds from which squawking marsh birds eyed them curiously.

Staring into the deep green swell, Allegra reflected on the strange adventures her stay at Santa Agnetha had brought. Only a month ago, she had been so fixed on submitting to a quiet, secluded life. Did such a life ever exist? Now she knew that however hard she might try to hide, if there were people about her, there would always be webs of desire and emotion to entrap her. The unsettling thought surfaced in her mind that maybe it was she who had brought some of this perplexity with her; that indeed, others only reacted to a strange readiness for experience they found within her. But she banished the thought immediately. No, Santa Agnetha was indeed a very strange place.

Most of the night Celina had sulked, twisting and turning on her own narrow bed, to which Allegra had banished her in preparation for today's duty. By the glow of candlelight she had cast baleful eyes at Allegra, creating an atmosphere of wounded pride. Glancing at her, as she stretched out provocatively with her hair down around her naked shoulders, and her gown hanging loose, Allegra had been strongly tempted to relent. How much more pleasant it would be to have company and stroll about the narrow *calli* of the city together. Perhaps she was being too harsh to the girl, of whom she was growing exceedingly fond. Yet she knew, when she consulted her head and not her heart, that Celina was best left supporting her alibi while she attended assiduously to her task. There would be other times when they might slip out together. And so, although it felt like a taut thread pulling painfully between them, she snapped it that morning, allowing Celina only the coolest of kisses upon her soft cheek.

At last they came in sight of the long sandbanks of the Lido. Pulling her cloak tight around the plain novice's costume, Allegra felt the change in the season blowing in from the sea. The long summer had ended; now the skies were a heavy slate blue above choppy green waves. No doubt winter would be cold and damp on the isolated island of Santa Agnetha; the ocean would rise and crash against the rocky outcrop and the winds would howl like furies. The misery of winter in the lagoon city was no doubt why the carnival was celebrated with such devotion. From her childhood, she remembered the perils of ice and snow, flooding and collapse that the change in season brought to a community living so precariously afloat a lagoon. Why should the common people not allay the savagery of winter with the spectacular festivity of carnival? Yet she knew it was more than that; maybe an age old fear of death which made them mad for a quarter of the year, which turned the world upside down in a frenzy of forgetful pleasure.

The familiar quayside slid into sight. There was the island monastery of San Giorgio, and across the narrow channel, the campanile of San Marco and the ancient domes of the Basilica itself. Soon they bobbed past tall galleys festooned with pennants and pale rigging, around which were gathered smaller craft and gondolas. At last the grey stone of the Riva could be discerned, and above it teams of sailors and workmen unloading goods from ships at the quay. Beyond that the crowds mingled all about the Piazza, a rainbow coloured throng crawling about the twin columns of San Marco and the pink arcades of the Doge's Palace.

Soon they were skimming along the narrow waterways which threaded like a labyrinth of watery veins into the heart of the city. Here, the boatman needed all his skill to circumnavigate low bridges and heavily laden boats, where vendors sold fruit and flowers and even food wrapped in cloths for hungry boatmen passing by. With a sudden swing, the craft swerved towards a mooring and with a sharp jolt, Allegra realised they had at last arrived.

'Until six, signorina,' the dour boatman uttered. They had fixed the hour to allow him ample time to visit his aged mother, this being his day's holiday. Although it was far later than she might have liked, there would certainly be time enough to see her duty performed to the last degree.

'Until six, signor. Here, at the steps.'

With a quick nod he was off, and Allegra found herself standing alone on a flight of ancient, water sodden steps, looking up at the crowded *calle* above her and wondering where exactly she might find Signor Bartolomeo. Ascending into the crowds, she was immediately overwhelmed by the bustle and noise. Already, she was attuned to the peace and tranquillity of the cloister; here people jostled and shouted, stopped to argue at street corners, shouted news of their wares or chattered ceaselessly as they ambled in pairs and groups. Amongst the swell of patricians, housewives, workmen, beggars and visitors of every hue from every land, Allegra felt herself to be but a plain and simple innocent. If she had but recently been rescued from an island of castaways, she could not have felt more awkward.

Her enquiries brought her out at the broader passage of the Merceria, where many passers-by lingered at the newly furbished shops, some with enlarged windows so that goods could be displayed. All of life was here; it was difficult not to taste the excitement inspired by the beautiful and fanciful objects for sale. Peering into one shop, Allegra found it to be the corset makers'; here were many grand ladies, their maids and children, all

123

surrounded by a mass of corsets hung from shelves in every stage of production. Her eye was caught by a pretty pink silk set of stays, as smooth as ivory with pearl buttons at the shoulder straps and rows of satin bows about the neck. If there was one thing she would change in her life as a nun it would be that, she thought. How she longed for the comfort of a well made set of whalebone stays. Every day brought an agony of chafed flesh and the careful insertion of little pads of cotton to relieve the pressure of stiff, ill-sewn leather.

After that, it was tempting to peer into each shop front. The rosary shop contained row upon row of necklaces all hung across the wall and a group of men busily grinding crucifixes and beads from every precious material. Shops full of musical instruments, fans, wigs, shoes, furniture, masks, books, cakes – every delight was arrayed for the loitering crowds. As the bells tolled four, she made a resolution to drag herself away from the very last shop. There, in a wide glass window with a card inscribed in French, was a large doll wearing a dress created in Heaven itself. The throng about it muttered and gasped; some who might have been dress-makers struggled to reach the front to make elaborate sketches for their clients.

Allegra stared at it as if it were an icon, trying to remember every detail to describe to Celina. It was of the new French style, in finest sky-blue taffeta embroidered all over in silver thread in a pattern of Cupid and Psyche. Wave upon wave of feathery lace fell at the sleeves and neck, and wide, imposing panniers held the fabric out to the sides to display every inch of the sumptuous ivory petticoat. On almost every inch was massed silver lace, blue rosettes and ivory bows. Beside it were two little shoes of embroidered satin, with diamond buckles and pink heels. To the other side was spread a pearl and ivory fan with a picture of Venus recumbent. The whole ensemble was like a feast to Allegra's starving eyes.

'Is it? No it can't be you. Allegra!' Looking about her, she could at first not find the source of that shrill voice. Then, noticing a gloved hand waving above the crowd, she pushed her way towards it. To her alarm, she found herself face to face with a sumptuously dressed young woman, replete with feathered tricorne hat and a cape of gold lace. Peering into the heavily painted face, she at last recognised her distant cousin, Spetzina.

'Mother of Mary, what are you wearing?' the fashionable woman pronounced, looking aghast at the dull brown serge.

'Keep your voice down, Spetzina. Let us get out of this crowd.'

'Domenico!' In answer to her call, a tall, masked youth detached himself from the fray and offered his arm to Spetzina as a model gallant. With some sense of growing discomfort, Allegra followed them, unable to ignore the finery of their appearance and even reluctantly noting the glances of admiration from those they passed. When at last they reached a quiet corner to their liking and turned to her, she wished more than ever that she had given them the slip before they ever saw her.

'Now,' the girl demanded, 'what in the name of the saints has happened to you? We know Procurator di Rivero is dead, but that is no reason to be hanging about dressed like a hired beggar at his funeral. What do you say, Domenico?' The youth had barely time to nod. 'Indeed, his virtue is that he never does have anything to say. Allegra, this is Domenico. My betrothed. Is he not handsome? Is he not like a young god? When we were at the Grand Duke's reception, everyone stared so, when the Duchess allowed him a dance. We looked for you there. Where were you? Surely you don't expect to get into society dressed in rags?'

Allegra was soon reminded of Spetzina's most conspicuous fault, present even when they had occasionally met as young children. So many questions – and no opportunity to answer even one. She chattered on for some time longer, at least sparing Allegra the bother of making a reply. The worst of it was, Spetzina did look well – flushed with pride and animal vitality of that sort best supplied by some pleasure, more leisure and even more money. Inwardly, Allegra sighed; she felt like Cinderella with no prospect of the Fairy Godmother ever making an appearance.

'I am to be a nun,' she cut in. 'It is a vocation. It is what I have chosen.'

Uncontrollably, Spetzina began to laugh. 'You?' she hooted. 'What in the name of the Lion do you want to do that for? A nun – I cannot wait to tell the others. Why? You are not so ugly as all that, nor penniless, I hope. What about the Procurator? Surely he left you something in his will? There is no need for drastic measures, my girl. Even with only a little money, there are ways to live well. There is always a good time to be had. Surely you have a little money?'

'Money, money, money!' Allegra could stand it no more. 'Does it not occur to you that by choosing to live in seclusion, it is just this avarice I am trying to escape. And pleasure? All of you, you are all set to drown in your pits of pleasure.'

'Allegra, are you well?' Spetzina's concern was yet more insulting than her condescension. 'Have you consulted an apothecary? Domenico, she is like an altogether different person. Perhaps her head has addled with the Procurator's death. What did he leave you, then? Surely he did not leave you penniless, to live in these rags? Have you lost your money somewhere? It has not been tricked away from you?'

'For goodness' sake, Spetzina, how can I convince you? I choose to live this way. And my guardian – well, he left me nothing of substance. In fact I am going to the notary this minute to dispose of it.'

'Dispose of it? That is a strange term. I hope there are no greedy old nuns after it. I have heard they will do

126

anything for money. It is a scandal. I hope you mean to bank it?'

'No. Dispose of it. I do not approve of what he has left me. I wish it to be burnt.'

Spetzina clutched at her betrothed's elbow in a great fit of agitation. 'Listen. Her mind has gone. She wishes to burn her legacy! Domenico, do something.'

With a great expression of helplessness, the seemingly mute Domenico looked from one to the other in great perplexity.

'Spetzina. For goodness' sake, there is nothing wrong with me but the possession of a spiritual nature. I am sure there are plenty of others who can more than compensate for my conscience with their love of money and frippery. The bequest is mine to do as I see fit. My God,' Allegra sighed in loud exasperation, 'I cannot wait to get back to the peace of convent life. I am late for the notary now. Goodbye.'

Without a backward glance, Allegra sped off up the *calle*, leaving Spetzina for once in her life open-mouthed and silent. Only as she was turning the corner did she hear her cousin shout after her, 'For someone with such a spiritual nature you certainly have an appetite for French dresses, I think!'

More heated and rushed than she might have wished, Allegra began searching for the notary. Only after a series of enquiries and a number of misdirections did she at last find the heavy, brass-embellished door of his office. After a space of time, a pale-faced clerk in a grubby white collar opened the door and she informed him of her appointment.

'Signorina Vitali, how gracious of you to call,' the notary bowed as she was ushered into his office. He was a small, round man, affecting the fashion for a doctor's wig, but otherwise dressed in the black toga and white bands of his office. He reached to take her fingers, which she somewhat awkwardly allowed.

'You received my message?'

Indeed he had, he assured her with another bow. 'But might I be permitted to check the details, signorina?'

Allegra sat at a worn wooden seat, drumming her fingers while the notary gathered a sheaf of papers across his desk.

'This property,' he began, 'is of considerable value.' He cleared his throat and averted his rather penetrating little eyes. 'I am afraid you do not understand the situation at all.'

'I assure you I do, Signor Bartolemeo,' she cut in. 'Now please tell me the arrangements you have made. I did expressly ask you to set in motion the destruction of that property.'

The notary shuffled uncomfortably at this desk. 'My dear girl,' he began. 'I see you are a simple creature. I know you seek to do good but, in doing so, you do evil to yourself and the interests of those who care for you. Certain items of your guardian's gift would raise a considerable fortune. It is my duty to advise you to keep them. Indeed – ' and here he looked a little sheepish – 'I know those who would buy, even myself. I would be more than happy to offer . . .'

As she listened, Allegra's blood began to boil. Furiously, she jumped up and walked across the room to the window. 'What right have you?' she finally spluttered. 'Where does it give you the right to disobey my orders? How dare you suggest purchasing those goods! Show them to me – I will set the torch to them myself!'

'Signorina, signorina,' the notary wheedled, standing up in great alarm. 'It is my duty as your legal representative to tell you the truth. It is a great pity, a great pity. Think of the money, then. Your convent might benefit?'

The thunderous look on her face was enough.

'But if your will is set, I suppose . . .'

'It is set,' she announced. 'Where are they?'

'Very well, very well.' Shrugging his shoulders he

reached for the door. 'They are waiting in the courtyard next door.'

Down the stairs she followed him, and out across the yard. Entering a back door they passed inside a vast and empty set of apartments which bore many signs of long neglect. But beneath veils of cobwebs Murano chandeliers were slowly splintering and the powdery dust of years obscured vast elaborate shields and escutcheons above worm-holed archways.

'It is one of the houses of the Barnabotti – the upkeep was too great. I lease it for a tiny sum.'

Allegra nodded, gazing at the fine rooms in admiration. She had heard of the great families whose fortunes now declined to such a catastrophic extent that they retreated with their ancient seals and ragged robes to the cheaper slums of San Barnaba. So this was what they left behind – the sad tatters of greatness, all falling into dust.

At last they reached a padlocked door, and beyond it lay the shadowy courtyard. Outside, the evening had grown colder and a chill breeze chased around the high walls. There, heaped in piles of crates and cloth bound parcels, stood the contents of her guardian's secret room. Allegra was not a little discomfited to see that most of the wrappers had been opened. Peeping from one cloth was a picture she had not seen before – of two young girls lying naked in a forest while a bestial satyr stood over them, his tail curled in coils around massive upright genitals. She quickly recognised the drawing of the two peasants, and modestly diverted her eyes from the depiction of the man's fearsome member. Glancing up, she saw the fat little notary watching her, clearly savouring her unease.

'Such masterpieces,' he crooned, lifting up the vast painting of the woman in chains. Again, the picture shocked Allegra; it was the knowing expression on the woman's face which assaulted the eye. As if in harmony with her unquiet mood, the flicker of lightning flashed across the dusky courtyard. For a moment the painting was fully and intensely illuminated. This was no victim, but a woman who delighted in offering the artist the symbolic chain in her hand, who professed a strange beauty in her willing submission to the eyes of others.

It was as if Allegra had developed a more knowing eye herself, for she could for the first time appreciate the lush desirability of the woman's body and admire the sumptuous curves of her breasts and thighs. She was indeed magnificent and deserving of the jewels which studded her naked skin. The intimacy of giving the body to another was something she was only just learning, but nevertheless now recognised.

'There is a small band of professional men,' the notary began. 'A small club, so to speak, who have particular interests. A figure in excess of a thousand gold ducats might be obtained. Just imagine the charity to be bought with such a sum.'

'No,' she began, though less certainly than before. 'It does not deserve to survive.'

'But the workmanship,' he continued, picking up a book of prints and leafing through it so she might not avoid seeing the incredible drawings inside. Again lightning churned in the darkening sky. It was as if the pictures would not stay in the shadows, as if they willed to be framed so brightly in flashes of sharp, white light.

'These works are from the far corners of the globe. France, Persia, Cathay, Ethiop. So strange and so wonderful.' He had the page open at a drawing of two nuns – she could see they were nuns from their veils and wimples but otherwise they were completely naked. She felt her cheeks redden as she saw that they were playing with some kind of implement shaped like a phallus and one was clearly reclining to take full pleasure from its ample proportions. If only, she secretly wished, she could be left alone to take just one private look at this incredible collection before it was destroyed. If he would only go away and then no one would ever know. There might be things she could learn, things she could even possibly try. Suddenly, she noticed that the notary was watching her with acute interest, a faint film of perspiration appearing on his upper lip.

'Very well, signorina. Two thousand gold ducats. That is a very great fortune. To destroy this collection – it would be an act of barbarism.'

Allegra bit her lip, pondering the offer. By her own foolishness, she was indeed very poor. And Spetzina's vainglorious words now rang in her ears – maybe they were not so foolish after all. Indeed, she was truly destitute: utterly dependent on the bed and board of the sisterhood. If these works were destroyed, she was condemning herself to a life of poverty and subjection. And two thousand ducats! She might even pay the convent a dowry for Celina and have plenty left besides to live upon.

And yet – to profit from depravity. The notary did himself no favours with his lecherous looks and sweating palms.

'The acts portrayed in these pictures – they are acts of barbarism,' she murmured. 'My whole life would be built upon corruption. It cannot be.'

'Signorina, I beg you. Think again. Surely your guardian did not intend that you throw his gift away like this?'

As lightning again flashed across the high pile of parcels and boxes she saw the bequest clearly – saw it indeed for what it was. 'My guardian,' she began wildly, 'would laugh in his grave to hear this. Do you not know, signor, that this is but a joke? From the very grave he mocks me, his bony jaw laughs at my discomfiture.' She found she was twisting her apron strings round and round very tightly in her fingers. 'If I destroy it, I am doing his will, which mortifies me. If I keep the goods it is against my nature. If I sell, I profit from corruption. What am I to do?' she wailed – not to the notary, but into the darkening air.

As if in answer, light drops of rain fell against her face.

131

The weather, which had threatened to change all day, had finally turned.

'Signorina, the goods – they must be sheltered.'

'No. Burn them here. Fetch a light.'

The notary stood in all perplexity, hopping from one foot to another.

'I beg you,' he began again. 'They are a treasure to the senses.'

'Sir, you have tinder?'

Reluctantly, he pulled his tinder box from his waistcoat. Eagerly, Allegra snatched it. In a trice, she had a spark, and reached for the nearest book. With a sudden brutal movement, she ripped out a page and a bright flame caught and flared. The picture of a naked woman at a mirror melted away into flame. Dropping the firebrand on to the heap of goods, Allegra felt a savage joy. Deep in her heart she wished she could burn everything bad and purify the whole world. For a few moments she knew the exultation of the zealot, burning the enemy, reducing sin to a puff of smoke and a pile of papery ashes.

'No, please, no, you cannot. This is profanity.' The notary was making ineffectual attempts to kick the flames out, but as he did, she lit another page and dropped that also on the goods.

It took some time, as she was so intent upon her task of flaming pages, to realise the very slight damage done. For as she set to torching the goods, so did the heavens continue to open, and for each lighted spark there fell a hundred drops of rain. Soon, as she tried to light a page, she found it too damp to take, and then in turn the tinder dampened and failed.

'What is this?' she wailed bitterly. 'Why am I forever doomed in my task?'

'Perhaps you must accept your legacy after all,' puffed the notary.

Signor Bartolomeo was hastily covering the open parcels and pulling over cloths to protect the collection from

132

the rain. Allegra watched him in despair. The very heavens had opened to prevent her from accomplishing her task. The Procurator was having the last laugh again. She might come another day to try again, but it would be different. She would never be so sure of herself again.

The rain was falling in heavy sheets, and in the distance came the rumble of thunder. The notary was growing frantic, skipping about in an attempt to protect the priceless pictures from the natural destruction of the weather. Suddenly, watching him, Allegra grew resigned.

'Very well. Take it inside.'

He looked at her in amazement, his face now streaming with water. 'What did you say?'

'I said, take it in. Whatever I want, nature will not allow it. For the time being at least, signor, protect my goods. I hear the bells toll six. I will send you word when next I can.'

The journey back across the lagoon was a miserable trial. High waves slapped against the fragile hull of the little boat, rocking Allegra back and forth in queasy motion. Outside, the swell had turned to darkest grey, echoing the glowering sky. Shivering in her thin, wet dress, Allegra found herself thinking of Spetzina and her rich clothes and warm dinners. And then there had been Domenico – yes, she could do with some warmth beside her and a pleasant gallant to take her arm. With a burning resentment, she saw the island loom ahead of her; now it appeared as grim as a prison, its black silhouette towering above the tumultuous night.

Only the thought of Celina and her warm, comforting body made her hurry as she crept beneath the rain dripping trees, seeking out the narrow window of their chamber. How cruel she had been to reject Celina the previous night – how welcome she would make her now. At last she slid over the stone sill and discerned the girl's rounded back beneath the blanket of her narrow bed.

'Celina,' she whispered, feeling affection flood from her heart towards the lonely figure. With gentle fingers she caressed the swell of her body beneath the bedclothes. 'I am back, my sweet, and aching for your lovely body. Move over, now. Let me in beside you.'

The figure turned slowly. For a long moment, Allegra could not quite understand what was wrong. Something in the shape of the shadowy face; the bulk of the figure; the different scent? Fumbling for the candle, Allegra could not light it, from a sudden trembling in her hands. The figure rose in the bed, a large shape looming in the darkness.

'Sister Almoro. Is that you?' The voice was loud, even gruff. It was not Celina.

'It is,' she stammered, backing off, feeling fear clutch painfully at her heart.

'You are to come with me. The Prioress awaits you.'

With a wave of horror, Allegra recognised the voice which spoke to her from Celina's bed. It was Sister Ino, who had witnessed her words of endearment to Celina. There could be no more lies left to spin; she was caught fast inside a web of her own making.

Chapter Ten

*D*own in the underground chamber below the chapel, an alarming scene awaited Allegra. Once again the sisterhood was gathered below the huge fresco of the Philomastrix, their pale faces suspended like masks in the gloomy candlelight. But they were not alone. The birching block which Allegra anticipated kneeling upon was already occupied. In a moment she had discerned the figure was a young girl. Then, slowly lifting her head, the girl turned to Allegra, imploring her with wild eyes. It was Celina; her mouth and limbs were bound but her eyes fiercely struggled to communicate some secret message. Immediately, Allegra attempted to comfort her friend, but with a harsh tug, Sister Ino held her fast by the arm.

'Ah, Sister Almoro. You have decided to join us?'

How she hated that name now. With an expression of loathing, she turned to the Prioress. Summoning a tremendous effort for Celina's sake, she feigned submission and threw herself down on her knees.

'I have indeed returned, Holy Mother. I beg your forgiveness for my absence. It will not happen again.'

'Indeed it will not. For your friend, here, has told us a great deal of your affairs. The opportunity will never arise again.'

·Hurriedly, Allegra tried to remember what it was she had told Celina of her purpose in visiting the city. She had said almost nothing. That was good, she told herself, as she studied the tiles on the floor and waited for the official pronouncement on her crimes. It was not long coming.

'Sister Almoro, your behaviour alarms and disappoints us. The list of misdemeanours already inscribed upon your slate would be enough to frighten almost any other novice into surrender. And yet – what do you do? Do you then decide to follow the paths of modesty and submission laid out before you? Do you submit to the iron rod of discipline? You do not.' The Prioress rose stiffly from her chair, and those gathered around her murmured a little and drew back. For the first time, Allegra felt a shiver of apprehension. Across the smooth stone floor, Celina watched her companion with eyes large with fear, her position rendering her completely powerless.

'Do you submit?' the old woman cried, her voice grown surprisingly strong with the power of her passion.

With her head still bowed to the floor, Allegra spoke. The atmosphere in the room was sultry and oppressive; she was desperate to be out of this place, and to free Celina too. 'I do.'

'Then you must prove it. For in submission there is love, and in correction, mercy.'

Allegra prepared her body for pain. Whatever whip or birch was laid upon her, she would bear it. It was physical pain only. Her mind was her own.

'The punishment I decree,' the old woman began in a loud and resonant voice, 'is a hard one. Triplefold it is, to test the will, the spirit and the arts. There are three parts to this riddle, and all parts must be accomplished. For the first part, you must solve this riddle: "As you beat, so you beat, man and woman both."'

Allegra looked around herself in complete confusion. She had expected the old woman to order a few dozen strokes to be delivered to her, or perhaps to serve the nuns in some depraved manner. But this? What was it about? To beat twice? To beat two people at once? She had no idea at all.

'And if I cannot solve this mystery?' Allegra asked, suddenly desperate.

'As I said, you must solve all three. If you fail? Well, then you cannot stay here. I will be generous and give you passage back to the city. And there you must stay – penniless and outcast. Oh, and your friend, of course, will go with you.'

So, she must condemn Celina as well. Celina, who at least was grateful to the sisters for her bed and board. Celina, who still had some small hope of escaping the place with dignity one day. Spetzina's words about greedy nuns rang painfully in her ears. Her dowry would disappear with her memory. If only she had not come back from the city – but then, what of Celina, an innocent victim left here to suffer alone?

As if losing interest in her, the sisters returned to their talk and strange ritual chants and Allegra was left to rack her brain herself. Thankfully, Domica approached her, masked as ever despite her modest gown and veil.

'You are allowed to look into the old armoury,' she whispered. 'It may help you.'

With a backward glance at Celina, who still lay bound across the block, Allegra rose and followed the mysterious nun through a low, metal studded door.

She might have expected a room of ancient swords and armour, and at first glance this was what she saw. Only when her eyes adjusted to the gloom broken infrequently by smoking tallow set in the walls, did she identify the strange implements that filled the low chamber. Across one wall were bunches of birches such as she had already experienced, along with flexible canes of varying lengths and curvature. Along the next, were a variety of leather implements: the tapette with its peculiar paddle shape and long fringed martinets and cats-o'-nine-tails.

Fascinated by this shrine to the nun's cruel goddess, Allegra inspected the remaining shelves. Buckles, bracelets, bonds of every type were available. There were even fine silk cords with ribbons and lace which would yet hold any victim still and secure. Next were masks; both black carnival masks and white waxen half masks, velvet masks that clung to the face and leather masks which bore strange, pagan countenances.

Clothes were there too: but such clothes as Allegra had never dreamt of. A corset of steel had pride of place, so fierce that its waist was barely a handspan; the breasts meanwhile showed only as two empty circles waiting to have willing flesh pushed through. Other strange corsets and belts were hung along the shelves. Unable to contain her curiosity, Allegra inspected the bizarrely formed leather stays, strange shoes and belts that formed the sisterhood's extraordinary collection. So interested was she that she forgot to be censorious. She could not quite believe that anyone could be so artful as to make these objects, which appeared so tantalising, offering she knew not what secret pleasures to those with the courage to use them.

'Ah, what is that?' she asked in a hushed voice. At first sight it was a sword belt, though rather broad and fastening between the legs as well as round the waist. Testing the scabbard, Allegra pulled out not a sword but a long, fringed martinet. It felt nicely weighted in her palm; heavy but flexible, as if it would spring gingerly through the air. Then, stifling a giggle, she saw what it was that was different about the belt. Growing like a false tail from the straps of leather crossing at the crotch was a strange appendage. Also of leather, it was a stuffed and rigid column, quite the size and shape of a well-endowed man. Laughing with delight, she reached out her fingers and felt its hardness: with her finger and thumb she could not circle its width. It felt satisfactorily

138

hard to her touch and it was impossible not to wonder how it might feel, were it used in the way it was clearly intended.

Smiling shyly, she turned to Domica.

'Is it what I think it is?'

The strange nun nodded.

'And is it used?'

Again, that oddly neutral nod.

'It would almost be like playing the man,' she speculated. 'How strange.' Then quickly she added, in response to a thought exploding in her brain like gunpowder, 'Is that it? To beat and beat? To be man and woman?'

Domica did not move.

'Please,' Allegra begged. 'What is it I must do?'

In answer, Domica walked towards the door, leading her back to the chapel. Hastily, Allegra picked up the strange belt and hurried after her.

Back in the larger room, the gathering waited for her. Making her way to the Prioress, Allegra lifted the belt for all to see, and presented it to the old crone.

'Here is the answer to your riddle,' she announced. 'As it beats, so it beats, man and woman both.'

The Prioress looked at her with surprising disdain.

'Not quite, Sister Almoro. What was it I said?'

Puzzled, Allegra tried her hardest to remember. She was sure the words were perfect.

'As *you* beat, so *you* beat. And what do you think I meant there?'

The small crowd around the old woman laughed spitefully at Allegra's despairing expression.

'I do not know,' she wailed. 'Surely your riddle is solved?'

'Indeed no. The solution is not yet complete. It is not yet enacted.' Pointedly, the Prioress lifted her eyebrows and looked over at Celina. There she still lay, gagged and bound, ready as any submissive victim for the scourge.

With a sense of fierce outrage, Allegra slowly realised what it was the sisterhood wished her to do. As if it had burst into flames in her hand, she dropped the loathsome belt on the floor. 'I cannot. It would humiliate me, which I can bear. But it would humiliate her, too. That is too much to ask.'

'And to be turned out like a beggar in the city. That would not humiliate her? Very well then. Let her be unbound.'

Like a well-trained soldier, Domica broke from the ranks of nuns and approached Celina's prone figure. Allegra could see her friend making an intense effort to speak, shaking her head and struggling, as if she were desperate to prevent Domica from freeing her. Confused and bewildered, Allegra called out to Domica.

'Stop! Hold a while. I need to think.'

'You have no time to think,' cut in the Prioress. 'The ritual must begin now, or you are both to be freed.'

But in this instant, Allegra had seen her friend's change of countenance. Now she no longer struggled; indeed, she looked at Allegra with willing, hungry eyes. Reluctantly, she decided that this was indeed what Celina wanted. How could she answer for the girl? Perhaps she would rather suffer this injury to her dignity and remain in the convent of Santa Agnetha than be cast out like a beggar. Only it will be hard, Allegra told herself, to hurt the poor creature in any way.

With all eyes upon her, Allegra threw down her cloak and lifted her heavy brown skirts to her waist. Knowing the ruffles of her shift would largely cover her nakedness, she slipped the heavy belt up and around her waist.

'The belt is worn naked,' the Prioress interrupted.

With a sigh of aggrieved impatience, Allegra began to undress. Anything, she told herself, to get this unsavoury act over with. Untying her skirt and petticoats, she let them fall to the ground at her feet. Then, with Domica's help, she unlaced her bodice and stays. Finally, she stood naked before them, her smooth flesh dappled in the candlelight. There seemed no response from the gathering, though she knew she must look a bizarrely erotic sight. Below her dark flowing hair, her rounded breasts swung freely and her hips flared fully below her waist. But from waist to groin she was encased in the strange leather belt from which sprang the stiff prong of leather, ever eager and ready to do her bidding. She found herself looking to the Prioress for guidance.

'As punishment for lying to aid your absconding, I decree thirty lashes to the flesh while she is beaten with the phallus. Begin.'

Quaking, Allegra walked somewhat unsteadily over to the birching block. She realised she had little idea of what to do. Never in her life had she beaten another person – and certainly never dreamt of physically taking one like a man. Beneath her bare feet, she felt the warm wood of the block and sensed the heat rising from Celina as she approached her from the rear. Very gently, she stroked the back of her dress.

'Is this what you wish?' she whispered so low that no one but Celina might hear her.

In answer, the girl nodded her head, unable even to make a sound, so securely did the gag seal her mouth. But even with permission, she could not conceive of how to carry out the task. Maybe in the privacy of their own room, she might have wanted to take the girl, or even playfully smacked her in a lover's game. But here – with dozens of eyes upon them – it was impossible for her to take on such a masterful role.

'Come along, get on with it,' the Prioress cried. A chorus of muttering rose from those thronged around her. Nervously, Allegra looked down at the prone girl, unable to tell how to start. Thankfully, Domica appeared at her shoulder, and with a crisp, dispassionate gesture, began to lift the girl's skirts in readiness. In a moment, the thin, creamy petticoat was pinned up high on to Celina's back, revealing her familiar plump little rear. Below, the bonds held her legs wide, so her stockinged thighs were parted at the top to show the slightest hint of soft, pink flesh.

It suddenly occurred to Allegra that this was how she must have appeared to the priest, Guillam. Anxiously, she looked over to the dais and soon found him there, white-faced and grim amongst the huddle of nuns. What must he be thinking now, she wondered? Did he, too, recall her own willing submission? How strange, even piquant, to have him watch her do the same again.

Unable to escape her duty any further, she unwillingly slipped the leather handled martinet from its scabbard. At least an arm's length it stretched; dancing slightly in the air with a fine tail of knotted thongs swinging at its end. Setting one foot before the other, Allegra lifted the handle and aimed, letting the tail of the implement fall with a sharp crack upon Celina's peachy flesh. She squirmed, and a little pattern of brighter pink almost instantly appeared on her rounded skin.

'Harder than that!' cried her holy tormentor. 'And it does not count if the whip falls alone.'

Exasperated, Allegra remembered the way in which the priest had approached her. Unable to resist glancing over to him, she let her free hand caress the girl's shapely buttocks, feeling a slight tremor as she let her fingers slip between the open cleft. With a mixture of both dismay and desire she found her fingers growing wet and slippery. There was no doubt that Celina was in a state of readiness. With her index finger she tried her secret entrance. It was hot and ready, dilated with desire, Celina flinched at her touch.

'Forgive me,' she whispered as she pressed herself down upon the girl, feeling the heated flesh beneath her gradually relax and succumb. Against her own naked stomach she could feel the rounded milky rump pressing against her hotly. With thigh against thigh she explored

142

the angle of the leather extremity as it pressed into Celina's flesh. Easing it against the slippery fissure, she was rewarded by a shudder of pleasure from the girl.

It had not occurred to Allegra that this would be anything other than a deeply humiliating penance, but now she quickly understood that Celina was frantic for satisfaction. Her spine arched and her whole rear end rose in eager expectation of penetration. Grasping the thick column of leather between her fingers, Allegra did her best to guide it home, parting the quivering lips to find that gently pulsing entrance that longed to be filled. As the thickened head pressed against Celina's distended opening, Allegra at once felt a surge of pleasure. Beneath her, the girl was wanton; completely at her mercy as she pushed her hips forward inch by inch.

So this was how a man must feel, she mused as the thick column bore down into Celina's delicate flesh, transporting her into a state of rabid delight. It was a feeling of power and subjugation, like a warrior astride a horse. Very gently, she began to rock back and forth, watching the shiny black column drive in and out of the luxurious pink labia. Soon she could see the black rod growing wet and slippery as the girl strained at her bonds to have it ever deeper inside her. Feeling ever more unsettled, Allegra obliged, pushing further forward, forcing the stiff leather phallus deeper and deeper inside Celina's willing body.

With a sudden recollection, Allegra grasped the martinet tight in her hand, and let it loose on the girl's pounding rear. Not breaking her rhythm, she let it fall again, and again. Soon she was rewarded with a rapid convulsion in the girl's loins. With skilful timing she let the whip fall lightly but sharply on her flesh and at the same time gave her a series of sharp, long thrusts that forced her entrance ever wider. She could see now that the girl was taking almost all of its length, from the round tip to the thick base that was stretching her ever larger. Then, with a spasm that burst through the whole of her body, Celina's climax quickly came. She seemed to grasp the delightful appendage deep inside her as she shuddered and writhed on its unyielding length. But as Allegra paused, the Prioress bid her carry on. There were still another fifteen strokes to render.

'I am sorry, I must continue,' she whispered.

Now she could see Brother Guillam, his face attentive and flushed as he watched the two girls. Inside, Allegra laughed to think of his discomfiture. She had no doubt at all that beneath his long robe he was again in an agony of frustrated desire. How he had ridden her that night – he was certainly no beginner at the art. Watching his face, she began to rock her hips again, aware of her breasts gently swinging as she took the girl again with measured control. Deftly, she used the martinet – not to hurt but to scorch her senses even further. Now she could see him lick his dry lips, swallowing in discomfort as she taunted him.

She knew that he, too, remembered. What was it he had done? Tightly, she grasped Celina's waist and pulled her back and forth, rocking her on and off the stiff leather shaft. The girl had clearly had little enough time to recover her last ecstasy before again she was being pushed to new heights of pleasure. Willingly, she was letting herself be used in this way, enjoying the strange experience of a never ending supply of hard penetration. Letting the martinet fall again, Allegra whispered encouragement to her friend. 'Come on, take it all, my sweet.'

Again, she manoeuvred it as far as she dared, letting her wild imagination conjure visions of herself playing the thwarted priest. How difficult it must have been for him, to have a creature such as this writhing on his sensitive member, driving him to the limits of his control. Why, even with a lack of feeling in the appendage she could begin to feel delicious sensations clutching her own stomach, emanating from the underneath of the belt where the rough straps rubbed between her legs. On and

144

on she probed, teasing and tormenting Celina with the rod's long and inflexible tip, searing her with its length and hard resilient width. Soon she realised that the steady movement caused complementary friction to the strap rubbing against her own receptive vulva. Again, she raised the whip, and again fixed on the face of the priest. For sure, he looked ready to swoon now, so closely was he watching the pair of girls in their unnatural and frantic coupling. With a gesture of abandonment, she tossed back her hair and let him see her breasts as they rocked rhythmically, her nipples stiff with excitement and eager to be touched.

If only, she thought, he might again take me from behind – while at the front I took Celina. Closing her eyes, she imagined him approaching her from behind. She remembered the long, crimson phallus that he had barely been able to squeeze inside her. She would enjoy being beaten again, and what a delight to give Celina pleasure simultaneously. Giving Celina yet faster thrusts, she pictured his bending her slightly and parting her legs, forcing the swollen flesh inside her and then the three moving as one, driving her onwards, forcing the leather phallus ever deeper into Celina's eager flesh.

Glancing down, she could now see that Celina's lips were swollen and puffy as her excitement reached another unbridled peak. Like a sleepwalker, she watched the strange black pillar pound back and forth inside the girl's rosy cleft. Even more strongly, now, she pictured the priest astride her rear, driving her on as she mounted the girl. She imagined him gripping her waist, squeezing her breasts, pounding into her. In parallel to her fancy, she drove into Celina, whose face was now glazed with lust and almost unconscious with pleasure.

Uncontrollably, Allegra suddenly felt the strap beneath her grow fiery and with a sudden movement, she pushed it harder into the centre of Celina's juicy cleft. Only a few more strokes remained, but as she delivered them, she saw Celina's neck arch and her face fill with bliss. From nowhere, it seemed, a pulse within herself now burnt hotter and hotter. The strap was wet now, sliding back and forth, tormenting her flesh. Unable to control herself any longer, she fell like a rabid dog on to Celina's back, clasping her own thighs around Celina's, driving the black tormentor as hard as she could into her flesh.

In a desperate attempt to relieve herself, she forced her own vulva hard against the girl's, so their juices mingled and the strap finally tightened so hard it rubbed her sex into spasms of climactic pleasure. Beneath her, she could feel Celina shudder and quake as she experienced the full length of the phallus, so hard and sharply had it been driven inside her. Allegra clung there on her back for a long, trembling moment, feeling moisture trickle down from them both, so intense had been their coupling and release.

Utterly humiliated, she pulled off the girl, watching the long, dripping length of the phallus free itself from the girl's body. In her excitement, she had forgotten the hostile audience who watched her every move. Somehow, she had completely lost control and made an intensely foolish spectacle of herself. She felt utterly ashamed of herself, and unable to face the Prioress. Slowly, with head bowed, she walked over to pick up her clothes and brought her cloak across to cover Celina.

'Very well, you have accomplished your task,' she heard the Prioress say. 'And learnt something of yourself as you did it, I trust. But now you face a second task and a second riddle. We shall see if you are capable of solving a greater mystery.'

Chapter Eleven

*A*t the far end of the island, where dark cedars cast shadows even at noon, lay the infirmary. Allegra and Celina followed the directions given them, scuttering down snakelike corridors where shadows jumped and danced in the candlelight like spirits of the night. Allegra felt sick with tiredness, her long day in the city already having drained her body of its usual reserves. Worse, she could not decipher the second riddle, which rang in her mind like a hollow, clanging bell.

> 'Raise the pennant on the slippery pole,
> Awake the sleeper and unlock the soul.'

Desperately, she wondered where it was she had seen a flagpole – but no, she could not remember seeing any in the place. Only as she and Celina had wandered in vain through the moonlit building had Domica again taken pity on them and silently motioned them down towards the softly lit infirmary.

At last they reached the heavily draped portals of the sickroom. Drawing back the curtains, they found a dimly lit chamber filled with empty beds.

147

'What do we do now?' Celina grasped her arm, pinching the flesh tightly.

Shaking her head, Allegra looked about her but there were no clues here. The beds were neatly made but resolutely empty, the floor was clean of all but strewn herbs and the shelves bore only a heavy load of strangely coloured apothecaries' vials.

At the far end of the sickroom lay another door. Uncertainly, Allegra walked towards it. Beyond the gilded crucifix set out on the door lay a small chapel where those who could not be cured were laid to rest. A grim depiction of a sainted martyr spread across the frescoed wall and massed candles were spread in rows about the walls. And there, before a modest altar, was stretched a figure on a low dais of snowy marble: a handsome figure in a velvet robe with hollow cheeks and sunken eyes.

'It is the Abbot!' Celina cried. 'Allegra, please come away.'

Horrified, Allegra unhooked Celina's arm from hers and crept towards the figure. His face was as pale as wax and appeared to be sleeping. Yet, with a sense of terror, she reasoned he was indeed dead, so strange was his appearance here, as if he waited for his own funeral. With a quick, deliberate movement, she reached out to his dry lips. There was no breath. Placing the back of her fingers against his cheek, she felt the cold pallor of death. But noting a slow pulse at his neck, she checked this too. There, in the passage of his humours, was a sluggish movement. Her heart froze, watching the insensible man.

'He is not dead,' she whispered, as if she feared he might be listening as she spoke. 'But why he is here, I do not know. Surely the sisters should nurse him? He might easily die on this slab of marble.'

'I cannot believe it,' Celina muttered. 'Surely our task cannot be here?'

As her friend spoke, Allegra could not help but agree in her heart. Clearly they had found the sleeper – but how to awake him? If his soul had truly left his body, who were they to bring it back?

'Surely we are not expected to nurse him?' Allegra murmured. Lifting his inert hand, she felt a dead weight, as if it were the hand of a graven image. There was not a trace of warmth in his stiffening fingers. Yet surely they could not leave him, in the chill and deathly chapel? At last, Allegra formed a grim resolve. 'We must carry him into the sick room.'

And so, with much fear and revulsion, the two girls raised the corpse-like Abbot, bearing his weight like workmen carrying a load upon their backs. Once he was upon their shoulders, they could drag him along with little effort, although both girls felt a thrill of horror as his head lolled forward against them and his jaw loosed to show long, almost canine teeth.

Once they had reached the sickroom Allegra looked about for somewhere to lay him out. There at the far end lay a larger than usual bed, hung about with thin muslin drapes to guard against the flies. With much heaving and dragging, they eventually lowered the prone man on to the bed and arranged his limbs to lie with some semblance of order.

'He still has not woken,' Celina pronounced. 'And if this did not wake him, what would?'

'Yet he is certainly connected with the riddle.'

They sat awhile, shivering in the gloomy chamber; the candlelight casting eerie shadows across the veil-like drapes about the beds. It was very still and silent; fears and fancies fluttered in their minds like cobwebs flying in a faery breeze.

'Look, it's the darkest point of the night.' Celina drifted over to the window. The night was as dark and obscure as blackest velvet. Silver moths quivered on the air, dancing at the window with finely veined grey wings. The moon was hidden and even the stars, which usually twinkled across the sky, were vague and distant. Suddenly Celina started back from the window in alarm.

Turning to her companion in dismay, she said, 'Must we stay here? Please, Allegra, let us leave this place.'

'If only we could. But we cannot ignore the riddle. The answer will come to us if we are brave and stay here.'

In a few steps the girl was over at Allegra's side, slipping her warm arms around her waist. 'It is a bad thing to sleep in the same room as a corpse. Do you not know that? There are many stories of their malign influence. He is but newly dead and this is the worst time of all, when the sun is furthest from us. Think of all the spirits that walk at night. Just now, a moth came to the window with such a ghastly face like a skull and two black eyes that looked straight into mine. Allegra, please, let us go. So what if we fail? I do not care.'

Holding a candle up to the face of the man on the bed, Allegra shook her head. Maybe it was the amber flame that cast a wholesome light on his skin, but somehow she could not shake off her certainty that he was indeed alive. 'I am as frightened as you, but I know he is not dead. I will try to rouse him. Get along to bed then, and I will do my best alone.'

But at this, Celina seemed even more alarmed. 'You cannot stay here alone with it! Do you not know that if you fall asleep, his spirit may return and suck away your soul? Allegra, do not do it. No, I will stay and watch over you.'

After much altercation, it was agreed that they would both stay with the Abbot but would try their hardest not to fall asleep. Celina's mind was addled with such tales of gravewalkers and hobgoblins that she very nearly persuaded Allegra to desert the sleeping man. But still Allegra held firm. At last they decided to rouse him, for Allegra's whole being was intent on confounding the Prioress.

First of all, they applied warm cloths to his brow and hands. But his olive skin remained cool to the touch. Next, Allegra tried to waken him with the strong odour of sal volatile beneath his nostrils. This time, there was the slightest flicker of response. Each time she tried, she saw his eyelids flutter, but his eyes remained firmly closed.

'He is most certainly alive,' she whispered to Celina, who stood above her, shading a candle in her hand. A sudden dull sound made them both jump. It was the convent bell calling four long tolls.

Desperately, Allegra rubbed his hand between her own palms. His flesh was lifeless, as white and smooth as soap. Lifting his sleeve, she rubbed again, trying to activate the humours that had sunk back into his soul and died. 'Maybe if we rub his heart?' she asked.

'Allegra, please. Oh, please do not do that. He is as good as dead. It is repulsive.'

'But the power of touch is well known. Many of your old wives cure ills with the laying of hands. Might we not do the same? What is it they do?'

'Usually, they burn herbs, I think. And rub oils into the flesh of the ill person. But no – you must not do that! Please, I am frightened already.'

Despite her fear, impatience finally got the better of Allegra. 'These fears of yours are childish,' she snapped. 'Think of a life of beggary in the city. Is that what you want? To sit in rags in the arcade with nowhere to sleep and the rough words and kicks of the other rogues as your only company? Come on now, where is your courage? This poor man is only ill – it is a common thing, to fall down and lie still like this. If you cannot bring yourself to touch him, then I will. Only help me, will you, for your own sake?'

Relenting, Celina went over to the rows of bottles and jars to search for some useful remedies. Desperately, Allegra tried to recollect all she knew of the healing arts. It was very little. Only her certainty that if the riddle had been set, there must be an answer, fired her determination. Soon they had a little collection of blackened herbs and seeds, some bottles of oil and a small brass burner to place above the candle. Looking about her, Allegra was struck by the strangeness of the scene: the prostrate

151

body of the Abbot, still dressed in his long clerical robe, the little pile of strange objects which suggested some strange witching ritual, and Celina, now translucently pale in the candlelight, sitting on the bed with a cloak of muslin falling behind her like a wedding veil.

Beginning with the herbs, Allegra placed them in the brass burner and heated them with the flame. Soon, a thick, sweet smell rose into the air, which caught at the back of the throat and quickly made their heads swim. Carefully, Allegra tried to direct the plume of smoke towards the Abbot, but still he did not stir. The worst effects seemed to fall upon the two girls, who felt the room dance around them.

'What is it?' Celina asked, with her fingers pressed to her temples.

Allegra only shook her head, too fuddled to answer, unable to order her thoughts into a coherent answer.

Celina was by now lying back on the bed, her eyes half closed. With a groan Allegra joined her, feeling the bed heave and rock like a boat on a stormy ocean. Closing her eyes was no good; strange shapes appeared in front of her inner eye. Trails of smoke coalesced into long armed phantoms, chasing each other through prickly-armed forests. Allegra blinked, slowly opening and shutting her eyes. Even with her eyes uncomfortably open, she found herself acutely aware of the walls of the sickroom; they bulged and receded, as if an ocean were swelling behind the plasterwork.

'It is not real,' she muttered, glancing over at Celina who lay like a waxen doll side by side with the sleeping Abbot.

For a long while they lay side by side: the stiff, corpse-like Abbot and the two girls twined about him. In Allegra's fevered mind phantoms played in the half-light; invisible spirits circled the trio, watching the pair who still lived slumber alongside the dead. She had the sense that something strange was happening around her but was unsure what. Every noise vibrated like a cracked bell in her ears; her fingers felt far, far away on the ends of her arms. As if in a fever, she wondered how it was she had arrived in this place. The riddle surfaced in her mind like an impenetrable iron casket she could not unlock. There was something she was supposed to solve, but the fabric which connected one thing with another was fraying and falling apart.

Only the mournful bell tolling five roused her from a weary half-dream. Shivering, she pulled a sheet about her shoulders and considered the task still to be resolved. By her side, Celina slumbered on, wanly beautiful with pearly eyelids, her yellow hair tumbling freely on the shroud of muslin. As carefully as she could, Allegra picked up the objects which they had collected but whose purpose now seemed more obscure. Staring into a tiny bottle of purple fluid, she found herself fascinated by the bulging reflection of a face in the curve of the glass. With a start, she realised that it was her own countenance staring back at her. Emptying a few drops of oil on to her palm, she again stirred herself to attend to her original purpose – to try to wake the sleeping man. 'Come along, Celina.'

Celina's eyelids fluttered, then, yawning, she roused herself and stretched. Laughing softly, she suddenly leant over and blew the candle out. 'You see,' she smiled, 'I am no longer frightened.'

Outside, a breeze had lifted, and autumn leaves tapped hesitantly at the window. Far away, the tide was turning, with a muffled boom from distant breakers. The grey veil of dawn was lifting. At last they could properly see the figure sleeping between them. In the pale light the Abbot looked calm and serene and handsome. Dawn had swept away the cobwebs of fear.

Leaning across the sleeping man, Celina pushed back her friend's unruly hair and kissed her. 'You know the answer, don't you?' she whispered conspiratorially. When Allegra failed to reply she continued, 'The source of eternal youth?'

'No.'

Celina rolled on her stomach, kicking her legs lazily into the air. 'I feel as if I have been travelling in a strange land of dreams. All the stories I was ever told unfolded before my eyes – of princesses and tinkers, of goblins and dragons. I remembered a story about an old, old Emperor in a far away land who greatly feared his own passing away. He so much wanted to keep back the effects of old age, that he slept between two beautiful girls every night. The young flesh animated his vital spirits and renewed him every day by dawn.'

Allegra gazed down on the sleeping Abbot. Could it be true? She thought about how his cold flesh had already been warmed by their bodies, of how any living man must certainly respond to two such ardent bed-mates. Cautiously, she reached out and touched his cheek. It felt cool, but not as cold as it had at first been. 'You are right. I am sure he will wake.'

'Shall we undress him?' Celina asked. She was by her side, her eyes glassy in the grey light her side. 'Or just lie beside him?'

'Maybe if we try to warm him.' Cautiously, Allegra lowered herself beside the sleeping man, and Celina did the same at the other side. It was strange to lie there, pressed hard against a man who might almost be dead. In the silence, they thought their own thoughts, puzzling over life and death and what it is that lies between.

'Is it witchcraft then,' Celina suddenly whispered, 'to use such herbs? My head is only just clearing.' Lifting her golden head, she gazed blearily across the solemn profile of the Abbot towards Allegra. 'I have also had such peculiar thoughts about the sisterhood. They would not put a spell on us, would they?'

'No. I think it is only the herbs – they make life a kind of dream. They open up the doors to many mysteries, to that strange place where dreams and stories live as vividly as you or I.'

'Surely he will wake now?' Celina extended her hand to her friend, who thankfully clutched it.

'He should wake, but there is no sign.'

Rather more languorously, Celina leant across his prone body and began to pull at the man's clothing, lifting his long, velvet robe to reveal a muslin shirt which fell to his knees. With a few quick movements she had his gown over his head and he lay very still and vulnerable on the bed.

'Here, let me have that,' she said, snatching the purple vial. When she unstopped it, a warm, spicy scent filled the air. 'Surely he cannot resist us?' she laughed, rubbing the oil quickly between the palms of her hands.

Sitting up beside her, Allegra was struck by the ordinary appearance of the room. It was a long and rather pretty chamber, the muslin curtains hanging like faery webs and not like ghoulish shrouds. Thoughts of spirits and witches now seemed as foolish as the ideas of children.

As briskly as a nurse, Celina began to rub the lotion on the man's broad chest. 'Look. There seems a little more life.'

Together they did their best to rouse the man, rhythmically stroking the oil into his pliable flesh. The front of his shirt was open, but otherwise he still lay modestly covered.

'Do you think it is healing, this stuff?' Celina asked. 'For I am still sore from that beating you gave me.' With a simultaneously innocent but crude gesture, she patted her own behind.

'My sweet, I had forgotten entirely. It has been such a strange night, like a waking dream. Shall I try it?'

Biting her lip, Celina continued her ministrations for a while. 'I don't know. Maybe it's blasphemous here.'

But there was something about the girl's coyness that inflamed her friend. The night's events had been oddly exciting without being fully satisfying. Here, in this secretive tent of muslin, far from the spying eyes of the sisters, they could spend a little time privately together.

'Here, let me help you,' she offered, easing the

bunched skirts upwards over Celina's poor reddened bottom. Tipping a few drops on to the heated surface, she pleasurably began to knead the warm flesh, feeling the girl gratefully sway her hips back and forth towards her. Meanwhile, Celina continued to stroke the Abbot, intent on her work as if nothing were happening to herself at all.

'Tell me,' whispered Allegra, as she playfully darted a finger towards the girl's inner thigh, 'when I took you – what was it like? Did it truly feel like a man?'

Turning around to face her, Celina's face was a little more flushed. 'I should say it was,' the girl murmured. 'Though pretty big and awfully hard. And you took me hard, too. You were not gentle.'

'Oh, I am sorry.' In apology, she caressed the girl more softly, letting her fingers linger gently where the instrument had before so harshly bruised her. 'And was it this broad?' Playfully she pressed two fingers deep into the yielding flesh.

'Yet more than that.'

'Like so?' Stretching three fingers to their widest span, she felt the girl tremble, though she still continued her ministrations towards the Abbot.

'I do believe you would like the same treatment again,' she laughed.

'I would not.' Celina's voice, however, was a little breathless.

Allegra had remembered now, that in their confusion she still wore the peculiar belt strapped under her petticoat. With a mischievous giggle, she began to raise her skirts.

The first Celina knew of it was when her friend's fingers quickly withdrew and the hard leather phallus bore down upon her. With a squeal of appreciation, Celina let herself be taken, letting her friend drive deep inside her until, panting rapidly, she fell forward on top of the sleeping man. With sudden, quick fervour, Allegra's passion erupted; she kissed the girl's shoulders and

156

neck and clutched desperately at her arms and breasts. In a few moments Celina's bodice was open and in a clamour of desire, Allegra kissed her nape and her back, squeezed her breasts, trying to sate the fire that had erupted in the new light of dawn.

Again, she felt an unnatural power as she bore down upon the pliant girl, watching the long, leather rod torment her to the heights of pleasure. But dissatisfied even with the extent of the hard pleasure she was receiving, Allegra could see the girl was taking even more delight from the prone figure beneath her.

'You are insatiable,' she whispered in her ear, leaning forward to observe. Whether indeed their proximity had kindled the cleric, or whether Celina had been for some time quietly nuzzling the man's parts, he now stood crimson and erect and ready for pleasure. As Celina crouched over him with her rump uppermost and Allegra took her from behind, the girl bent over secretly, taking the fleshy member into her mouth, kissing it and sucking it in a paroxysm of pleasure. Not for long could she stand this double indulgence. Grasping her hips, Allegra aimed the long phallus deeply into Celina's cleft, forcing her to bear down on to the sleeping man so she received the fullest benefit of both. Almost instantly her hips buckled and shook, momentarily stretching rigid before she relaxed contentedly into Allegra's arms.

'You are wild,' Allegra told her, 'the greediest girl I have ever known.'

Like a gourmand contented at a feast, Celina lazily blinked. 'Why do you not have him?' she said. 'No one will ever know.'

Allegra looked at the long red member, its head now swollen purple, still wet from her friend's kisses. 'I could not,' she demurred.

But in a moment, her friend's arms were about her, her lips were kissing the soft skin at her throat and her fingers were avidly unfastening the laces at her front. 'No one would ever know,' Celina whispered. 'Here are

157

you a novice, yet in their midst you could enjoy a man's flesh. And no one will be the wiser – not even him.'

As she spoke, she awakened the fire which slumbered in Allegra's flesh, exciting her skin with short, sharp caresses. Pulling Allegra's breasts from the tight stays, Celina kneaded the sensitive spheres, making her friend gasp with delight as her nipples lengthened and swelled beneath the assault of finger and tongue.

'Go on,' Celina murmured in her ear, pushing her forward towards the red shaft which stood so tall and erect from the parting of muslin and black velvet.

'I cannot.'

But as Allegra hesitated, Celina was undoing her resolve, sliding her fingers between her thighs and teasing her lips with tender promises of pleasure still to come. Playfully letting her fingers slide around Allegra's secret entrance, Celina began to harry her victim, all the time leading her hand to the swollen rod which stood so firm. Finally, Allegra let her hand be led to the healthily reddened penis; with a sudden burst of pleasure she grasped it and felt a warm flood of lust fill her loins. It was true – private as they were here, she must have it inside her. Though still wearing the belt, it was easy to slide that to one side, and, with her back to the sleeping man's face, clamber astride him so his member jutted between her parted thighs. Holding it steady, Celina guided her friend downwards, until, with a spasm of bliss, she felt its flaming tip pierce her, then stretch her and finally pound deep within her.

It was like making love to two people. For as she rode astride the motionless phallus, neither would Celina let her be. Where the man lacked kisses and caresses, Celina made up for this, clambering across his thighs to press hard against Allegra, guiding her back and forth on the slippery rod. It was clear that Celina was transported just by observing the scene, enjoying watching her friend's aching slit bear down on the stationary cock.

Eagerly, she partook as well, caressing her in those

many ways which she knew would drive her quickly to the edge of rapture. Squeezing and stroking Allegra's buttocks, she increased the pace of her friend's thrusting, stroking her lips where the wide member forced them brutally apart. As the pace increased, Celina took Allegra's breasts and pinched the nipples hard, making Allegra cry out in both pain and dizzy pleasure.

Only when Allegra grew flushed and breathless, did Celina throw off her last few garments and grasp the leather penis which still bounced from Allegra's crotch. 'Let me be with you,' she groaned, sliding her thighs wide around Allegra's waist. With barely a second's hesitation in the rhythm of their coupling, Celina had mounted the false member and was riding too, driving her own willing flesh hard on to the spiky leather. Face to face, they kissed each other in a frenzy of lust, tongues probing hard into each other's mouths and fingers exploring every cranny of flesh.

With a pang of delight, Allegra felt the stiff rod of the Abbot twitch inside her. It had stood manfully for some time now, plunging deep inside her as her sensitive skin rippled and squeezed around its girth. Looking down now, she saw the wonderful sight of the reddened base of this true member disappearing inside her wet and swollen interior. At the same time, the cruel black phallus was tormenting Celina, stretching her wide around its base where her juices foamed with pleasure.

'Push against me,' Allegra begged, pulling her even closer. For even though they might both be pleasured by a male instrument, still she wanted to feel the soft, yielding pleasure of the female. Only by experiencing the deepest penetration could they make their two swollen lips graze one against the other. The effect was like sun on glass. While the Abbot's member seemed to be buried so deep within her she could feel the swollen head throbbing inside her, she still pushed hard against Celina's beautiful pouting lips.

In the agony before release Allegra grasped Celina,

pulling her down hard against her eager vulva, burying the leather probe unmercifully deep inside her. But with a wave of fire, their two burning clefts made frantic contact and, grinding one into the other, convulsed in an agony of bliss. Moaning, panting, their breasts kneading hard against each other's, their swollen lips rippling, they climbed the last few steps to rapture.

'Yes, he is here,' Allegra moaned, as pleasure erupted like a wave from the pit of her stomach to the ends of her fingers, 'he is with us.' For in the tumult of pleasure, she felt it – a hot surge in her loins, a spasm and release.

'Hurry, he is waking,' Celina giggled, noticing his eyelids fluttering.

'Help me, then.' Together they rapidly pulled down his tunic, trying simultaneously to pull on their clothes. In a few seconds all looked neat; his hands were folded modestly across his stomach and the two girls looked only a little dishevelled, as if they had indeed spent a sleepless night nursing their pitiful patient.

It was not a moment too soon. Tossing his head from one side to another, the man gradually wakened, his clear blue eyes finally meeting those of Allegra, who gazed at him somewhat abashed.

'You have slept for a long time.' Celina offered him a sip of water, for which he was clearly grateful. In reply he mouthed a phrase which at first they could not decipher. At last Allegra guessed that he asked for how long he had slept.

'It has been five days,' she said gently. 'Do you remember nothing?'

Thankfully, he shook his head, gazing with gratitude on the pair of novices who had so dutifully nursed him back to health.

'Then we must tell the sisters,' Allegra announced briskly, 'for we are truly grateful at your return to life. It is a great deliverance, for all of us.'

160

Chapter Twelve

'*I*t looks like a city of gold.'

The two girls had walked out to the shore, where the sun was now setting in a scarlet mass of radiant, gold-flecked clouds. The city itself glowed across the water, a luminous shimmer beneath the distant mountains.

'It is more lovely at a distance than close at hand,' Celina murmured. 'I dread being sent back as a beggar. What you said, it frightened me. What if we cannot solve the final riddle tonight? I should never have believed we might solve the first two.'

But Allegra was silent, wandering off alone to gaze out at the limitless water, her heart asking questions as deep as the very ocean she contemplated. There were more puzzles here, she reflected, than the riddles of the Prioress. Since sleeping so soundly most of the day, she had awoken in this mood of puzzlement. At this very moment, she compared the glamour of the city, with its rich mixture of vanity and beauty, with the very different glamour of the spiritual life that had so attracted her. Nothing was as it seemed. The city appeared to be made of burnished gold, but on closer inspection the traveller would find only solid, impenetrable stone. As for the sisterhood, its harshness and purity were rare things indeed in a world of hollow vanity.

Allegra stretched out her hand to her companion and Celina approached across the sand, falling gently in beside her. As they walked together, their two frames knitted one to the other, as comfortably as a baby folding into a mother's arms.

'Where would you rather be?' Allegra asked. 'Over there, or here on the island.'

'Here of course, in the care of the sisters. I have nowhere else to go.'

'And if you had somewhere to go?'

'It would depend upon who was with me, of course.'

It was as they took a late supper that they were called. The activities of the last few days had left Allegra with a new and vigorous appetite. Together, they had been feasting on cold chicken with fried polenta and some apples newly dried for the winter.

This new vitality seemed also to be benefiting Celina; no longer did she look translucently pale, like a frail aristocrat unable to stand the summer sun. There was a pink bloom to her cheeks and the long day's slumber had filled out the hollows in her cheeks and below her eyes. Replete with food as a traveller about to set off on a long and arduous journey, Allegra watched a dark figure approach the kitchen. It was one of the sisters crossing the garden.

'Sister Ino,' she whispered, nodding to Celina. Allegra's heart began to beat as if she were being called upon to fight or run a race. Quickly, she squeezed Celina's hand beneath the table, and in her turn, her friend squeezed it back. Whatever else, they would stand together in this trial.

As before, they were led down and down into the underground chamber. There was an air of occasion about the room tonight; a brazier burnt at the front of the hall and an ornate stone font stood beside it. Behind,

162

the sisterhood sat in a huddle of chairs, as if they had but recently witnessed some kind of entertainment. Allegra shuddered to think of what it might have been. Although the pain she had experienced at the sister's hands had mostly been to her pride, she did not doubt that they would brand and mark any they believed in need of punishment.

Sister Ino pushed them towards the centre of the floor, beneath the undulating painting of the Philomastrix. Her overturned crucifix was laden with flowers tonight, as if it were some feast day. Side by side, they faced the Prioress.

'So, I believe you have helped our Abbot to better health. That is good,' she said, as if bitter aloes were in her mouth. It was clear she had not expected success. 'And so you come with high hopes of succeeding with the third task. Well, do not expect to. I concede you have shown some wit and ingenuity in your attempts so far, but you have also had a large measure of luck. You will have no luck tonight.' Like a reptile, she licked her thin lips, watching them all the time with contempt.

'Again, you have until dawn to succeed. The task I set you is to find for me this thing:

<blockquote>
Crossed I am held,
Unmarked I am strapped
Untied I am bound
Unloosed I am trapped.'
</blockquote>

Allegra listened in complete bafflement. She guessed it to be some kind of instrument – but it might be any of the strange implements in the armoury. Then she remembered the riddle of the flagstaff, and even of the strange belt. Neither had suggested an obvious solution. Celina, too, looked completely bemused and even a little frightened.

The old woman smiled her terrifying smile. All of the company watched them with wry amusement as the

Prioress concluded. 'Until dawn, then.' Gathering her robes about her, she suddenly remembered one more item and raised her palm to attract their attention.

'You have some assistance tonight. Brother Guillam has volunteered to help with certain aspects of your task. There really was no great need, but I am persuaded that his strength may be needed. Very well, Brother. Proceed.'

Blushing slightly at the subtle admonishment, the young priest broke ranks with his spiritual family and approached the two girls. Remembering the frisson that had already passed between them, Allegra nodded shyly and lowered her face. But he set his face to ponder the distance without a sign that he had ever seen them before.

As before, once the riddle was set, the sisterhood returned to other discussion. Completely ignored, the three huddled together, anxious to make a start.

'What do we do now?' Celina wailed hopelessly.

'The armoury, as a start?'

Brother Guilllam nodded curtly at Allegra's suggestion and together they made for the low iron-studded door. Once inside, they wandered about the laden shelves, picking up strange implements and testing manacles and bracelets.

'It is some kind of restraint, I think.' Allegra was examining a set of silken bonds that hung on a large iron hook from the ceiling. 'What was it? Straps and bonds and traps?'

'And yet,' the young priest added as he joined her, 'each is with an opposite. There is something of a paradox here. As if the straps exist but at the same time do not.'

Absent-mindedly, he caressed the silk cord, testing its strength. When his hand brushed against Allegra's, she started and blushed but he appeared not to notice.

'Each of the first two riddles had to be enacted,' added Celina. 'When we find this restraint, maybe we must try it.' She was smiling now, as she picked up long feathery lashes and tested them in her hand. Not having been inside the armoury before, she was avidly curious, picking up some of the strange clothes kept here for unknown purposes – iron stays and corsets, wide leather belts and transparent, silky blouses.

The need to enact the riddle was something she had already wondered at, and was indeed already contemplating as she watched the intent young priest search this erotic chamber of delights.

'I can see nothing here,' he concluded, after looking quickly across all the shelves. Reluctantly, they returned to the main chamber, which now lay empty and expectant of their next move. The coals still burnt in the brazier and the candles as thick as a man's arm gently flickered, but all of the sisterhood had left. In keeping with her mood of defiance, Allegra sauntered over to the Prioress's vacant chair. It was as fine as a throne, an oaken seat inlaid with mother of pearl and gilded across the back. Resolutely, she sat in her enemy's seat. Closing her eyes, she thought hard. If she were the Prioress, what riddle would she set? Feeling this elevation above all others, sensing the desire from this throne to play off one against the other like puppets, she set her mind to work.

Guillam meanwhile inspected the brazier, disturbing the coals with a poker. 'This is hot. Hot enough to melt iron.'

'But what do we do with it?' Allegra asked, still with her eyes resolutely closed. 'What metal is there in the room?'

'The poker itself, some tongs, the candleholders, nothing else of interest.'

'Here,' began Celina, who was sitting on the edge of the birching block, 'are the metal rings which hold the straps.'

They were all silent for some time, contemplating any other uses for the fire.

As a thought occurred to her, Allegra rose and joined

Celina at the block. Sure enough, metal rings held the leather straps which had previously bound them both. 'Do you know anything about knots?' she suddenly cried out to the young priest.

'A little. What have you found?'

Joining her at the block, they tried and tested the four rings for some time, until with a sharp twist, Guillam showed them how the rings could be unloosed.

'So, we have four metal rings,' Allegra announced. 'But where do we put them?'

'And how can someone be untied but bound?' asked Celina

'It may be, as your friend here suggests, something to do with the knots. There are various types of knot – a slip knot for instance – which can grow tighter or looser with use. To leave the skin unmarked is easy, for we have a variety of soft fabrics.'

'And the frame itself? Something to be crossed?' Allegra asked eagerly.

'I have an idea of that,' he replied. 'While you collect the bonds, I will improvise.'

'Still, I do not understand,' persisted Celina. 'It doesn't make sense.'

'It will. Come with me,' Allegra said.

Taking her friend by the elbow, they re-entered the armoury.

'Why is he here?' Celina began immediately.

'To help us.'

'But we don't need help. We have solved the others alone.'

'What is it? I hope you are not jealous?'

'I have seen him look at you when you cannot see him. Some priest he is, to lust after you like a deer in rut.'

'And to lust after you, too, I am sure. That is what comes of a hot-blooded youth being forced to stay celibate. Come on, Celina. Choose some ties that would not mark the skin. Of as thin a fabric as possible.'

With a sulky pout Celina began to search, but Allegra

could see her heart was not in it. 'What about these?' She was holding a set of pink silk ribbons that looked far too delicate to hold a person's wrists.

Holding out her wrists, Allegra said, 'Try them.' With a few twists, the ribbons crossed and re-crossed the white skin of her wrists. As a trial of strength, she tugged. 'No, they are sharp and bite into the skin. There must be something else.'

Next they tried some soft deerskin buckles. But again, they left a red mark on the skin, growing harsh once the leather tightened. Finally, Celina picked up an odd set of restraints that looked like something that a horse or dog might wear to pull a sled. Made of soft nap leather on the outside, the inner surface was covered in even softer fur. Even the fastenings were fluffy loops of fur that slipped back and forth as easily as any knot.

'I will try them on you,' smiled Allegra, reaching out for Celina's delicate hand. In a trice Celina's two narrow wrists were secure in the soft fur bindings. Her friend pulled them tight so she could not move.

'How does that feel?'

'I cannot move – but there is no pain. It is as soft as snow.'

With a yank of the strap, she pulled the girl closer. 'And could I do as I like with you?'

Celina made a pretty play of struggling, but still managed to position herself below Allegra's mouth so as to be suddenly kissed. Playful as it was, their position with the one bound and the other in control suddenly excited them.

'I think you like it,' Allegra whispered, as she looked greedily down at the girl's dishevelled dress. With a poke of her finger, she pulled the girl's bodice apart to appraise her pretty breasts. Giggling, Celina tried again to struggle free but the bonds held her fast. 'I think I like it too.' With the ties held fast in her hands, she caressed the soft bulge of Celina's breasts, feeling the nipple stiffen through the fabric of her dress. 'Are you not a silly girl, to think I would prefer that priest to you?'

'I don't know,' breathed the girl.

'Well, I would not. For you have attributes,' and here she squeezed the whole, full spheres of her breasts, 'which he has not.'

'It is ready.' It was Guillam. Silently, he had crept into the room without either girl noticing. Allegra caught a fleeting expression on his face of avid interest; his eyes had narrowed with attention as he peered at their play and his cheeks were flushed. But in an instant he disguised his curiosity. Turning round, he led them back into the large chamber and hand in hand they followed.

He had constructed a large X-shaped frame in the centre of the floor. It took the girls a few seconds to realise that it was indeed the Philomastrix's overturned cross that formed the basic structure. To each of the arm ends was attached a ring of iron and the whole thing was suspended from a set of ropes that hung from the candelabra hooks in the ceiling. Once the fur-lined ties were knotted loosely the whole structure was ready.

'What now?' Allegra asked, but knew the answer.

'We have time to try it,' Guillam said.

She could see Celina's lovely mouth forming that foolish pout once more. She loved her friend too dearly to let her feel any pang of jealousy. 'Celina, you must try it.'

'Not I. It is for you, Allegra.'

'It is for one of us. You must try it first.' Taking the girl in her arms, she kissed her full on the mouth. As she expected, Celina was ardent to respond, though too proud to agree in speech. Kissing Celina's lips and throat, Allegra began to slip her friend's bodice and shift off, while the young priest looked on. Whether it was this audience which aroused her friend, Allegra did not know, but Celina responded like a harlot. Pulling at her bodice, she soon had her breasts hanging free, and

168

eagerly let Allegra rub and fondle them while she untied her skirts.

As she was revealed in all her lovely, smooth nakedness, it was evident to Allegra that some play-acting was at work here. Celina was flaunting her sensual beauty, letting Guillam see the full extent of her loveliness. And he, meanwhile, was almost rigid with excitement as he watched the girls at play, his breath coming fast and unevenly as he took in Celina's deliciously pointed breasts and smooth, rounded rump.

He was at first lost for words when Allegra asked what they might do next. 'Let her try the restraints,' he croaked.

Somewhat amused, Allegra helped Celina down on to the large cross, so that her arms and legs were opened in the shape of a large X. As she eased the fur ties around Celina's wrists, she whispered, 'I think he wants you, too.'

Celina's pout straightened somewhat into a mischievous little smile. It was true. The priest could not take his eyes off the delectable feast spread before him. With her arms raised above her head, Celina's breasts were swollen and rounded above her ribs, the pink nipples long and stiffened and aching to be touched. Even worse, the arms of the frame held her legs crudely wide; her ankles were bound apart to reveal the lovely pink cleft damp and ready at the core of her being.

'I believe it is customary to raise her,' Guillam said and grasped a rope, the whole frame lifted into the air, swinging before them like a giant candelabra. Squealing a little, Celina clearly enjoyed the odd sensation of being lifted on the instrument. For a few moments, she rocked back and forth.

'Well, why not begin?' Allegra invited. It did not need a second request for Guillam to reach out and tentatively caress Celina's small foot, then lowering his head, he kissed it. Meanwhile Allegra played with her breasts, pulling and teasing them until soon the girl was panting and aroused.

Looking down, Guillam had moved between the open cross of the frame, indulging himself in the luxury of Celina's milky thighs and open fissure. Again, he bowed his head as a supplicant, setting his mouth greedily at her lips, kissing and sucking until Celina could not help but moan in ecstasy.

'Let me have you both,' she whispered, and with a quick adjustment to the ropes, the rear end of the frame was lowered. With her head now lower, she begged Allegra to strip off too. As Guillam satisfied her with his eager tongue, so did Allegra tear off her clothes and gratefully slide above her, so that her aching centre might also be released.

With a sob of gratitude, Celina buried her face in the hot lips which her friend spread for her. Soon her tongue was at work, teasing and flicking, then driving hard at her entrance like a tiny, stiff member that drove her friend to distraction. The girls were rapidly engrossed in their pleasure, Allegra astride with Celina's tongue driving her again and again into a state of rapture. Below, the priest echoed her skills, worshipping her honeyed centre with his lips. Unable to take any more, Celina jerked her tongue in unison with the priest's probing explorations.

As the crucial second approached, he quickly slid his fingers deep inside her and gave her a fast, hard series of thrusts. Stretched wide and defenceless as she was, the girl felt a wave of unstoppable pleasure build in her pelvis. Like a flood the dam broke and, crying out loud, she experienced a climax as powerful as any coupling could give her.

'Now we must relieve our friend,' Allegra whispered to Celina. In a few seconds she was free of the bonds and they had persuaded Guillam to try the frame. Despite all his protests that he wished to avoid the restraints, it was still peculiarly easy for the two girls to overpower him.

With a few second's work, they had tightened the fur ties around his ankles and wrists. Lowering the frame, they let it swing at the height of their waists.

'I believe he is a very bad priest,' began Allegra, picking up a switch from the birching block and trying out the angle in the air. She was naked still, and she could see his eyes travel rapaciously over her body. He was painfully excited but not a little frightened of the power of the lust in which he was drowning. Letting Celina play the strumpet, she played the mistress. A soft blow of the switch to his thighs made him twitch, but without a doubt the pain was not too great through his robe.

'Let us see what lies beneath,' she cried, and lifting his hem with the switch, she let it trail over his knees to his thighs and over his great distended member.

Unable to resist, Celina reached out to play with it as soon as it emerged. Stooping to squeeze the long, crimson shaft between her breasts, she was rewarded with a groan of rapture from the unfortunate priest, who looked wildly from one naked girl to the other. Soon Celina had succeeded in making his penis twitch with anticipation, as she rolled the long muscle between her small fingers and gently squeezed his hardening scrotum. To keep him alert, Allegra applied the occasional smarting sting with the switch, tormenting him with insults and remarks about his lack of control.

'It is true,' he moaned, 'I cannot bear it. Please,' he begged 'let me have some release.'

'Shall we?' Allegra asked her friend with a mischievous wink.

'Oh, I don't think he's ready yet,' said Celina, stretching his penis as long as it might go. 'We must make him bigger than this.'

With a groan, the young priest let them continue their frolics, as they rubbed and squeezed him into a state on the constant edge of climax.

Finally, Allegra joined her friend at the juncture

between the man's legs. 'What does it taste like?' she asked.

At this Celina tried it, lowering her plump lips over the distended purple head. When she did not rise, Allegra too, began to kiss the base, licking the sensitive shaft and the heavy, bursting balls. Almost screaming with desire, the priest begged them to finish. He was wriggling in his bonds now, his hips twitching with pent-up desire.

'In our own good time,' Allegra lectured, giving him another taste of the switch on the base of his member. With a cry of lust rather than pain, he tried his best to lie still. But it was no good – for too long he had suppressed inflamed fantasies, reliving in secret the wild rites he had witnessed. When the two girls again administered their tongues and lips to his stiff, engorged phallus it was too late. With a spasm of deliverance his torso lifted to force his penis hard into their mouths and then again and again he discharged his load, groaning and sobbing at the power of his release.

It was with a deflated member that he dismounted, quite unsteady on his feet and trembling at the force of his long-repressed climax.

'And now you must experience the bonds,' Celina said.

With a few quick adjustments Allegra slipped on to the frame. It was not uncomfortable and felt oddly liberating as it swung in the air, leaving every sensitive part of her naked and exposed.

'I have brought something I know you want,' Celina confided. Laughing, Allegra looked about her. But it was with the greatest surprise that she saw Celina held the leather belt with the strange appendage. How many times she had pleasured Celina with it – but never had she wondered how it might feel herself.

'I don't know, Celina,' she began, suddenly unsure whether she wanted the long, black rod to be plunged inside her.

172

'There is no choice.'

'But I want you as you are.'

'And not know how it feels? Besides, I will be the man now.'

It was impossible to argue with the girl. She had strapped on the wide belt around her slender waist and where her reddish hair generally flowered, the black snake of leather now swung.

As cool as a man, Celina leant between Allegra's legs, caressing her swollen breasts which stiffened and jerked beneath her nimble fingers. It was impossible not to be aware of Guillam watching them too. He was standing close, as still and rigid as a soldier but his eyes were black as night. Like Celina, Allegra felt an upsurge of wantonness as she felt the priest's eyes gorge upon them, so every touch and lick administered by her lover was magnified in pleasure. Knowing every way in which to torment her, Celina positioned the false member close to the girl's lips where it teased her slippery opening with promises of hard and unyielding penetration. As she leant forward to suck each crimson nipple to the point of pleasurable transport, so did Celina begin to nudge the long piece of leather into the easy parting that led to the very entrance to her being.

'I cannot bear it,' Allegra moaned, feeling the cold, solid pipe work its way nearer and nearer her opening. It was like a penis but harder, so that when it passed inside her she felt her muscles grip it and find a resistance which was both strange and wonderful.

Celina was no beginner with the implement. Using the natural rocking motion of the frame, she stood still and let Allegra swing back and forth on the leather penis. Barely a few thrusts brought it deeper inside her, as it forced her slippery flesh apart to pound onwards and upwards. In a state of rapidly mounting excitement, Allegra watched the girl ride her, her breasts swinging back and forth and her face growing flushed and masterful with excitement.

'You must take more. You have given it all to me.'
With that she pushed yet more inches into Allegra, so
that it felt as long and stiff as a candle pounding back
and forth inside her.

To her surprise, she saw Guillam appear behind
Celina. In only a few minutes he had recovered his
manhood, which now stood erect once more and ready
for action. Breathlessly, she watched as he manfully
parted her legs from behind and penetrated her as she
stood. Now, Allegra could see him cramming her breasts
into his splayed fingers, forcing the pace as he thrust
inside her like a wild man. Each thrust of his bore Celina
down upon her friend, so soon the false penis was being
used at its full length, pushing back and forth as Guillam
set a rabid pace. It was almost too much to bear; the
leather device rammed into her with massive, dizzying
force.

Leaning forward, with a face suffused with lust, Celina
crawled on to her friend's body, so their breasts rubbed
hard against each other and their tongues could mingle
ecstatically. Allegra felt overwhelmed, as if satisfaction
could never be greater. Over Celina's shoulder, she could
see Guillam's face wet with perspiration as he grasped
Celina's upturned rear and rapidly pumped hard inside
her. The whole mix of sights and sensations, sounds and
scents made Allegra's senses reel. She could feel Celina's
tongue at her throat, her hardened nipples jutting pair
against pair, and the long leather penis stretching and
pounding within her like a well-aimed cudgel. With
rapidly increasing pants for breath, she felt a climax lift
within her like a giant wave.

'Press hard,' she whispered to Celina, who obediently
ground her vulva hard against the swollen bud at her
centre. One stroke, two strokes, at the third, everything
seemed to squeeze together. She was aware of the rigid
head of the phallus tormenting her deepest flesh and
Celina's wet slit pressing into hers. Then, with a groan
from Guillam, she felt him twitch and bear down. For a

174

moment they all lay there together, feeling satisfying runnels of moisture run down their thighs. Like one creature, the three pulsed with sweet after-spasms of gently released muscles.

With a sudden flash of torchlight, they became aware of others in the room. Stiffly disentangling limb from limb, the three eventually stood, naked and slippery. The Prioress and her company had drifted back to their places at the front of the chamber. How long they had been there watching, the three did not know.

'I see you have been keeping amused,' the Prioress said wryly. 'Above the ground the dawn has arrived. Now, which of you will give an account of your actions?'

Chapter Thirteen

'We have solved the riddle,' Guillam began, although Celina shot him an evil look.

'As you can see,' she interrupted quickly, 'Allegra and myself solved it easily.' They were both standing naked, quite unashamed before the assembled company. Only Allegra picked up her clothes and began pulling garments hastily about her shoulders.

From her viewpoint on the dais, the Prioress watched them with a barely suppressed glimmer of satisfaction. 'Explain.'

'Well, this is the cross,' began Celina, pointing to the frame, 'and of course the ties do not mark.' Suddenly puzzled at the whole solution, she paused, trying to remember how the riddle fitted together.

'Let me tell you,' said Brother Guillam cut in. 'The ties are slip knots, so that as the victim is bound, the ties unloose.'

They waited in uncomfortable silence as the Prioress considered. It had not been like this before; each time she had quickly, if reluctantly, confirmed their success.

'So what is the solution?' she commanded.

Somewhat feebly, Celina waved towards the frame.

Guillam stood stock still, his naked form glowing amber in the torchlight.

'I am afraid I must tell you,' she began, in a maliciously crooning tone, 'that you are wrong.'

Allegra could hear Celina gasp with astonishment. She had listened to enough of this travesty. It was time to speak. Slowly walking forward to the Prioress, she straightened her clothes and ran her fingers through her hair. Barely a handspan from the old woman, she halted.

'I have not yet given the solution.'

'You? And what do you suppose it to be?'

'The answer is this. You asked us what it is that holds us, which binds us and traps us. My companions are not the fools you imply them to be, to point at this device. Yet, as you well know, Holy Mother, that is too simple a solution. Brother Guillam is correct to suggest the bonds that held us grew loose as we struggled. Indeed, I quickly noticed that the more fiercely the victim struggled, the looser the bonds. Why then, I asked myself, did the victim not free themselves? Am I close to your solution?'

With a grim aspect, the Prioress nodded.

'There were no physical bonds or ties that held us tonight. Only one force kept us bound. It is the same answer which underpins both of the previous two riddles. Lust. Lust is the answer to your riddle. It does not mark, nor tie – but it traps. Am I correct?'

It took only a moment for the Prioress to recover her composure. But in that moment, Allegra could see fury flame across her face and then as quickly disappear behind a mask of composure. A sudden twisting of her fingers further suggested the restraint of a sudden flare of violent feelings.

'Very well,' she announced slowly. 'I see I must congratulate you, Sister Almoro. You have indeed won our little game. Not for you, the cold byways of the city. You have indeed earnt yourself a place in our order. From this day on, you have earnt the right to our virtues

177

of purity and discipline. You have fought with our enemy and won understanding. Welcome.'

At this she rose, and with all good grace, extended her hand to the girl. Flinching only a little, Allegra stepped forward, kneeled before her on the hard floor and kissed the great ruby sparkling on her ring.

'Thank you, Holy Mother.' Staring hard into the old woman's rheumy eyes she tried to penetrate that reptilian exterior. Standing, she felt her head swim with weariness, but forced herself to continue. 'But I am afraid I must decline your offer.'

Behind her she could hear Celina gasp with surprise. 'No, Allegra,' she whispered urgently. The company of sisters too, murmured their disapproval, like a flock of startled pigeons.

'What did you say?' demanded the Prioress imperiously, gripping the arms of her chair.

Taking a long breath, Allegra began to explain her new understanding. Once she began, the words tumbled out, but she knew she had never spoken a truer word. 'When I came to you, I was a fool,' she began. 'The world of the physical, the world of the flesh – they were repugnant to me. Yes, I was frightened by them, by what you know as the enemy named lust. What a monster it seemed to me then – so enormous, wild and irresistible. Quite rightly, you tried me and tested me. That which I feared was indeed within my own self. Like a hunter who fears the wild creatures of the night, I became a coward, fearing instead the very act of hunting itself. But your riddles have taught me to tame those creatures, to welcome them and love them. Now you want me to trap them in the cages of discipline and obedience.'

The room had fallen absolutely silent; all that could be heard was the slow clink of embers dying in the brazier.

'You see,' she continued, 'I cannot be a nun. What attracted me was fear, but you have saved me from that. My pride was brittle: the mask of a fool. You have helped me to learn that I need freedom. Yes, I respect

178

your discipline and your harsh rites. For those I will always be grateful. But no, my way is back in the city where I can be free.'

'And I suppose you think this is some way of getting your dowry back?' the old woman snapped.

'No,' she replied quickly. 'The gold is yours. That is small payment for what I have learnt.'

Behind her, she could hear Celina groan, calling out to her to reconsider.

'Very well,' the Prioress agreed, though somewhat surprised. 'You are free to go.'

With a rapidly beating heart, Allegra gathered her skirts and returned to the others. Facing Celina was not easy.

Still naked as a child, she glared at Allegra as if she was a lunatic. 'How could you?' she seethed in a loud whisper.

'Celina, will you come with me?' her friend asked, offering her an outstretched hand.

The Prioress interrupted, calling out to her, 'You may stay with us here, Sister Dorico. You will be safe in our care.'

But with a resigned groan, the girl took Allegra's hand and kissed her on the cheek. 'Let us not be parted.'

'And you, Brother Guillam? Surely you cannot stay here now?'

As naked as Adam, he stood, hesitantly biting his lip. He was no more than a boy, she realised for the first time; like Celina he was probably an outcast from his family, given to the nuns to be fed and clothed and cruelly used. But his answer belied any attempt to understand him.

'I will stay. Today the enemy you described overcame me and I must do long penance to beat him out from within me. But I will overcome this foe. I will not be trapped in this cage of lust.'

'But it is a cage one chooses to enter or leave,' Allegra began, before seeing he was resolute. 'Very well,' she agreed, kissing him chastely on the cheek. 'I wish you well, Guillam. Do not punish yourself for being only what you are. I will always be a friend to you, should you seek me out.'

As they left, he looked after them, suddenly confused by Allegra's kindness. But the Prioress shot a glance of disapproval at him as sharp as any arrow. 'Clear this up, Brother,' they heard her shriek as they mounted the stairs. As obedient as a well-trained dog, he set to work, picking up the bonds which had restrained him and tidying them neatly away for the sisters.

Dismounting from the boat, the girls found the city veiled with a silvery rime. The massive stones of the quayside were black with ice and all around them the arches and bridges, columns and balconies of the city were dressed in icy, sparkling frost. It was hard not to think of the convent's raging fireplaces within its thick, protective walls as they slithered up the steps.

'Where are we going?' Celina complained, pulling her thin cloak tight around her shivering shoulders.

'You will see.'

Allegra had at least benefited from reclaiming her clothes from the convent store. The black taffeta was hardly a winter dress, and her cloak was more of an ornament than a comfort, but at least she had the satisfaction of looking like a lady. Poor Celina's clothes, when they had at last found them, were the threadbare garments of a neglected child. Reluctantly, she had kept her brown skirt and cloak. As they walked into the Piazza, Celina hung back a little, until her friend had to remonstrate against her for her slowness.

'Come along, you may get lost. That is the last thing I want. Walk with me, arm in arm.' Then Allegra noticed her friend was peering into the dark openings of the arcades. Catching a movement in there, she suddenly recollected why Celina would be so curious. 'Do not worry,' she laughed, 'we will not need to sleep in there.

180

I am sorry if I frightened you with tales of beggars and rogues. We are not reduced to that, yet. I have an idea.'

With a very loud sigh, Celina let herself be led forward. She shook her head as they entered a narrow *calle* between two high buildings. But Celina's fears were substantiated when Signor Bartolomeo's clerk told them that his master was not available. It was almost carnival, he explained, as if to two children, and from the start of the carnival the office would only be open for necessary business.

'I have most important news,' Allegra urged. 'He will wish to know immediately.'

The clerk was reluctant; he had clearly received orders to keep all business as far away as possible from his master.

There was no alternative but to do business Venetian style. From what little was left in her silken pocket, Allegra transferred a couple of sous to the clerk's hand. 'Blessings for Christmas, Signor.'

The transformation was immediate. 'It comes back to me that in an urgent situation he may be disturbed. This is urgent? Very well, you will find him at 2971 Castello.'

With the address burning brightly in her mind, Allegra set off once more.

'Why do you need to speak to him?' Celina asked. 'Should we not find a place to rest?'

It was beginning to snow as they set forth. Beneath their feet the slippery *calle* floors were treacherous, and the steps of frequent bridges lethal. Huddled together, their hands growing chapped and raw, they did their best to find the house, soon wishing they had asked for clearer details of its location.

An hour of cold and shivering wetness brought them out into a deserted piazza so like a hundred others, with an ornate, carved church, a fountain at the centre and row upon row of very tightly locked green shutters. They had seen the number 2962 some way back – the labyrinth that formed the backways of the city could baffle even long-lived residents. At last they saw a movement at one of the heavy doors. Stepping into the snow was a man in a legal toga, accompanied by a servant who held an umbrella carefully over his powdered wig.

'That must be it,' breathed Allegra, as she scampered over to the door. Rapid inquiries confirmed that it was indeed the Quill and Powder Club, refuge of judges, notaries and advocates. A liveried servant let them in.

Signor Bartolomeo was tucked well away from the perils of the weather. Sitting by an open fireplace, he was contentedly reading his gazette while a cup of coffee steamed lazily at a little card table by his chair.

'Signor, forgive the intrusion.' Allegra swept a couple of chairs over, so they might join him. 'I urgently need to take your advice.'

'I'm sure I don't know how I could be of service,' he stuttered, reluctantly putting his newspaper to one side.

'You will be pleased, I assure you. As I remember, there was a certain set of items left me as a legacy in which you were interested?'

'Indeed.' He patted his lips with a napkin and looked pointedly at Celina.

'A trusted friend.'

'Some coffee, ladies? Some cake?'

Warmed by the fire and gallons of strong, bitter coffee, Allegra began to outline her plan. 'Can you assure me, Signor, that you can legally secure the bequest for me? Make it totally secure. Draw up a paper to that effect. As the sisters have my dowry, it is all I own.'

The notary puzzled over this for a little while, asking for dates and other details of the paper she had signed at the convent.

'You see, I would like to help you share the collection,' Allegra urged. 'For a price.'

'Then name your price.' His small eyes narrowed. She was sure he was trying to conceal his tremendous desire

182

for the goods. 'I suggest the following. You secure my
ownership of the goods and we continue to store them
in the old palace by your office. You and your connois-
seur friends may borrow, indeed use, the collection as
you wish. It will be easy enough there, only next door to
your business.'

He was clearly hooked, though he tried to stifle the
glint in his eye.

'In return, my terms are small. You pay me a rental –
a small amount, say fifty lire a quarter. Also, you let me
live on in the Barnabotti palazzo to guard my collection.
It is empty now, so no loss to you.'

Sipping his coffee, the Signor considered. For a small
fee he would secure access to the best private collection
of curiosa in Europe. And it would be there, next door
to his office.

'Done,' he said.

'An advance on rental?'

'Certainly.'

With a deliciously heavy coin of silver in one palm and
an ornate key in the other, Allegra led Celina once more
out into the snow. It had settled now like a cloak of
ermine; the little piazza glittered in the moonlight and
the air was crisp and sweet. Pulling their cloaks tightly
around themselves, they lingered for a few moments to
admire the twinkling solitude. At the twin windows of
the parish church the amber glow of candles cast a
homely glow. Above, the sky was heavy with iron grey
snow clouds which scudded across the moon. The peaceful air was resonant with hushed, icy beauty.

'Come along,' Allegra called to her friend. She was
transfixed, her face rapt with emotion as she studied the
tranquil scene. 'I must show you our new home.'

For the first few weeks they did not venture far. The
rambling Palazzo Raffi needed airing, dusting, polishing,
washing and scrubbing. They set up their quarters in

one of the front rooms where the narrow gothic windows were not so large that they might let in too much cold air. The frame of a bed was the starting point, and over subsequent days, as the fifty lire piece was changed down into smaller and more useful coins, they haggled for linen and rugs and an easily mended feather-mattress. Soon they learnt who would deliver firewood, where milk was to be got and which taverns provided a hot meal on the owner's plate for a few sous. Discreet inquiries to Signor Bartolomeo led them to house sales where no more than an ancient housekeeper presided over salons of old-fashioned porcelain, candlesticks and silver.

Now it was not the insistent convent bell which woke them before dawn but the clarion bells of the city which gently lured them awake well past the start of the day. Stretching and lazing in the vast feather bed, they listened to the scurry of the wooden pattens of those citizens who were forced to scuttle to work. But for most of the city, the carnival was a holiday; shops reduced their hours of business and the offices of government only opened by appointment. Nevertheless, more money was made then than throughout the rest of the year – it was simply so much more enjoyable to don a mask and coax money from the masqueraders directly.

It soon became apparent that the notary was an expert in the shifty underworld of ill luck and repossession. It was no accident that he had acquired the rental of the Palazzo Raffi. At first it seemed a tragedy to the girls that so many of the old families were reduced to selling their goods for the price of the food to keep their kin alive. Some of the nobility whose names were inscribed in the Doge's Book of Gold had declined in number to a single, infirm member. When that last representative died, whole estates and palaces were quietly put up for sale.

'Why is it, Signor, that you deal so much in death?' Allegra asked a few weeks later, as the notary dropped in to borrow a few items for his club. Her guardian's collection was now housed in the former library. It was a little shabbily hung, but at least the gentlemen visitors could take their choice from the shelves at their ease. Celina and Allegra also occasionally visited and learnt a great deal too.

'That is the purpose of the law, my dear, to set out the accounts, both for birth and death.'

He was somewhat engrossed in a book spread on his lap. The girl could just see a set of illustrations concerning a woman and a many-armed god. In some of the pictures he was making very immodest use of his dozens of fingers.

'But the old families – so many are dying away. If I think of my own, there is only Leon and myself left.'

At the mention of Leon, the notary turned the book over on his lap. 'Your cousin? Well, he is a case in point. These families – your good self excluded – have run their course. Money made in the old days from merchanting and business has been squandered. Good blood squandered, too – diluted in cousin marrying cousin and brothers sharing wives. They will not marry outside their kin for fear of losing wealth and yet by mixing similar blood they breed poorer and poorer specimens. Your typical noble is no better than Leon.'

'Have you seen him?'

'On odd occasions. He was not impressive over the will. He tried to have your dowry returned, but I would not hear of it. Now there is the Palazzo di Rivero falling to rack and ruin. The servants dismissed and no use made of his place in senate. As a senator he could at least do as the rest and bribe his way into a useful position in government, but no, he does not care to be up before noon or in from the whore house before the dawn.'

This was sad news for Allegra; while it had not been her own home, her guardian's house had once been a kind of home. She wondered what had happened to the servants, and how long it would be before Leon fell into the state of ruin which brought gentlemen like Signor Bartolomeo to take a particular interest in his affairs.

'Now, I have news to cheer you.'

The little agreement between Allegra and her notary had bred nice, easy relations between them. They both considered each other useful people to know.

'A certain marquise has had the misfortune to pass away in this cold snap. An old lady, certainly, but once a favourite at the court of the old Sun King. They say she had such clothes laid by that were the best produced in France. And costumes for balls and carnival as were once written of in the Paris newspaper.'

Already, Allegra was clapping her hands with delight.

'They are in my custody until the will is read on Sunday. With carnival upon us, you might borrow – let me see, what would you need? A full costume each from the collection? If you give my name to the servant they will let you have your pick.'

It had been hard to ignore the carnival gathering speed around them. From Saint Stephen's day the citizens had donned dominoes and masks and even the thousands of visitors to the city had hired and begged costumes from their hosts. Venetians favoured traditional roles: Harlequin in his diamond patterned suit and sweet, untouchable Columbine. The mad University Doctor and the Brigand, the white faced Pierrot and silly, egg throwing Signor Punch. Already Allegra and Celina had marvelled at the glorious costumes of the rich. Wrapped in dominoes of gold cloth and masked in black velvet, the nobility of Europe glided into ballrooms and masques like glorious phantoms of another age. Together they had looked at the clothes stalls for suitable outfits but they were far too late to find anything of quality. Every costume of distinction or interest was already hanging on another's back.

Taking a gondola to the old marquise's house, the two

girls could barely stifle their excitement. Beyond the heavy drapes of the craft, they could see the crowds out in masses along the quays, gathering for a bull race, or off to watch the acrobats at the Piazza. Without even masks, the two friends had felt oddly out of place in the city – even the watchmen wore masks of devils and the old man who swept the alley wore the bib and costume of a child. As they slipped through the water, Allegra pointed to a beggar, huddled beneath an archway. So mad was the city for carnival, even the destitute were masked.

Inside the marquise's house they found a series of elegant, faded salons. Far up, beneath the rooftop, lay the stores, where costumes had been packed in oaken chests strewn with bunches of dried roses. The first beautiful outfit they found was an English riding habit of green velvet.

'Can you not see me, riding a chestnut mare?' Allegra cried, holding the costume high to her breast.

Next was a court dress. It was quite out of fashion but so studded with jewels and feathers that it stood up alone, as if the marquise had only just that hour stepped out of it. The first of the masquing clothes was the dress of a shepherdess. With a striped silk petticoat and pink rickrack laces, they pronounced it to be divine. But then the treasure trove tumbled open – the costumes of Turkish slaves, goddesses, vestal virgins, Amazons. Then there were the personages brought to life from pictures: the black velvet of Mary Stuart of Scotland, Rubens' wife with her white feathered hat, the burgundy velvet of Signorina Borgia. In an ecstasy of dressing up, they paraded before the mirror. Almost dancing with excitement, Allegra began to realise the nature of the mask.

'We might be anyone we like when we step outside.' Carefully, she slid a black velvet mask across her face. Only her eyes twinkled through the slits. She felt secretive, wild and free. She looked at Celina, who was

187

pulling a glorious confection of blue silk moiré about her shoulders. Masked, she might be a princess or a cowman's daughter.

The light was fading and the lamps at public shrines were being lit before the girls had finally decided. At last they swept out, to join the throngs in the darkening byways. At the head was pretty Columbine whose traditional dress was of the finest satin, printed in a diamond-shaped pattern of reds, and greens and blues. The skirt fell in three tiers from a tiny waist and old-fashioned puffed sleeves were slit to show fabulous satin undersleeves. At her neck was a coquettish spiked ruff of finest lace, below which her breasts were bare to the tightly laced bodice. The effect was completed by a little scarlet half cape at her shoulders and matching cap with three nodding feathers.

Behind was a sensual odalisque, whose oriental shift wafted transparently over her lovely form. With a patterned brocade skirt and fur lined cape, the effect was of a character from the *Thousand and One Nights*. On her golden hair an aigrette of jewels was set at an angle and a girdle of gold kilted up her gown to show sheer, damask trousers. With a half-corset squeezing her waist, the effect was dazzling. In a pair of Moroccan embroidered slippers, she floated along the slippery *calli*.

The final touch was a pair of coquettish masks. Columbine's eyes glittered behind an eye mask of ebony silk and the odalisque smiled through a peacock feather guise.

At the Rialto market they halted, surveying the rings of torches around fortune tellers, mountebanks, tumblers and quacks. In the far distance they could see fireworks lighting the sky. A bonfire raged in the piazza and the sweet scent of roasted meats drifted on the air.

'Where do we start?' the odalisque whispered.

She was trembling now, with the fierce excitement of it all.

'We must start at the centre,' Columbine whispered, squeezing her arm. 'Let us first see the nobles at play. With a mask the Ridotto is open to all. Perhaps we might win at the tables tonight.'

Chapter Fourteen

*T*he old patrician at the doorway of the Ridotto welcomed Allegra and Celina with a slight incline of his head. All summer the lavish doors of the gaming rooms were closed to any of less than noble birth, but come carnival the mask not only erased individual faces, but also the divisions of class. It was impossible not to notice a flutter of interest from the gentlemen in the salon as they approached.

'May I be of assistance to you ladies?' the man wore the red robes and cap of a cardinal, from which Allegra construed he must be of the opposite type.

'You may, sir, for we are unfamiliar with this place. Are the gaming rooms here?'

She had quickly looked about, but could only see the fabulously costumed crowd gossiping in groups, sipping cordial and eating from great plates of iced fruit.

'I would escort you, signorinas, only then I would lose the pleasure of listening to your fair voices. The gaming halls are strictly silent,' he said, with a shake of his head, 'and I should very much like to converse awhile with you.'

It was an interesting game, Allegra thought, to try to penetrate the mask and guess at the age, type and countenance of the man. However, she noticed Celina standing quite dejected and alone a little distance away. It was poor manners indeed of the cardinal to pay court only to one and ignore the other.

'It is the silence of the tables which calls us, signor. Our conversation must end here.' With a slight bow, she took Celina's arm, and moved forward into the crowd. In only a few more steps they were assailed, this time by a man all decked out like a wild man, hung with animal skins and bearing a cudgel.

'Why, I do know you,' he began. 'And you too, my pretty Turk.'

'Sir, you do not,' snapped Allegra. It was clearly a common line he was spinning. Besides, she knew it was poor manners to expose a mask.

At last they reached the far end of the room, and indeed the level of chatter was here diminished. Another patrician in his long wig sat at a heavily curtained entrance. Before him was laid a table on which were set great piles of coins and counters.

'Sir, may we observe?'

With a bored nod he let them through.

The chamber was not as the girls had imagined it. Where excitement and liveliness might be expected there was silence and concentration. Many of those at the tables wore the white skeletal masks called *volto*, which hung upon their black hoods and capes like the nodding heads of spectres. The most richly dressed nobles walked idly amongst the tables, their dominoes heavy with gold and fur. Both girls wondered how they could bear the weight of damask cloaks, fur muffs and stiff, panniered dresses. All were masked, even the children selling cordial and the servants sweeping the floors. A soft, hissing sound floated on the air, and a less frequent metallic clink. It was the sound of cards falling one on another and the ceaseless exchange of coins.

Promenading from one group to another, Allegra tried to follow the games but soon failed. Choosing instead to study the players, she soon noticed the companion to her character lounging at a table with a group of richly apparelled masqueraders and some heavily powdered patricians. Though dressed as the servant Harlequin, the man's costume matched her own in its sumptuous style and richly printed fabrics. Noticing her interest, he made Harlequin's ornate, ridiculous bow towards her.

Unable to resist, she found herself smiling. Beneath the costume he looked a fine man, with curling fair hair beneath his plumed cap and a pleasing shape. Unlike many of the lesser Harlequins she had noticed, he had no hanging paunch and his shoulders were pleasingly broad. His hands, too, were well formed and neat as they laconically threw down cards.

Silently, he motioned her across. Inwardly pleased, she stood beside him. In the way of a mime, he motioned her to choose a card, which he then threw down. A few moments later, a pile of coins was pushed towards him. This mummer's show continued for a while and each game his winnings grew. At last, he motioned his resignation from the game and with his friend, a swaggering Scaramouche, rose from the table and escorted Celina and Allegra to the salon.

'I thank you, mademoiselle, for your lucky choice. Now I must help you spend your bounty.'

His voice was not as she expected. It was melodic, with the accent of a Frenchman. Yet, it was certainly the voice of a gentleman. She smiled and asked how that might be.

'You have won almost ten gold ducats. What better place to spend it than the Serenissima on a carnival night? Look, the moon is up. Where would you care to spend first?'

Despite protestations that it was he who had won the money, he politely and calmly insisted. Looking to Celina for support, she got none. Clearly the Scaramouche had taken her fancy; he was also a tall, dark-looking man, dressed in a striped doublet and hose with a great satin sash across his chest and a large iron sword hanging from his waist.

Over the next few hours they did their utmost to spend the money with the greatest enthusiasm. They ate roasted nuts in the Piazza, threw coins to the child tumblers, bought an ivory fan and paid for a song to be sung to them by a band of Neapolitan balladeers. For a few sous they all had their fortunes told, and Allegra heard that she would never want for money. 'That is true,' she laughed to her companions, 'if I hang about the Ridotto each night.'

Although she found the Harlequin well mannered and civil, he was yet no sighing lover. He carefully directed the proceedings and seemed to stand back a little, enjoying the night by giving her pleasure, as if for himself, he had seen it all before. He was proud, too, and would not take any but the best place in the crowd at the bull races when they began near midnight.

'It is not worth staying for unless we have a good place. The rabble may squash together, but I could not see two such elegant ladies pushed about by the crowd.'

Pushing a few sous into the hands of a ragged attendant, they mounted a wooden dais on which were a series of tiered steps. Next, he attended to bets, and Allegra divided the remainder of her cash for the four to wager. Without a second thought she placed her money on the blue bull from the San Marco district of the city.

It was as they waited for the animals to begin, that he asked her why he had not seen her before at the salon.

'Why, sir, we are but newly out of our convent.'

A flicker of interest passed behind his mask. 'And which is that? Santa Virgilio?'

The place he mentioned was an institution frequented by daughters of the nobility. It was known for its laxity and elegance and not at all for its religious order.

Smiling, Allegra corrected his opinion. 'Not at all. We have just escaped from the harsh sisterhood who live on the rock of Santa Agnetha. Indeed, this is our first night of carnival.'

'You cannot be,' he cried incredulously. 'A pair of real nuns. On your first night of freedom?'

'I am afraid so,' she grinned.

'Forgive me, I thought you were two senator's daughters tasting the low life. Your clothes, you see. But,' and here he thought of his words carefully, 'did you not pine for masculine company while you were shut away?'

She knew what he meant, and decided to tease him. 'Desperately,' she said, squeezing his hand. 'To be locked away on a miserable island without any sight or sound of a man – it was terrible. And to think that the pair of us were too young when we left the city to ever have been in the company of men at all. It has almost been too much for our young bodies to bear. You see, it is an unnatural life, without a man, if you understand me.'

By his open mouth, she guessed the Harlequin understood her drift. She could see that Celina was doing her best to smother her laughter but the Scaramouche, too, was dumbfounded by their good luck.

'So,' began the Harlequin, slipping his arm about her waist, 'are you enjoying yourself now?'

'Indeed I am, sir. But I should hope this is only a prelude to the incomparable pleasures we may sample later on.'

Again, it amused her to see his Adam's apple bob up and down as he swallowed rather quickly.

'And you,' the Scaramouche asked Celina, 'surely you were not incarcerated in this terrible place as well? Such loveliness must fade without the appreciation of a male eye.'

'Indeed it would,' she agreed with a straight face. 'For I had only my friend here to share my chamber, and what good is that, you may ask?'

'I do commiserate,' the Scaramouche said, 'for anyone might see you were made for a man's pleasure.'

With her eyes rolling upwards to heaven, Allegra at

194

this point considered dumping the patronising pair, but by now they were entirely hemmed in by the crowd. As the bulls were led to the starting point by their masters, the throng pushed and shoved to get a sight of their favourite.

As they watched the proceedings move forward at an exceedingly slow pace, Allegra felt her partner sidle behind her, his arm still tight about her waist.

'Your costume is very fine for a runaway nun,' he said. 'I hope you are not teasing me.'

He had begun to kiss the back of her neck below the pretty ruff, taking advantage of the press to bear against her with his body. She swung around, still pressed up close to him.

'I swear on my friend's life, we have just come from Santa Agnetha. In truth, our friendly notary arranged our costumes as a favour. They are from the estate of a dead marquise.'

'I swear you are as resourceful as your character. Like Columbine, you are clever.'

'And are you then like your character Harlequin?'

'How's that?'

The character was known both for his dense brain and his bawdy appetite. In kindness, she elaborated on the latter.

'Do you desperately want your Columbine?' she whispered.

'Of course,' he answered hoarsely.

'It has been such a long time,' she sighed elaborately, and pressed her cheek to his shoulder, laughing to herself.

'I am a gentleman,' he announced. 'I assure you I will more than compensate for any lack you may have experienced in the past.'

Yet when he wrapped her in his arms and began to nuzzle at her ears she could forgive at least some of his conceit. Although his mask made his kissing a little cumbersome, still it added to the piquancy of the situation. As he was not sure of her, so was she not at all sure who he could be. The most likely was that he was some young dandy on the grand tour, visiting the city as part of a liberal education before he took up his dull life in some dull province. His ready profession to being a gentleman suggested this.

'And you?' she whispered. 'Are you a visitor to the city?'

Idly, she let him slip his fingers in through the gap in her skirt. He was stroking the soft taffeta lining, trying to find the heat of her flesh. As he pressed up hard against her back, she leant upon him, enjoying his attentions as they stood so boldly in the crowd.

'You will see when we retire,' he murmured, his fingertips working through a layer of lace. Looking across, she could see that Celina was similarly at play with the Scaramouche, who was openly caressing the thin fabric of her costume. No one cared or noticed. The crowd of revellers were drunk on either wine or excitement, so happy were most to be gathered in such a city on such a night.

As the bulls assembled at the starting line in the Piazza, the crowd began to clamour. Each beast bore a rosette of a different colour, representing the different districts of the city, and therefore separate cheers rose from the crowd as each bull-bearer lifted his colours.

'It is like the circus in ancient Rome,' murmured the Harlequin. 'This is what I like so much about this place. It is a society without needless controls. Licence is all. What do you say, my errant nun?' As he spoke, he succeeded in breaking through the protective tissue of lace. With firm, seeking fingertips, he began to stroke her rounded flank.

'I say – what are rules but a restraint? Are not restraints on a creature a means to train, but once trained, to be thrown away?'

'I think you are exceptional,' he murmured, but

196

whether this was spoken in reply or as a response to his eager explorations of her body, she could not tell.

With the thunderous boom of a pistol the race began. Suddenly the air vibrated with the clamour of the crowd, bellowing, shrieking and whistling for their own runner. From their high viewpoint, Allegra could see the bulls begin their circuit around the square. Some were indeed running, but others were puzzled and sniffed the warm air while one or two pawed the ground in anger. As if their cries could indeed communicate with the animals, the crowd only roared louder, jostling and waving arms in the air in desperation.

The Harlequin, however, was intent on more immediate business. Having explored the neat roundness of her rump, he succeeded in twisting a little and pushing a part of his arm through the slit in the skirt. As the crowd pressed about them, he secretly continued his explorations, parting the warm cleft he found between her thighs and sending forth a tentative finger to test her resistance. She did not resist.

'Look, at last blue is moving!'

With a prod from the bull master, at last the gigantic black creature was trotting towards his fellows. Eagerly, Allegra strained to watch, though still pleasantly aware of her companion's attentions. He meanwhile was scorching the nape of her neck with his kisses, pressing his weight against her.

With a wave of her arm, she cried out, 'The blue is coming. Look! Look!'

The lumbering creature of San Marco had trotted up to the leaders and now a few of the larger animals were galloping around the fountain, much to the delight of their supporters. Ten circuits were to be made; now the race had actually begun, Allegra was rigid with excitement.

'I cannot bear it,' the Harlequin groaned, drawing her attention back to his caresses. With a deft pull at her dress's opening, he pulled the seam apart and grasped

197

her hips with both of his hands. Allegra no longer cared. She was confident no one could see, for no one else would watch anything but the race. Only when she felt the moistly heated top of his member burrow against her thighs did she glance backwards towards him.

His eyes closed in ecstasy as he guided his cock towards her pliant flesh. There was a sudden surge of the crowd and an observer might have noticed the Harlequin stumble a little against the back of his thickly clothed companion. But Allegra suddenly gasped at the pressure. With one deft movement he had entered her, not gently, but a half-shaft. Smiling to herself, she set her feet firmly on the dais and let him continue. There was noise and hubbub enough about them to be private, but indeed, at the last count, she did not particularly care.

The race had been proceeding to the point of five circuits when one of the leaders grew tired. Pausing in his stride and pawing at the cobbles, he began to swing his horns from side to side. In the blink of an eye, the situation changed. With a rapid charge the beast roared towards the crowd, his head down and horns shining in the torchlight. Screams of terror rent the air as onlookers pressed back. The bull masters flocked together with long spears to try to drive the raging bull backwards.

Taking advantage of the commotion, Allegra's lover threw aside all pretence. Gripping her hard around the waist, he pushed even harder at her entrance, forcing his wide girth forwards until she could not help but cry out with pleasure. As she had guessed from his stature, he was not inconsiderably endowed and now he was struggling to make her take him as she stood.

She could hear him panting by her ear until, with a deft movement, he quickly lifted her an inch or two in the air and pulled her swiftly on top of him. This time she could not stifle a sharp cry. His bulk was tormenting her most sensitive, deepest part. As he began to thrust in short, sharp movements he made her want to scream with pleasure. Instead, she used every effort to remain silent, slowly twisting the fabric of her dress between her fingers as waves of delicious pleasure built and built in the pit of her stomach.

Perhaps it was her last little cry that attracted him, but suddenly she noticed the Scaramouche watching them both intently. He was standing next to Allegra and Celina was beyond him, completely intent upon the race. It was his eyes she could see behind his mask, glittering as they flickered over her. By now she could hear the roar and cries of the onlookers but otherwise, she could no longer follow the race. The Harlequin was like a bull himself, hard and assured as he charged, using force and not subtlety to master her. Now, as she felt his friend's eyes upon her, she felt his passage inside her grow easier as her juices uncontrollably lubricated his way. As if from a long distance, she heard a wild roar and screaming rise to a crescendo and in doing so, heard too a cry of rapture break from her own lips.

At that moment the Scaramouche reached out and took her arm. Gratefully she took it, convinced that any moment her legs might collapse as his friend's wide phallus thumped on and on inside her. But instead of allowing her hand to rest gently on his arm, he quickly pressed it against his groin. Clearly the effect of watching their coupling had been profound; his cock too was massive and stiff beneath his clothes.

Gently, Allegra closed her fingers around the bulky shape. For a second she closed her eyes behind the mask, concentrating on the ample shaft of flesh ramming into her from behind. At the same time, she let her fingers explore the shape of the rounded tip and shaft that continued to swell and stiffen beneath her touch. The effect was immediate. With a shout that any in the crowd would have taken as a victory cry, her legs buckled beneath her as a climax tore through her body, leaving her almost senseless. Catching her in his arms, the Harlequin grunted as he tried to extend her pleasure for a few more seconds, driving her on with thrust after thrust until she could bear it no more. Unhanding his friend, she pushed both away; despite his protests, she pulled herself away from the Harlequin, leaving him dangling in the cool air.

Opening her eyes, she could see that the race was over.

'Please,' he groaned, trying to regain entry.

'You may finish later,' she commanded. 'Now put it away.'

Dolefully, he acquiesced. A quick glance at the Scaramouche confirmed that he, too, was now composed, chattering to Celina who had noticed none of this. With a quick readjustment of her gown, she stood up straight and looked about her. 'Who was it won?'

'The blue,' muttered her companion, as the crowd began to break and scatter.

'San Marco. That is mine,' she smiled. 'I quite feel like the cat who got the cream tonight. I cannot shake off my good fortune.' And with a little kiss on his mouth, she patted the swelling within his costume which plainly would not subside.

Inside the discreet gondola that the Harlequin immediately hired, the two couples lounged on padded velvet couches. Although the boat carried a lamp at the front for the gondolier to find his way, inside it was deliciously gloomy as they groped in the dark. Soon it was difficult for Allegra to breathe, so ardently did her companion press his kisses on her. Curiously, she peered at the other pair; she was pleased to see that Celina was enjoying herself. The Scaramouche was eagerly enjoying her delights, caressing the white glimmer of her neck and throat as Allegra knew Celina liked and slowly turning his attention to the pretty pale spheres of her breasts. With a glimmer of disappointment, she realised that the two men would probably want to part ways when they arrived home. Looking at the three, she considered that it was Celina who most attracted her.

200

Reaching across to caress her friend's bare arm, she gave her a little conspiratorial squeeze. 'I am sworn to keep a watchful guard on my friend,' she announced to them all. 'Wherever we go, we must all stay together.'

'But come along,' the Harlequin complained, 'that is hardly fair.' He certainly looked disconsolate, no doubt wondering if he would ever get the opportunity to rid himself of that unseemly bulge.

'You forget she is new out of a convent. It is my duty to protect her. We will stay with you, gentlemen, but will not be separated.'

'It is a condition,' Celina chimed in, 'or we will go home now.'

The Harlequin snorted contemptuously. 'You are not little girls, you know. Hanging about the Ridotto, you must take the consequences if you meet two young bloods such as ourselves. If you had wanted to play the nun, you should have told us earlier.'

'What do you say, Scaramouche?' Allegra gave him a little half smile that held much promise. Then she reached down in the darkness to appreciatively brush her fingers across the site of her earlier caresses.

She soon realised that he did not possess the density of his companion.

Taking each girl by the hand he said, 'My friend, why have one, when two are twice as good?' Then the three laughed merrily, much to the discomfiture of the frustrated Harlequin.

It was with some relief that they arrived at a fine set of rooms. Allegra had been dreading an hotel, for no other reason than that it might be very solemn and they would need to behave respectably. The Harlequin's rooms were comfortable, filled with elegant French chairs and bureaux and gilt Venetian mirrors before which candles softly burnt. No servants were in evidence but a fire slumbered in the grate and a tray and glasses stood waiting on a card table. Escorting them inside, he offered wine and biscuits and then announced their first task from the middle of the room. 'And now, as we are in private, it is time to unmask.'

'Is it?' Celina asked as she reclined on a narrow brocade sofa. 'May we not stay in disguise? That way we might never know each other. I think I prefer it that way.'

'And yet,' Allegra chimed in, 'I am certainly curious now.' She could see the outlines of the faces of the two men, but their actual features eluded her still.

'If we were to do it,' said Celina, 'how would it be done? One at a time or all together?'

'Revelation is an interesting topic,' broke in the Scaramouche. He had just entered the room with a second jug of wine. 'For the utmost piquancy, I believe the mask should be the last item to be removed.'

The two girls laughed while the second man still looked as if he had not yet been told the joke.

Still intent on teasing him, Allegra joined him as he threw himself down on a rug by the fire. 'And would I know your mood better if I first took off your mask – or your breeches?' she whispered.

'You are very bawdy for a nun,' he complained.

'Too bawdy for you?' she asked, kissing him and then watching for his reply.

'No, no. I do not know what I say. My mood is disturbed tonight. I had thought we might complete what we began earlier, that is all. I am disappointed. I apologise.'

Glancing over at the other two on the sofa, she saw that at last they were beginning to grow amorous. Celina was sitting across the man's knee with her lavish gown falling in glittering cascades to the floor. He had succeeded at last in freeing her breasts from the gossamer silk of her bodice and was caressing them appreciatively. The Harlequin had not even noticed yet, that licence was there to be taken whether they shared a room or not. He was such a dolt – but then she remembered the feel of him inside her. Idly, she let herself roll against his stomach and heard him groan with desperation.

'What a tease you are,' he complained, 'one minute a bawd and the next a nun.'

'Do you know that you talk too much?' She sidled up to him; it didn't feel uncomfortable, lying at full stretch on the rug.

'But what am I to think? Which are you?'

'You think too much. Do as before. Just feel.'

Rather more tremulously, he began to caress her, kissing her neck and mouth and breasts. The poor man really is in torment, she concluded, as his mask slipped a little and she saw his cheeks flushed with excitement. Gently, he tried to ease down the shoulders of her bodice and she had to show him how it unlaced at the back. At the same time she kicked off her skirt and petticoat, letting them lie in a mound of rich fabric on the floor. At last she lay down in only her stays and chemise.

Ferociously, he kissed her breasts where they arched above the tight stays and kissed her stomach and her thighs beneath the thin muslin.

'My bedchamber,' he said, 'is through there.'

'No, let us stay here, where I can watch Celina.'

The other pair had progressed at a similar rate, so part of Celina's clothes now lay on the floor beside the sofa. She was still sitting on the man's knee but he had freed her breasts from the corset and was kissing the pink nipples feverishly.

By chance she caught Allegra's eye. 'Allegra, would you help unlace me. I fear it is beyond them both.'

With a giggle her friend jumped up and moved over to the tangled pair. Kneeling down on the floor, Allegra set to, unlacing the half-corset, bending close to the man's knees as he watched her with surprise. From behind her, she heard the Harlequin call out with impatience. Languorously, Celina pressed her back towards her and without shame, Allegra kissed the soft arch of her back and slid her hands round to her friend's

203

breasts. She felt the man slide his own hands away, making way for hers.

'Let me unlace her,' Celina whispered to the man. Without protest, he let her slide off his knees. Together on the floor before his feet, they knelt together as Celina slowly unlaced the pretty pink stays which Allegra had chosen with her outfit. As the garment slipped to the floor, Celina took her in her arms and they kissed each other passionately.

This was the piquancy Allegra had been waiting for. Now she could taste the man in her friend's mouth and feel the warmth where he had rubbed her breasts. At last she felt hungry as she clutched Celina through the thin shift, aware of the man's interest through half-closed eyes.

'*Mon dieu*, are they whores?' she heard the Harlequin ask, aghast.

'No my friend, they are undoubtedly what they claim to be. Our luck is in. A pair of runaway nuns.'

Allegra was aware of the Scaramouche slipping down on to the carpet beside them. Silently, he slipped his garments off and she looked with interest at his hard, muscular body. His member was as strong and shapely as she remembered it; like a stem of flesh it rose tall and stiff from a forest of hair. Very gently, he kneeled and nuzzled Celina's back, not intruding upon the girls' lovemaking, but adding to it, caressing Celina's rear and thighs while Allegra sucked her breasts. Dizzy with pleasure, Celina moaned, parting her thighs to show them both the lovely flower of flesh at her centre.

'May I?' he asked Allegra quietly.

'Of course.'

As he moved down to caress and kiss her slippery cleft, Celina pulled at her friend's thighs. 'Let me taste you,' she whispered.

It was what Allegra wanted, to feel the expert little tongue and soft friction of lips coaxing her to dizzy pleasure. Moving astride Celina, she parted her own lips with her fingers to feel the sensation even more strongly, rocking slightly so that every lick or caress caused waves of pleasure to build from her vulva to her tingling pelvis. Below her she could see the man pleasuring Celina in the same way, bending down on all fours as he buried his face in her, moaning a little as he sucked at the sweet honey she knew so well.

In a very few moments the girls had reached their first peak of pleasure. Allegra watched as Celina's back suddenly arched and her pearly thighs locked ecstatically around the man's shoulders. It was not only exciting but somehow tender to watch her friend receive pleasure from another. When the man raised his face she smiled at him with real affection.

'Would you change places?' Celina whispered.

Gratefully, the man bestrode her, stifling a cry as her lips slipped over the end of his bulbous penis. Allegra knew she would now be in ecstasy, tasting the man, rolling his sensitive tip in her pretty little mouth, wanting to kiss it, lick it and suck it until it was all inside her. As she slipped her own mouth over Celina's secret place, she was overwhelmed with the taste of the man's mouth again. She was happy that her friend was being transported to a state of bliss. Playing her favourite tricks, she flicked her tongue quickly over Celina's sensitive bud of feeling. In answer Celina raised her hips, aching for more, wanting to press down hard while her own mouth was deliciously full.

'For God's sake, man,' she heard the Scaramouche saying.

Raising her head a moment, Allegra saw the Harlequin standing by the sofa in a daze, watching them with his hand moving rapidly up and down his own member.

'Join us,' Allegra called. Slowly, like a man walking in his sleep, he stumbled towards her. With a groan he fell down behind her and grasped her rounded bottom. Not knowing what to do first, he squeezed her hanging breasts, her flank and then slid his hand between her legs to find her hot and moist centre. Carefully, Allegra steadied herself on her knees and presented herself for his entry.

As she felt his wide girth press against her entrance, a giddy pleasure swept her away. Above, Celina squirmed with pleasure, her nipples hard and pointed as she floated from one peak of pleasure to the next. The Scaramouche had moved now to kneel at the side of Celina, though she still was pleasuring him with her mouth. His organ hung like a vast, purple fruit, shiny and mottled as she sucked on it like a starving woman.

As the man behind her settled into his stride, Allegra allowed herself to fully enjoy the sensation of his rhythmic thumping. Again, as his long member reached its limit, she felt his swollen testicles banging against her and she longed for that luscious moment when he would release himself into her. Instinctively, she reached out and grasped Celina's lovely breasts, squeezing them hard as she knew the girl liked and pressing the bead-like nipples hard between her finger and thumb.

It was too much for her friend to take, with a breathless gasp she pulled free of the man and pushed against Allegra's stiff little tongue. With slippery fingers, Allegra sought out her entrance and let her friend twitch and spasm on three stiff fingers, thrusting hard into the heat of her body.

Feeling her own body about to topple into an explosion of release, Allegra searched hungrily for the kneeling man at Celina's head. Immediately he understood. So, as his friend continued the hard, full thrusts that were driving her relentlessly to rapture, so the darker man scrabbled towards her, offering her the bounty of his swollen genitals which dripped with Celina's saliva and drops of his own uncontrollable fluid. With a sigh of completion she took it into her own mouth, trying to contain both thrusting members, wanting to be tormented and filled by the pair at once. The penis inside her seemed to have melted into a burning spear, jabbing relentlessly, almost lifting her upwards on its unwieldy length. The other man's member seemed sweet and salty, making her jaw ache as she tried to contain as much as she could. A deep fire of satisfaction rolled through her; behind her closed eyelids she saw the scarlet of her own blood coursing fast in her body.

Just as she felt she could take no more, she became aware of Celina wriggling beneath her. Their two tongues met hungrily at the base of the man's shaft; at the same time she could suddenly feel her friend's hand slip downward, rubbing her own stretched vulva with slippery fingers. The sudden friction drove her over the edge. For a long second she felt her body float away and then return, exquisitely conscious of the two shafts simultaneously filling her and her beautiful friend caressing her too.

As if in response to the intense spasms of her passage, she felt the man mounted behind her increase his speed. A gasp and groan told her he had held his self-control for as long as he could. With a series of short, stabbing thrusts he reached his climax.

Still trembling from the force of her convulsion, Allegra tried to disentangle herself from the knot of different bodies. The man behind her had withdrawn and thrown himself exhaustedly on the sofa. She wanted very much to join him. But as she pulled free, Celina whispered to her to stay just a little longer. Locking her arms around her friend's neck, Celina kissed her sweetly and pulled Allegra on top of her so that their two open clefts locked one against the other. Celina's own was sticky now, but that only seemed to excite her more; rubbing back and forth, she was clearly close to release.

With something resembling anguish, Allegra looked over to find the darker man. Still he was unsatisfied, his member now violently engorged as it swung in front of his stomach. For a second he looked at the two girls, cradled in each other's arms, their hips grinding into each other in search of deliverance.

Then, seeing his way into the puzzle of flesh, he slid gently above them and with a quick movement pierced Celina's ready flesh. With long, leisurely thrusts he bore down on the two girls, pressing them harder together as they simultaneously pushed swollen lips against swollen lips. Although he had entered her friend, Allegra could feel the barrel shape of the penis brushing past her own lips. Again, the nearness and tangle of all their bodies excited her. Their juices were mingling and it was hard to tell where one of them started and the other ended.

Pressing her own swelling breasts into Celina's she felt their nipples jar and rasp; again, though she would never have believed it, she felt herself hungry for satisfaction. To her utter delight, she felt the man above her shift and then, miraculously, he slid his cock from Celina to herself. As easily as wave of the hand, he entered her sticky passage, easily travelling the length of her with his inflamed, vein-engorged member.

Beneath her, as her breath grew faster, she could see Celina's face. Like Allegra, Celina was transported, still rubbing her vulva hard against her own bucking flesh, feverish with desire. It took only a dozen skilful thrusts and Allegra was again moaning with need, barely aware now of what it was that was doing this to her, her heart thumping as once again her entrance squeezed like a fist around the man's penis, her thighs running with juice she knew not from where.

Later, when they untangled, she saw that same expression of satiety on Celina's face. They were both utterly satisfied; the man they called Harlequin had been roused again and had once more taken Celina, spreading her thighs as she sat on the sofa, taking her fast and hard while the others bathed. Allegra was profoundly exhausted, but oddly happy and content. In the bed chamber, she curled around Celina and the two men curled around each of them, one on each side. It was light outside and the birds were singing a welcome to the new day. Defenceless and free, they threw aside any remnants of clothes and looked curiously on each other's naked faces. Their masks lay trampled on the floor, crumpled and tarnished, along with any other false disguises of the night.

Chapter Fifteen

*A*llegra was awoken by the sweetly bitter scent of coffee. Rousing herself from a tangle of sheets, she remembered the circumstances of the previous night with a sudden flush of embarrassment. Wriggling beneath the counterpane, she found the fluffy hair and soft body of Celina.

'Wake up,' she whispered. 'What are we to do?'

With a long yawn, the girl stretched and pushed her head above the bedclothes. 'Mmm, coffee. Just what I need.'

Reluctantly, Allegra followed her lead and showed her face.

The Frenchman who had dressed as Harlequin was pouring glasses of coffee from a silver pot. Quite shyly, Allegra looked at him, unmasked. His face was smooth and rather delicate; his eyes were a pale grey in the light. She was pleased that she liked his face; it was odd to see that last of all.

'And you, mademoiselle?' he asked her. She took a glass of the acrid liquid and sipped it, watching him closely.

Almost immediately, they were disturbed by the second man, whirling into the room in a uniform of the

hussars. 'Greetings, ladies,' he announced, sweeping off
his fur cap. 'It is with the greatest regret that I leave you
so suddenly – but duty calls. Captain Milovski of the
King of Poland's own guard at your service.'

Bowing, he took their fingers in his and kissed them
with much expression. In his braided jacket and cloak he
looked handsome enough to thrill any woman. Allegra
recognised his easy charm and assurance from the previous evening, but noticed that the mask had covered a
few ugly white scars to his face. Still, they gave him a
brave, slightly tragic appearance.

'And your names, signorinas?'

Celina was clearly besotted. Almost trembling with
excitement she told him her name. 'Celina Bartoli,
signor.'

'And Allegra di Vitali.'

He had taken both of their hands in his.

'Celina and Allegra. You will let my friend have your
addresses? I can only leave you on that assurance.'

'Yes, of course,' breathed Celina. Then he was off, with
a swirl of his military cloak.

'Alexei is an oaf,' the other man began. 'Do not be
seduced by the uniform – he is a glorified valet. They
will play with their decanters and corks till dusk.'

But the two girls ignored these ungracious remarks
and finished their coffee.

'Myself, I will be at my letters and then I am summoned to the ambassador at two.'

'Ah,' Allegra asked politely, 'you are attached to the
French court?'

If she had suggested he caught rats beneath the arches
of the Rialto he would not have stared at her with such
an expression of disgust. 'The court? That gathering of
putrid whoremongers! What freeborn Frenchman in his
right mind would consort with those puffed-up
wretches? No – it is the Venetian ambassador I visit. The
ambassador to the free Republic of Venice. Would that
the land of my birth could boast the title of free Republic

211

and not be ground down by the weight of fat Louis. To think of that doltish creature who calls himself our king and his stupid, diamond crazy wife. No, there is work to be done in this haven of the free. Great deals to be struck and secret plans to be made.'

Then, remembering himself, he clumsily tried to draw a veil over his activities. 'Of course, these are only interests of mine, private interests I indulge. You will not repeat this, will you?' he asked, with a sudden, desperate air. They were enjoying his hospitality; it would have been hard indeed of them to tease him.

After the young man they learnt was named Phillipe had excused himself, they dressed.

'Do you think they will call on us, Allegra? A captain attached to the King of Poland. What a catch! Oh, will they not think us strange, to have no servants?'

Indulgently, Allegra smiled as she watched her friend fuss and fret over her hair and complexion. 'I think they like us well enough as they find us. Do you think this one is a spy?' she wondered out loud. 'Perhaps he is not such a fool as he first appears.'

Alexei and Phillipe did indeed call upon them that very evening. Dusk was already falling in the narrow *calli* around the Palazzo and the stars twinkled brightly in the frost. Although the snow had dispersed, the stones underfoot glittered with ice.

'I have brought you ladies a small gift from the royal household,' Alexei announced, producing a bundle from beneath the folds of Scaramouche's cloak. 'In Poland, our winters last half the year.'

Inside the bundle were two full-length cloaks, one of a ruby colour and the other of sapphire velvet. Each was lined with the softest, warmest ermine. At the throat were gorgeous golden clasps.

'It is the loveliest thing I have ever worn,' said Celina, as she kissed the Polish captain, and then for good measure kissed Phillipe as well. At last, as the fur slipped over their shoulders, they were warm, however cold the weather might turn.

There was much outside to warm the heart, if not the flesh. At the wild beast show they found a strange creature named an elephant, which was as large as a carriage and had a gigantic nose and feet like the trunks of trees. Many of the ladies screamed a little to see such a monster, but Allegra thought him a gentle, curious beast.

Finding themselves with an appetite for dinner, they stopped at an hotel where the cook brought them platters of roast lamb and goose with jugs of malmsey wine. Later, as they pressed through the crowds, they stood at the edge of the quayside, watching firecrackers light up the heavens in bursts of red and green and gold. Around them, the throng contained every gradation of society, from masked beggar children selling sweetmeats, to the great powdered members of the nobility with their liveried flunkeys making way for them through the crowds. Between the two extremes were the ordinary citizenry: the wives of artisans all dressed up as Mary of Medici or Isabella of Spain, with their children waiting on as attendants in homespun livery, gondoliers or grocers dressed as Pantaloon or Monsieur Punch and the young apprentices kitted out as any bizarre character, pelting the crowd with bonbons or flowers or eggs filled with rosewater.

'You are very fortunate to have such contented people,' Phillipe remarked. 'In France the people starve in the fields, while the court gluts itself on banquets where most is left for the pigs.'

'And you?' Allegra asked, straining on his arm to watch the fireworks.

'I am born noble but my family can no longer afford the millions needed to keep up a front at Versailles. I pity the common man. It is time for change. Not just for the rich and poor, but for church and followers, men and women. Do you not deplore the heavy bonds of marriage

213

that hang like chains around men's and women's ankles? Most women are simply passed from ownership of their father to their husband without ever a glimpse of freedom. Yet you Venetians celebrate love outside of the stifling dungeon of society. Look at your carnival – this licence would not be allowed in France. Your people are well fed, take ample holidays and can mimic their masters without fear of being cast away in the Bastille. There is freedom to mingle, to make love and change identity without a care. If the state is like a rack, holding the oppressed down, exerting more and more strength, in the end the mechanism will finally break.'

'So, you have a philosophy of freedom?' she asked, suddenly interested in his fierce speech.

'Of liberty.'

'Ah, liberty,' she said, feeling the pleasant shape of the word form in her mouth. 'So, there is a philosophy of liberty?'

'It is spreading all across Europe, across the world,' he whispered.

Smiling, she continued to watch the fireworks burst in the sky, casting deep reflections of red and gold across the still waters of the lagoon. An idea was slowly flowering in her mind, a strange awakening of understanding. Something of the racing blood and thrill of the hunt that was the carnival had roused her. If this was liberty, she loved it. But she could only cherish it because she had known a lack of it. Still she was grateful to the harsh schooling of the Prioress; without passing through harsh oppression she might never have treasured liberty.

Towards midnight, as before, the byways became even more crowded. Hearing a band of musicians playing in a nearby square, the four tried to squeeze through the throng to reach it. Ahead was a group of guildsmen, all dressed in the striped livery of their butchers' trade. Apparently the worse for wine, they stumbled and shouted along their way, waving and shaking fists at passers by. The trouble began when a stout, purple faced

214

butcher stumbled against the steps at the canal and then, with a long, wobbling motion, finally plunged into the freezing water.

Aghast, Allegra unhooked her arm from Phillipe's and stopped to see him pulled out, dripping freezing water and weeds on to the cobbles. Imagining some affront from an innocent Pantaloon, the sopping butcher began a foolish, drunken brawl, which was as quickly ended as it began. But as she turned, about to speak to Phillipe, Allegra found herself alone.

For a few long minutes she looked about in the crowd, sure that her eye would suddenly alight on him and all would be well. But as minute after minute passed, she realised that she was indeed alone. Flustered, and cursing her own foolish curiosity in watching the free performance, she pushed her way onwards into the square. The band were playing on a small stage and laid out before them was a sanded area where a cluster of ponies huddled, dressed in sparkling saddles and reins. Wherever she looked, Allegra saw a Harlequin or a red-cloaked Scaramouche, or indeed, a fair haired odalisque. But they were never exactly right – the Harlequin would turn and present an odd, swarthy countenance. Or the odalisque would be fat or red-haired or a trifling youth.

Resignedly, Allegra watched the entertainment begin, scanning the crowd each few seconds but never finding her friends. They had had no deliberate plans for this evening – perhaps they were searching for her, or had gone home to wait or tried somewhere else. As a group of acrobats began their miraculous dancing and leaping from pony to pony, she began to abandon her hopes of the evening. There was nothing to do but retrace her steps to the Palazzo and wait for them all to return.

'Signorina, do take care.'

She had been so deep in thought that she had not even noticed a weary team of performers carrying a makeshift stage through the crowd in a direct line towards her. A strong arm reached out and pulled her clear of the heavy wooden planks.

'My apologies, sir. I am not myself.'

His arm stayed fast on hers. He was costumed as an English tar, in striped jerkin and wide pantaloons. At his narrow waist was a wide red belt.

'May I help you then? Take you somewhere?'

His accent was foreign, but she did not know from where. The mask was a grotesque white *larva*, with the long, phallic nose of a Punchinello. It was impossible to know whether he was trustworthy.

'No, no, signor. I am waiting for my friends. They will be along any moment.' And so she was obliged to stay a little longer. As she watched the acrobats in their spangled hose and pointed caps, she found herself unable to help enjoying the show. A little child with streamers flying from her hair was the notable performer – she was thrown from horse to horse and always landed gracefully in her companions' arms. As a finale she tumbled and somersaulted from one horse to the other, spinning like a ball through the air, only to take her bows from atop a heaving saddle as the multitude clapped and cheered, throwing coins into the ring.

'They were good, don't you think?'

The sailor smiled; she could see good, straight teeth in a strong, weathered face. She allowed herself a condescending little nod.

'May I escort you to your friends?'

It was quite some way back to the Palazzo. Already, she had begun to wonder at the solitary journey back alone through crowds that now seemed to have gained a more desperate, rowdy air.

'Where are you going next?' she asked.

'Wherever you command me,' he replied with a small bow. 'So long as we do not have to find your friends.'

She could not help but smile; he had the easy manners of a scoundrel, she decided, but did not like him any the less. 'There is a place by the Campo Raffi,' she explained.

216

'If you could accompany me there, I should be forever grateful.'

Thus they began their journey, arm in arm through the heaving, jostling alleyways. Allegra was soon pleased that she had found a trustworthy companion, for it was the night of many contests between the guilds of Venice and it seemed a great excuse for many bands of men to get drunk and hang about at corners, berating each other and making the types of remark to passing women that they would blush at if their wives could hear. There was only one problem in accompanying Ricardo, as she soon learnt he was called – his liking for drink.

As they passed the first tavern, he suggested a quick jug of wine. Allegra agreed to take a glass, and soon they were on their way again. But at the next, he insisted again. Once more, she agreed to take a small glass, having acquired a taste for the warm, syrupy liquid that made her glow warmly beneath the fur cloak.

'Your friend cannot think enough of you, to let you alone for a second,' he announced. 'The most beautiful Columbine in Venice. Anyone can see you have been badly treated. I would not let you stray one pace from my side.'

It is the drink speaking, she thought, but let him chatter on. It was warm and snug in the tavern; revellers were crowded at tables in the candlelight. There was a strong smell of woodsmoke and pungent liquor in the air. Allegra loosened her cloak and let the fire heat her skin.

'Why should he have you,' announced the tar, 'when he cannot look after you? Why should you return to him?'

'I belong to no one,' she said quietly.

Puzzled, he shrugged. 'You may say that, but you will find your excuses rather than come home with me.'

There was an unspoken challenge in the air; not with this young fellow, but with Phillipe. He might well speak eloquently of freedom between men and women, but he would no doubt expect a certain fidelity. She wondered if it was that peculiar Italian type of fidelity that involved much constancy on the part of the woman and much dalliance on the part of the man. Besides, the strong spirits were warming not only her body but heating her ardour, too. Here was a handsome man; his body had a pleasing shape and his gallantry appealed to her slightly tarnished vanity.

'I have no excuses,' she heard herself say. 'Where is it you live?'

If he was bemused, he did not show it. 'I am here with the ship *Fortuna*, docked at the quay of the Slavs. We are here for a refit, heading for Crete. As to where I live, it is on board with a dozen others, but I am not quartered with the common men. I am apprenticed by my uncle to learn navigation.'

Taking another deep draught from the jug, he licked his lips and looked directly at her. Raising his fingers to her bare breast he let his index finger run down from her throat to the deep cleavage pushed upwards from the stiff satin of her bodice. 'So,' he asked lazily, 'will you come with me?'

'Why not?'

Below the frosty stars, he took her into his arms. They had boarded the massive hulk of the ship by a wavering plank, laughing all the while at the dark water lapping below. But finding lamps lit and voices below, Ricardo had put his fingers to his lips and guided her over the deck to a low wooden platform. Sheltered from any breeze, they could lie there beneath the towering rigging, feeling the slight rise and fall of the ocean. He felt strong and wiry, as if the muscles in his arms could hold her fast in a vice of pleasure. His mouth tasted of sweet liquor as his tongue plunged into hers, seeking and probing as he caressed her shoulders beneath the cloak of fur.

'We must be quiet,' he whispered, as she heard herself

218

moan quietly in his ear. 'We do not want anyone to join us.'

Trying very hard to be silent, she let him slip his fingers inside her clothes. He was breathing very hard as he explored her warm flesh.

'Your hands are cold,' she giggled.

'I am surprised any part of me could be cold,' he whispered, as he pulled at the silk laces to her costume. It opened quite easily, and her breasts spilled whitely into the moonlight. Cupping them in both of his hands, he kissed them slowly, while she closed her eyes and let the welcome dam of anticipation build at her centre, enjoying the slow sensation of being deliciously teased. For a while he suckled at her breasts, sucking them until they were hard and burning in the night air. Then, pulling himself on to her, he pulled her skirts upwards and found the warm skin above her stockings, stroking it eagerly. She could feel him pressing against her pelvis: a hard, exciting pressure which she returned, arching her back to rub violently against him.

Below deck, she suddenly heard the clink of glasses and they halted. But a moment later, the soft murmur of voices drifted across the air. Sinking back on to her, Ricardo reached down and held her thighs apart, trailing his fingers across the soft skin where her garters pressed into the pliant flesh. Already, she felt tremors of fire burning in her stomach. A moment later he was kissing her breasts, but at the same time pushing away her petticoat to find the heated cleft below.

With a sigh his fingertips met her luxurious centre, probing the soft lips like oiled silk. She did not know if it was the speed of their encounter, or some strange attraction between the two of them, but she could barely wait for him to satisfy her. As his calloused fingertips stroked and squeezed her inner lips, she felt herself part her legs like a harlot, wanting him to take her with all his force. Looking down, she could see her stockinged legs stretched out palely in the darkness and him

219

between them, eagerly trying to undo his breeches. At last he released his gently swaying member. Taking her hand, he guided her to it and she felt the heat rising from it and the taut pressure of the tight skin around the head. Gently, she pressed it to her slippery centre, feeling exquisite bursts of pleasure as it pressed against her pleasure bud. Very slowly, she led it to her entrance which tingled with anticipation.

Now it was his turn to groan. Panting in her ear, he begged her to let him in this very second, for he could not bear her torture. Pushing her slippery fissure downwards, teasing him mercilessly, she let him wait just a little longer. Then, wrapping her thighs about his strong hips, she relaxed and let him slide into her in one long and luscious movement.

Lying back on the wooden platform, Allegra closed her eyes the better to feel every movement of his long, agile member. Soon, she felt him get into a striding rhythm, pulling back and forth like an oarsman, driving her aching passage wild. Pulling him hard inside her, she crossed her ankles behind his buttocks and let herself slide back and forth on the platform, slipping on and off his heated phallus with hard, slapping thrusts.

It was impossible to stay quiet. Even he was groaning now with exertion, pulling himself upright all the better to target her as she rocked back and forth on the relentless pounding length of his cock. With a stifled cry, she felt herself grow dizzy with sensation. Looking down she could see her nipples hard in the cold as they rocked back and forth. She knew it was only seconds until her moment of release.

With a loud cry she felt Ricardo shudder and throw himself forward upon her. Desperately, she tried to use his last few movements of spasm to bring herself to the crest of her own wave. But it was no use, in the wildness of his excitement he had climaxed and was rapidly growing soft inside her. Biting her lip, she resolved not to complain. Maybe, she wondered quickly, it was a punishment for her own licentiousness.

'Is that you, Ricardo?'

'Who's that?' she whispered. While they had been distracted someone had come up on deck.

It seemed that Ricardo was either too exhausted or confused to answer. Struggling to pull down her petticoat, she pushed at him to get off her. It was then she realised he was a leaden weight upon her.

'Get off!' she hissed.

Very slowly, he collected his wits and began to withdraw. But already she could see the dark silhouette of a figure against the rigging, groping towards them.

Clumsily, Ricardo slumped against the platform. So that is it, Allegra thought – he has had too much liquor. Hastily, she tried to gather her skirts and pull them down over her thighs. It was too late. Already the onlooker was upon them, peering into the darkness.

'Ricardo? Who is that with you?'

'It is me,' Allegra replied resignedly. 'And he is drunk, so do not bother questioning him. Who are you?'

'Arturo Carvese. Second officer of this ship.'

It was difficult to be dignified with her clothes spread over the platform, but Allegra did her best. 'Ah, his friend. Then will you help me? As you can see, signor, we have had a little *amore* but the drink has got the better of your friend. If you could lift him, maybe I could free my skirts?'

Arturo struggled awhile to oblige her, but could not help but stare at the open bodice and expanse of white leg still glimmering in the moonlight. At last her skirt came free and he sat down beside her.

'If I can assist you in any way,' he began. 'To escort you back, or – ' and here he swallowed, 'in some other manner?'

'By which you mean?'

She could just see Arturo in the darkness and already

a thrilling prospect seemed to open up before her. It was dark, she was masked, and no one need ever know.

'If I could help to dress you,' he began, but instead of closing her bodice, his hand slipped over her warm, bare breast. Frighteningly quickly, she felt her body respond to him. Waves of pleasure engulfed her as his fingers found her hard nipple and his soft mouth sought out her lips in the darkness. I do not even know him, she reproached herself. But her body knew otherwise; it responded as if he were an old, habitual lover.

As his fingers retraced those of his friend, her back shuddered once more and her thighs spread greedily. She was already sticky from Ricardo, but deep inside she felt a heat like a furnace craving for more and more. Without a thought for modesty, she reached for the fellow's breeches and felt a satisfying swelling beneath her questing fingers. He meanwhile was fondling her breasts which was pleasuring her in giddy waves of excitement. As he slipped between her legs and unfastened his breeches, she sighed with pleasure, raising her knees on to the platform, wanting to be taken up and filled with him.

This time there were no romantic overtures. Sensing his opportunity, Arturo seized his ready member and slid it hard into her wet passage. With an extraordinary thrill of excitement, Allegra felt it push its way into her, pushing its wider girth into the already heated enclosure. With a gasp of pleasure she pushed herself upwards on to her palms, so she was sitting half-upright on the platform while her new lover stood, using each thrust to push a little further inside her, his wider girth causing her spasms of delight as he eased his way deeper and deeper. He was strong and assured, probing her every inch with his solid, insinuating rod. Suddenly, with a cry of frustration, he seized her by the waist and lifted her physically off the platform.

The next moment she was hanging around his waist, his arms holding her tight around the small of her back, as he stood, bearing her full weight. The effect of this position was immediate. She felt herself impaled on his bulky penis; the tip seemed buried deep within her, tormenting her womb. A pleasurable ache erupted deep in her stomach as he lifted her up and down on the spike of flesh, driving her wildly on and on until she could feel nothing else but that pounding of slippery, swollen muscle. With a cry like silk torn into pieces, a white flash exploded deep in her body, erupting outwards until even her fingertips tingled pleasurably. Uncontrollably, her inner muscles spasmed around him, and slippery juices dribbled down her thighs. Gently, he laid her down and she felt waves of peace tremble through her being.

If she had imagined this would be the price she had to pay for satisfaction, she was wrong. Barely had her breathing slowed a little, than he was taking her again. With the virility of youth, he slid easily back inside her and again she felt herself slide back and forth on the hard wood. She could just discern his face above her; handsome and impassive in the moonlight, intent on his task as he kept up a strong, urgent rhythm.

With a glimmer of surprise, she felt her body begin to respond. As each thrust ceaselessly ground on inside her, some secret spark awoke. It is torment, she thought one moment, and then the next she thought, this is bliss. Again, she remembered the darkness, the strangeness and her mask. No one need ever know, she thought, as she raised her knees. Ferociously, he reached out, catching her swinging breasts, scraping her jutting nipples with his rough hands.

Allegra felt herself propelled onwards, unable to stop the journey of pleasure on which she had embarked. Deliriously, she reached downwards and felt the satisfying slap and friction of his phallus pounding inside her. She could feel her own wetness now, a swimming softness as the hard muscle bore on and on inside her. She felt as if she were floating now, on a strange river of thick, syrupy liquid. Closing her eyes, she felt her knees lift as every instinct still screamed within her to take more and more pleasure.

A sudden heat brushed against her face. Feverishly, she opened her eyes; at first she puzzled at the shape beside her, then slowly realised that Ricardo had roused himself and was kneeling beside her. With the hot anguish of a fever she grasped his hips and searched with her mouth for the feast she knew she would find. As she closed her mouth around his awakening member, a powerful spasm gripped her body; the taste and sensation in her mouth sent her crashing into the deeps. Far away, she was aware of an inexorable pounding, on and on into her convulsing entrance. Even as she recovered her breath it went on and on, like the mechanism in a giant engine.

The night continued. In a place somewhere like fevered sleep, Allegra existed, half-dreaming, half-watching, as the act continued. She knew that Ricardo again took her, but did not know who it was whose phallus she greedily sucked. The fire inside her was raging uncontrollably; at the barest touch her limbs trembled and her blood heated as if it were molten ore. She no longer cared who it was who took her, or how she was taken. However wet or soft she became, still the heat grew and exploded in her veins again and again. She was dizzily aware of men about her, of shadowy forms with hard, unmerciful sexes, who touched her and stroked her, who lifted her thighs high in the air and pushed themselves gratefully inside her.

New flames burst inside her; she was aware of being turned on her stomach and held suspended on her quivering limbs. Suddenly her buttocks were parted and a fiery male rod plunged inside her rear so hard she cried out into the whispering night. By now her body was so wet with sliding juice the shaft pushed onwards into that strange, virgin territory and soon the pain subsided. Tight and fierce, the shaft drove inside her, until surges of fierce, scalding sensation rippled up and down her spine. She was suddenly aware of a pair of thighs before her face, of her hair tangled and falling before her eyes. She heard a grunt of untamed pleasure as her swinging breasts were seized and another phallus pushed between her smeared and sticky globes.

Again, she had moved past reason. Crying out like a cat in heat, she surrendered to the sublime pleasure of the moment. Hands were everywhere: caressing her swollen breasts, stroking her sticky rear, grasping her ankles and probing that soaking, exquisite flower at her centre which welcomed them all and still squeezed and released and burnt at the highest plateau of sensation. Never had she imagined such heights could be reached from physical coupling alone. It was something primitive and secret, she knew. It was something which had been practised in the ancient times in dark caves by masked figures. It was frightening and raw and dangerous. But it was also the wildest, most powerful pleasure of her life.

It was after dawn when she crossed the city. She had woken in a tangle of clothes and limbs and quickly struggled out to get home. Her only chance to bathe had been at a bucket on the deck and there she had rapidly sluiced the worst from her legs and stomach and breasts. Now, as she darted across deserted squares, frightening only the pigeons and the occasional vagrant, she felt drunk with life. Her limbs still trembled and her clothes were trampled, but deep in her soul she felt radiantly alive.

'Allegra? No, it cannot be you!'

Turning rather unsteadily, she found herself face to face with her cousin Spetzina. With a slight twinge of regret, she realised that she had lost her mask somewhere on the deck of the *Fortuna*. Spetzina too, had changed. The rich silks and velvets had been replaced by a dull black dress. Over her head was a black lace veil, which she now cast back across her hair to reveal two round, reddened eyes.

'Spetzina, what has happened?'

'He has left me,' the girl wailed, using the tip of her veil to mop a sudden, dripping tear. 'You will not believe it, but my betrothal is over. That rogue, that scoundrel, Domenico – Allegra, you will not believe it – he has left me for another!'

For a moment Allegra steadied herself against the wall. Then she remembered the poor henpecked creature her cousin had captured to fetch and carry for her and shook her head. 'Who is he with?'

'Some girl from the country, some meek and mild child who has no breeding but ten thousand lire as her dowry! To think – I was almost married, Allegra. What am I to do? In the name of the saints, I am off to pray for a husband, but who knows – maybe I am too old? Oh no, I could not be a shrivelled nun like you! But what has happened? You look – quite different. My God Allegra, you are not turned whore in desperation?' Spetzina reached for a black lace handkerchief and blew her nose loudly.

Allegra shook her head again. 'Why do you care for a husband? I do not. I have swallowed my pride and taken my guardian's bequest and am comfortable enough. It is the carnival – enjoy yourself.'

Spetzina, who had been looking at her cousin a little more closely, backed away a little. 'Allegra. I do hope I am mistaken as to your tone. Maybe the nunnery has indeed addled your head. I hope you are living respectably.'

Still drunk on lust from the long night, Allegra lifted her head and laughed. 'Respectable!' she proclaimed. 'Of course I am not respectable. You mean, do I hide from my own true nature and fear the enquiries of others and grow old and unhappy by burying my true self deep, deep down in my soul? Of course not. I am an honest woman and worthy of respect from only my equals.'

226

'Allegra,' her cousin hissed in a tone of reproach, 'you do not know what you say.'

Although she knew her gown was stained and her hair hung in rats' tails about her face, still Allegra felt a heady pride. 'There is a new philosophy,' she hissed back. 'Of liberty. Try it. And if you find yourself so unhappy in your lack of a husband, I recommend you a place to distract you from your woes. The convent of Santa Agnetha. They would welcome you, Spetzina. If you cannot afford the dowry, I promise you I will pay it for you. I should enjoy the spending of it more than anything in the world.' And standing aside, she let Spetzina continue her tearful way to mass. 'Take the advice of your priests and counsellors, cousin. A spell on the rock will soon help you forget your injured pride.' Then, turning on her way, she felt the new sun alight on her unmasked face and laughed out loud, all the way down to her own door.

Silence filled the high chambers of the Palazzo Raffi. With barely a sound, Allegra tiptoed up the curving stairway to her chamber. Heavy drapes covered the windows and around the bed, rich hangings fell to the floor in twisted skeins of faded damask. Raising the edge, Allegra looked at the three sleeping figures, their arms and legs curled each around each, their faces unruffled and noble in sleep. As she undressed and bathed, she felt no jealousy, only a serene contentment at Celina's undoubted pleasure. Then slipping in amongst them, she cradled herself against their warm, salty flesh and slept.

Chapter Sixteen

The two men did their utmost to entertain Allegra and Celina during the long cold of the carnival. When the lagoon froze solid they learnt to skate on iron runners sent from Poland and when the snow fell they stayed in bed for lazy hours, sharing each others' bodies and feeling no mistrust or envy, only true affection. With a bank of logs roaring in the library fireplace, they spent winter evenings looking through the late Senator's collection after the gentlemen's club had taken their pick. Above them hung the painting of the woman in chains, her eyes meeting those of the spectator with an expression of languid challenge. Now, Allegra loved to stare at the image. The jewels were wonderfully painted against the soft skin; the woman's body invited the observer to admire every tiny fold and delicious cranny.

'This is a novel idea,' Allegra began, turning the pages of an old album bound in fine, gold tooled leather. 'A brothel where the men serve women. That is the place for us, Celina.'

Her friend was reclining across the sofa, her golden hair flowing freely across Allegra's lap. Her lips curled into a greedy smile around her small white teeth. 'It should do these two good, to have to perform extraordinarily well, so that we might choose them again. No slacking in their duties, or we should choose another pair of handsome fellows the next time.'

Alexei looked up from a portfolio of drawings he was leafing through on a rug by the fire. Rolling over on to his stomach, he kissed the corner of Celina's silk slipper. 'And what duties would you give me, cruel mistress?' With a gentle kick she dislodged him and he pretended to pant like an thirsty dog.

'There is such a place,' Phillipe cut in, turning a book of sensational tales upside down across his knee, 'and it is in this city. But perhaps it is unwise of me to tell you,' he added, lifting his eyebrows in Allegra's direction.

'There cannot be,' cried Allegra excitedly. 'We must go there this instant.'

'Yes, Allegra, yes,' cut in the other girl.

'You are both insatiable,' said Phillipe, in mock dismay.

'I am sure you should hope so,' Allegra replied, 'so we will not tire of you after we have had all we can at this place. Tell us about it, then.'

'All I know is that it is frequented by ladies, often ladies with an aged husband or in some other way unable to take a lover in the usual way. I believe it is in the Calle Cretori. There is a back entrance which is very discreet. But you could not go – of course you could not.'

'What is the cost of this taste of paradise?' Allegra asked. It was the girls' only lament that their income from the collection was small. It was not that they wished to be extravagant, only that they disliked being occasionally obliged to Phillipe and Alexei for the cost of entertainments.

'I am afraid it is a whole gold ducat a night, my dears. Rather beyond your means, I think. And do not even think of asking for a loan – you must make do with us for the moment. Though I imagine, if it were cheaper, they would be running down there tomorrow night, Alexei, while we are engaged with your regiment.'

'Why is it so dear?' Celina complained. 'I am sure most fellows would work there willingly for scarcely any money.'

'It is a shame,' said Allegra, stroking her friend's hair and winking secretly at her all the while, 'that we must stick at home like two old spinsters tomorrow while they get drunk and have a glorious time.'

The Calle Cretori was a dark, shadowy crevice close by the clamour of the Rialto bridge. In heavy black lace dominoes and masks, the two girls slipped up to a narrow door, not long after nine o'clock when Alexei's regimental banquet was due to begin. With a tentative knock, they waited, watching carefully that they were not followed. A small window slid aside in the door.

'Yes?' came a surly voice.

'We are here on business,' began Allegra. 'On the recommendation of a lady friend.' The bolt was eased back, begrudgingly it seemed. With a grunt, a surly doorman led the way. Squeezing each other's hands, they went inside. Passing up the long, threadbare stairway, Allegra remembered her promise to Celina that if it was tawdry or in any other way unsatisfactory, they should leave at once. But at the top of the stairs, they found themselves in a delightful, airy salon. A delicate lady with elegant, powdered hair and a pompom of feathers greeted them warmly.

'My dears,' she smiled, her dark little eyes glittering in her powdered face, 'welcome to you both. Do not have a care in the world. Your cloaks? Some tea, perhaps?'

In a very short while, they were seated with the bird-like Madame Escolier drinking tea from Meissen china and feeling strangely as if they had, indeed, simply called on her to discuss the news of the day. Then, with a sudden gesture of sympathy, she placed her hands on each of theirs.

'What is it, my dears? Awful, gouty old husbands? No lovers good enough for your parents? Possessive fathers? Or uncles?'

'Not at all,' replied Allegra, suddenly inspired by her recent exotic reading. 'We are both to be married soon, to two brothers from the Ottoman. Our father, who trades with the sultan of that country, received the strangest letter from them, making it clear that they expressly did not expect us to be virgins by the date of our wedding. Not only that, but these two would be mortally offended if we were not most proficiently skilled in the arts of lovemaking by the time of our arrival in Constantinople.'

Madame Escolier's eyes were round with amazement. 'By the Saints, what heathens!' she pronounced. 'Surely your father does not agree to your coming here?'

'No, no, of course not,' Allegra replied, smoothly enough. 'Only it is our secret wish not to disappoint them. They are the idols of our hearts and so rich besides, they have diamonds as large as goose eggs to give to us and palaces with hundreds of rooms to live in. Will you help us, please?' she begged, pressing the woman's little hand.

'If that is what you wish,' she concurred. 'But there is a fee.'

'What would it be for, say, one night's – education?'

'Well,' she considered, 'I have two good and very gentle fellows free tonight.'

'Oh no,' Allegra interrupted, before she could stop herself, 'that would not do. Our betrothed are soldiers, rough and ready types. Maybe it would be better if we could try a few? Different types, for example?'

Madame Escolier pressed her lips together, considering the odd request. Then greed got the better of her conscience. 'Two lire a night. Each.'

'Very well.'

231

So, as Allegra had guessed, Phillipe had exaggerated the cost to put them off. She had enough and plenty more in her purse.

Madame Escolier led them into a small bedroom with very fine pink damask hangings and a large bed with piles of cushions and dainty gilded mirrors set about the walls. It was indeed a room arranged for lovemaking.

'You may have this room,' the woman said to Celina and led Allegra onwards, but the girl quickly replied, 'No, we will stay together.'

Madame Escolier's eyebrows raised.

'Please,' Celina added. 'I am not as bold as my sister. I should rather not be alone.'

'But the bed – there is only the one.'

'If we are to learn quickly,' Allegra cut in, 'it will be better to stay together. What do we do now?'

'You choose your companions, of course.'

A smile played on Allegra's lips as they followed the woman through a narrow corridor. How often was it the man who chose his consort, like meat from a market? She was looking forward to choosing her produce like a careful housewife. It was like shopping, she decided, and that was something women were very, very good at.

But the first couple of men were disappointing. Reclining on narrow beds dressed only in breeches, one was far too young and the second was somewhat oily and unattractive. The third was promising: a black-skinned Moor with rippling muscles. The next was a strong looking fellow with a pleasingly embarrassed look, as if he would rather not be where he was. Celina giggled at his discomfiture when he would not meet her eyes. In response to her laughter, he blushed crimson, turning away. A few more were too old or too ugly or too young. Then at the end was an olive-skinned fellow with a ready, white-toothed smile and another Moor with a ring through his ear. Allegra informed the woman of their choice.

'Four? All together?'

'We have only one night, madame. And that night is running out quickly.' Then, collapsing with laughter, they retired to the pink damask room.

'Oh goodness, Allegra, what do we do now?' Celina was pulling at her cloak, anxiously trying to get herself prepared for an onslaught.

'Listen, silly. It is for us to decide. I mean it, truly. No need to impress them or care a jot for what they think. Let us drink some wine and consider slowly and at leisure how we can have the best time of our lives.'

When the men arrived, they found their clients demurely playing cards around a table. They were dressed in lace-trimmed morning gowns and only thin folds of silk covered their corsets and chemises. Nodding politely towards them, the two delightful creatures indicated that the men should join them in their game. Somewhat perplexed, the four slumped into chairs and waited.

'Wine, sirs? Do help yourselves. I shall deal you each a hand.'

Allegra dealt the cards speedily.

'We are playing faro. After each game there are forfeits. Begin.'

Still the men looked baffled but, with good grace, began to play. The first to lose was the olive-skinned youth; grinning, he bowed to Allegra and asked what his forfeit might be.

'I will choose,' interrupted Celina, tossing her loose hair back over her pearly shoulders. 'Allegra. Let me think now. He can do anything I want?'

Her friend nodded.

'On the floor, my man, and down to business.'

Sheepishly, he sank to his knees and crawled beneath the table. With a little rearrangement of her petticoats,

Celina let his mouth find her most intimate place. The remaining five continued with another game.

Celina's game was not so good this time; her eyes acquired a glassy look and at times her breath was short. At the end of the game, she grasped the edge of the table and looked at Allegra with a kind of desperation.

'Our friend here has contrived to lose,' Allegra said, nodding towards the larger Moor, whose game had been quite atrocious. 'Do you have a penance for him?'

Celina was already flushed; her eyes moved languorously to the man and she smiled like a greedy cat. 'Stand behind me – so,' she demanded. 'Here, do this.'

As he stood at the back of her chair, she guided his long, black fingers to her open chemise. His fingers cupped her bare breasts, fondling and stroking them gently. The others watched for a few open-mouthed moments until Allegra announced the start of the next game.

This time as they played, it was a little more difficult to concentrate purely on the game. Celina was distracted and threw down any card. And yet the second Moor appeared to be in competition with her to play even worse. From below the table, there was a tell-tale sound every so often, and at times Celina could not help but allow a heedless sigh to escape from her dry lips. Above, they could all see her pointed breasts grow flushed beneath the twin attentions of the man's nimble fingers; her nipples were hot and hard, even the pink aureole growing red and swollen. Allegra felt a frisson of excitement as she watched her friend grow ever more agitated. It delighted her to watch the girl enjoy and be enjoyed; her every response fascinated Allegra. The Moor rapidly lost the game.

'Do you have another forfeit?' Allegra asked quizzically. Celina's shoulders and breasts looked ravishing as the dark fingers caressed their marble whiteness.

'I shall retire,' Celina replied breathlessly, 'to the bed. You,' she added to the recent loser, 'come with us.'

Laughing quietly, Allegra watched the four cross over to the plump, pink bed and collapse in a heap of bodies. Soon Celina had them busily arranged as she wanted – the olive-skinned youth still doing sterling duty with his tongue between her milky thighs and his two comrades paying attention to her breasts with their dark fingers and darting tongues. It was to a chorus of animated moans and cries that the remaining two continued their game.

'Does it trouble you?' Allegra asked the shy-looking youth as he stared down at his cards. He was facing the bed and it was hard for him not to look at Celina's lovely flesh spread openly for the men to taste and enjoy. Only inches away, the other youth's head was buried far into the creamy flesh of Celina's thighs; her legs were stretched wide with her silken stocking slipping down to her calves in the tussle. Her gown had disappeared; only her satin corset pinched hard at her waist, giving prominence to the twin orbs which the two other men were sucking and caressing. In her transport, Celina was fumbling with the breeches of the nearest of the men and had already freed his large coffee-coloured phallus; her fingers were exploring its length, jerking back and forth.

'No, signorina,' he mumbled. 'It is only work to me.'

'Ah, work,' Allegra echoed. 'How dull for you.'

Their game continued in a desultory fashion. Eventually, to a crescendo chorus of cries from Celina, the young man lost. Tapping the cards against the table top, Allegra asked him, 'If it is only boring work, why do you look at them?'

He was indeed, quite clearly discomfited. Tiny beads of perspiration had broken out on his forehead; indeed, he looked desperately uncomfortable. 'I am not,' he stuttered. 'I said, it is only work.'

'But you lost the game,' she remarked, leaning back into her chair and lifting her fingers quizzically to support her chin.

'You play well.'

Laughing a little, she gave him a long, searching look. 'I think I play well, too. So I know we must finish by the rules. Your forfeit – what should it be?'

'Whatever you please, I am at your service,' he muttered, gazing down at his knees with every appearance of crushing embarrassment. Allegra thought that she had never seen such a surly, reluctant lover.

'Would you come with me?' Rising, she bid him walk across to the bed. The four lovers were now as deeply entwined as skilful acrobats. The smaller of the Moors was clearly joined with Celina, thrusting into her with his dark and powerful tool. The air was warm and scented with perfume, sweat and the salty odour of sex.

Quickly Allegra wrapped the lacing from her corset about the youth's wrists and bound him to the bedpost. Now he could not avoid watching the coupling, though he still tried to avert his face.

'Are you really so bored?' she giggled, sidling up behind him and pressing herself against his back. He was deliciously trapped, trying not to watch the others and suddenly very fearful of what this strange girl might make him do next. Slipping her gown to the floor, she rubbed her naked breasts against his back. He was very warm; she could feel the heat of his skin through his thin shirt. He flinched as she caressed him. Grasping his waist, she whispered in his ear. 'Would you like to do that to her? Look how she arches her back to feel every last inch of him. How wet she is. How eagerly her mouth seeks the other man. How she pleasures all three!'

Slowly, she slid her fingers downwards. His breeches were swollen hard with desire. Teasing him, she brushed her fingers across the bulge. 'You ask how you might please me? No doubt you imagine I would like a quick coupling here – the usual trade, I'm sure – and then you're done. No,' she laughed, 'that is not what I want.'

As her delicate fingers again played with the mound at his crotch, he groaned loudly. Through half-closed

236

eyelids he was watching the four on the bed. 'What do you want with me?' he asked, his voice thick with emotion.

'Just to play,' she whispered. 'Just to play with you for a very long time.'

He shook his head, unable to understand her. Releasing his stiff, unyielding cock from his clothing, she cradled it in her hands, feeling a throb like a heartbeat passing through its length. His breath was uneven, like a man encountering mortal danger. Suddenly, he struggled to loose the bonds at his wrists.

'Calm down,' she crooned, though she still caressed his phallus in the most tormenting manner. It was like tugging the string of a stiff, unwieldy puppet. When she squeezed the end of it, he almost screamed.

'Let me go!'

With great dexterity, she fondled his engorged member until droplets formed on the swollen tip. He gasped with excitement, but as the muscle twitched, she withdrew her hands.

'Please,' he begged. His eyes were full of the love-making on the bed in front of him. At his back he could feel the girl's body pressed against his, enticing him with its heat and soft curves. 'I beg you, finish me.'

With a series of firm smacks to his penis, she admonished him. 'You are not so very good at your work now, are you? I thought you wanted to please me?'

'I do,' he groaned. 'I will do anything.'

'Then you must cool off awhile, until I choose to release you.'

It was a hard task Allegra had set him. Barely inches away from him, on the bed, Celina was gorging herself on a feast of pleasure. The olive-skinned youth was now upon her, his muscular rear rising and falling like a dolphin riding the ocean. One of her hands was squeezing the Moor's stiff phallus against her breasts, which rocked rhythmically above her straining ribs. Suddenly her blue eyes sought out Allegra, then moved to the anguished face of the bound man. Maybe it was the sight of him, trussed and helpless, his member twitching without hope of release, that sent her spinning over into the deeps of a climax. Her eyes blinked, losing focus on the room and her attentive lovers.

With a gasp of anticipation, she bore down on the stiff cock between her legs, and with eyes tightly shut, the convulsion tore through her. The captive at Allegra's side struggled for release; rattling the bedpost and cursing beneath his breath. Allegra did not know if he would have thrown himself down at her feet or thrown the other man aside and lunged into Celina himself. She was enthralled by his painful frustration. Pressing in front of him, she felt the stiff appendage jab hotly against her thighs. Deep inside herself, she felt a giddy excitement melting her flesh to liquid. Her hard nipples trailed across the heat of his bare chest. His face was pale with anguish.

'This is no good to me,' she whispered mischievously. He gasped as her fingernails brushed against his most sensitive, taut flesh. 'I am afraid,' she pronounced very slowly, letting the sentence linger in her mouth, 'I must find my satisfaction elsewhere.'

As Celina raised herself up from the bed to find the ewer of water to bathe, Allegra slid on to the mattress to take her place. It was like lowering herself into a bath of hot, feverish sensuality. Three sets of hands moved across her body, softly but eagerly, pulling aside the thin muslin of her chemise and skilfully unlacing the cords of her silken stays. Fingers caressed her throat and shoulders, her distended breasts, the curves of her buttocks, her thighs and stomach.

Surrendering herself to every delectable sensation, Allegra closed her eyes and let herself drift into that other country of utter, raw sensation. With an involuntary shudder of excitement, she felt the wiry head of the Moor brush against her thigh as his kisses grew closer and closer to her quivering centre. As his tongue inched towards the expectant swelling at her vulva a cry issued without words from her throat. It came into her mind: I can take what I want – there is no one here to stop me.

With eager fingers she reached down and raked the man's hair, pulling him deeper against her, as blissful sensations burst again and again like bubbles of pleasure from the pit of her stomach. On and on it went, this juicy devouring of her being, while the others sucked at her breasts and kissed her lips and neck, until she felt a wild desire to be filled and filled until she could take no more. The Moor guessed her readiness, and through half open eyes she saw him pull away and grasp his long black tool and steady himself, ready to take her.

'No,' she moaned, though her knees were raised apart, 'not yet.'

Startled, he looked at her with wild, lust-crazed eyes. Eagerly, she reached forward to take his massive penis from his own grasp. It felt heavy and solid in her hand, which in turn looked pale and small against its girth. Inside her stomach, she felt knots of lust twisting round and round, her muscles tingling with fiery excitement. I can do as I wish, she thought, and though it was agony to do it, she held off him still longer.

Slipping down the bed, she dipped her face downwards and smelt his raw, salty sexuality. Then she parted her lips wide over the fat bulge of its head. The sweet, briny taste was like an elixir, making her drunk with lust. Her mouth strained wider to take more of it, her fingers milking the shaft, feeling the ripeness of his swinging testicles, desperate, it seemed, to discharge. As she bore down ever lower, the two other men's attention turned to her wriggling upended rear, as they caressed and kissed every inch of her body.

Soon, as she gorged her mouth on the one man, she felt the others drive into her silkily receptive cleft, until she could no longer differentiate between tongue or finger as they throbbed inside her wet and ready entrance and even in her second, most secret passage. As she frenziedly rubbed her lips up and down the weighty column of flesh the Moor reached out and grasped her breasts. She was on fire now, every touch driving her closer and closer to an explosive pinnacle of excitement. Teasingly, he pulled on her lengthened nipples, which jutted out stiffly, almost too sensitive to be touched.

'Take me,' she demanded, reluctantly withdrawing the delicious flesh from her lips. Greedily, she looked at its brown, shiny wetness, where her saliva now mixed with the first milky drops which he had been unable to hold back. Lying back on the bed, she flaunted the scarlet gash at her centre, so wet and shiny like a painted mouth, the lips puffed and swollen with desire. As he moved towards her, she felt her muscles expand and contract with excitement, so ready was she for this, so pent-up with a craving and hunger for this wild, name-less heat.

As the Moor's bulky phallus slid against her entrance she twisted a corner of her chemise round and round in her hand. She was reeling with excitement, feeling her own saliva dribble from his cock on to her parted cleft. But now that she was ready, she was rigid with arousal, her muscles tightened inflexibly. Try as he might, he could not force himself inside her. Desperately, he pushed his slim black fingers down inside her, almost forcing her to climax on the stiffness as they thrust pleasurably inside her. But when he withdrew his fingers, again he could not manoeuvre the bulk of his member inside the ecstatic grip of her entrance.

'You must help, my friend,' he croaked to the olive-skinned youth. The next moment the second man was kneeling before her, his crimson tipped stem at the ready. 'Make a path for me.'

As if in a delirium, Allegra was aware of the two men pulling her thighs wide while the third parted her lips and aimed his member at her over-excited channel. Again, there was a resistance, but this time he grasped her buttocks and squeezed his way inside. So locked had she become that he could barely work his way into her, but the effect was a mixture of tantalising impediment and glorious release. With a few thrusts, he broke through, easing more and more of his shaft inside her. With a sudden, juddering movement, he gave her the full length of it and she seemed to fall, her body flung into a spasm of ecstatic release, her muscles suddenly squeezing so hard he cried out as if she held him like a vice. Withdrawing, the others looked at his dripping and reddened member. Then the first Moor sprang down to take his rightful place.

Again, as he guided his fearsome tool towards her entrance, Allegra felt an excitement build in her loins like a fire catching on paper. He was as well endowed as any man she had ever seen; his cock swung darkly against her thigh, like a great tube of muscle throbbing with blood and power. With a moan of ecstasy, she felt it batter against her slippery entrance. Again, he bore down on her, jamming the rounded head hard against the small, fleshy fissure. She wanted it so much, wanted it inside her, swinging to the very hilt. But again she could not take its girth, though her juices ran across the head like salty dew.

'My friend,' groaned the Moor to his countryman. 'You try.' And so the second Moor took his place, raising his dark weapon at her crimson gate. Uncontrollably, she met his thrust, and after a few gentle attempts, he slid inside her. Now at last she could feel the hard flesh drive inside her; lifting her legs, she pulled him as tightly as she could into the soft inner hollow at her centre. Crying out without restraint, she urged him on, feeling him slap against her buttocks, letting any of them, for she knew not one from another, caress her and fondle her as she experienced complete abandonment.

Whether it was the result of desperation or frustration, she no longer knew or cared, but she became aware of her thwarted lover kneeling astride her. His member was stiff and engorged, the veins standing up in patterns along the shaft. Ecstatically, she let him push it between her breasts, and then unable to stand the temptation any longer, she pulled it gluttonously to her mouth and let him take her that way, feeling both cocks moving inside her in rampant, ecstatic unison.

Almost immediately, the taste and sensation were too much for her – with a cry of unbridled bliss, she succumbed to wave upon wave of pleasure, her head flung back as the two pounded on and on, riding the tide of ecstasy. In answer, she felt the phallus between her legs suddenly spasm, filling her with a delicious stream of juddering heat. Lying panting with her back arched ecstatically, she wanted it to go on and on forever.

'Do you still want me?' The Moor was still astride her, his cock newly free from her mouth. It was engorged, hot and hard. Now, if ever, she would be able to take him. Could she bear any more? She felt a spasm of delight twitch between her legs as her eyes travelled along the pole of flesh, from the heavy, bloated testicles to the purple tip which oozed desire. She could feel a wanton dampness beneath her on the sheets, but still her eyes greedily gorged on him, imagining being impaled on something so harrowing and huge. With a nod of her head, she let him slip down between her thighs for the third time. She felt lax and ready now, from the other men, and felt she might take anything. Eagerly, she watched him nudge the purple head against her lips.

'Here, I will help.'

It was Celina, slipping behind her so that Allegra could sit up and lean against her. She smelt fresh and lovely; her hair falling in golden waves before Allegra's face. They moved to the edge of the bed, and as Allegra sat half on Celina's lap with her legs spread wide, the Moor had a better vantage point to enter her. Allegra was almost faint with desire. This, to have Celina so close as he took her, was itself a kind of paradise.

'Here, let me guide you,' Celina whispered, as she slipped her fingers around to part her friend's engorged lips. The delicate fingers gently massaged her friend's slippery passage. Allegra could tell that the girl was excited too, as her fingers teased the rim of her entrance, raising ripples of pleasure so deep and powerful that she feared her frame could hardly bear it. Then Celina grasped the head of the Moor's shaft. Her fingers ran admiringly along its full veined length; it was surprising he had the self-control not to forget himself there and then as the two girls played with him.

As if mating two hesitant creatures, Celina expertly pulled the coffee-coloured phallus towards the slippery little gap, directing the bulbous head downwards. With a cry of pleasure, Allegra felt it press against her, double its force and then ease its way an inch inside her. She was aware of Celina's little hands stretching her lips, easing the shaft inch by inch inside her. In front of her, the Moor was steeling himself to retain control, beads of sweat breaking out on his forehead like raindrops.

As three, then four and finally five inches rammed their way inside her, Allegra felt herself being stretched exquisitely. Gasping a little, she wriggled on to it, watching Celina stroke it gently into her. Still disciplined, the Moor's member compressed into her tightness, pushing a little further each time. Six, then seven, then eight. Allegra thought she couldn't take much more. Still Celina's hand was pushing it further, jerking the big black shaft back and forth as it gratified her friend into a state of oblivion. Then, as the Moor began to move faster and faster, shooting back and forth, Celina withdrew her hand and began to squeeze and rub Allegra's breasts, all the time watching the girl as her face grew flushed and her moans grew louder.

From a sudden pressure on the mattress behind her, Allegra suddenly realised that one of the men had joined Celina on the bed and summarily mounted her. Though she still clung to Allegra's breasts, Allegra could hear the girl cry out as she presented her rear to her lover and he slid easily inside her. Again, Allegra felt the same wildness that she had experienced on the boat – a smell of lust like sea salt, a knowledge that here, in this wild coupling was something ancient and good. Glancing quickly over her shoulder, she could see Celina bent over, the second Moor driving into her smooth white flesh, pounding at her rump. Before her, her own lover was at last gaining the relief he deserved, his face almost blank as he strove with every nerve to hold off until she had reached her climax. There was one thing missing, Allegra's feverish mind told her.

'Unbind one of his hands,' she cried, pointing to the youth still tied to the bedpost. Quickly, the olive skinned youth complied. Then, with a sudden gesture, she reached forward towards her captive and felt his phallus rub ecstatically against her breasts. With her eyes, she devoured the bound youth. Over the passage of time his discomfiture had grown. He now looked undeniably agonised by frustration. The congested penis that rose from his groin was scarlet in colour and twitching with unrelieved excitement. An exhibitionist glee filled her; she raised her knees to better enjoy the Moor, knowing too that her mental prisoner would witness the cruel eroticism of her enjoying every inch of her lover in close, exquisite detail.

Allegra was now so slippery, he could indeed manoeuvre deeper and deeper inside her. Though she had thought all her capacity for pleasure might be reached, the massive rod of flesh tormented her with its ceaseless driving, stretching her further than she had imagined was possible. Looking down, she could see it riding back and forth, the thick black shaft wet and slippery as it forced her lips apart.

A sudden motion made her look up to her prisoner by the bed. At last he was unable to stand his torment any further. With his one, free, feverish hand, he grasped himself and ecstatically rubbed himself up and down. He was watching Allegra fixedly, watching the intense responses of her body, watching the ceaseless pounding

244

of the Moor's weighty cock, watching her pleasure as she drove him to this final, pitiful state.

'Lift me,' she whispered to the Moor. He did so, grasping her waist to impale her again and again on the thick bulk, which rubbed again and again over the delicate skin inside her. She was inches now from the bound youth. Wild with lust, his one free hand yanked at his body in a frenzy. She could feel eyes upon her, watching her, staring, enjoying her pleasure.

Feeling the cock buried inside her grow too much to bear, she began to cry out, pressing back against Celina, feeling each stroke burn inside her. She could no longer get her breath; her eyes closed tight. He was driving her down on it hard, she could feel the very shape of it, stretching her with its magnificent size. When her climax burst inside her, the room seemed to spin, so violent was her release. As she gripped the Moor's vast member in her convulsion, it was not only him she thought of, but her eyes fixed quickly on the sight of her poor, pitiful prisoner, his hand jerking back and forth like a puppet. With a tremor he groaned; from above she could feel his hot rain pattering softly on her ecstatic, blissful face.

Slowly recovering, Allegra stretched her limbs and lazily looked around the room. Her captive had slumped to the carpet, curled up in his nakedness. The others too, were dozing quietly close by her. Allegra's mind wandered over the last few hours, wondering how it was she had attained such a potent summit of pleasure. She smiled to herself to remember the youth's frantic eyes as he watched her – and yet, there had been more than that. The sensation of being watched had been so strong, almost as if she had been a naked performer on a stage, posturing for the front row. It reminded her of something very long ago, far away in the past.

Very gently, so as not to disturb the others, Allegra lifted her hands, letting them trail across her damp thighs. Play-acting a desire she could no longer feel, she began to stroke her own breasts, squeezing them in the palms of her hands. She could hear the other men breathing gently around her; it seemed that all but her had fallen asleep. Through half-closed eyes, she gazed at the walls; damask hangings were draped across most of the facing wall, along with gilt candleholders and mirrors.

One of the mirrors was particularly striking; its shape was that of a laughing satyr, his open mouth forming the glass in which her own side of the room was reflected. Above the looking glass the foreshortened face of the satyr contained a long, hooked nose, two blackened eyes and a pair of impish horns. With a counterfeit sigh of self-indulgence, Allegra faced the mirror, parted her thighs and began to rub at the top of her legs. There was no sound but for that of the sleepers around her.

In a pose of extreme wantonness, she lifted her hips a little and pretended to caress her swollen vulva. Then it happened. Without a sound, she felt a presence like a shadow crossing the sun. Raising her eyelids imperceptibly, she saw the glint of human eyes flicker behind the eyeholes carved into the mirror. Her heart beat rapidly as she continued her pretence, her mind racing all the time to decide what it was she should do.

Then, in the quietness of the room, she heard a sound. It was a long, beseeching sigh, as her watcher moaned to himself behind the thin fabric of the wall. It was too much. Trying not to move too suddenly, she lifted herself up and yawned, then sauntered over to the ewer of water. From there she noticed the olive-skinned youth suddenly stir. Whispering, she called him over.

'Come out into the corridor,' she hissed, pulling her thin gown over her nakedness.

'What is it?' He had followed her out into the dimly-lit corridor. The whole place was silent now, for it was not that long until dawn.

'There is someone watching from behind the wall. Do you know who?'

His astonished face told her that this was not a custom of the house, to charge men to watch the activities in the bedrooms. 'No. Let me think. This room is at the end of the building. They must be watching from next door. It's an empty house. The filthy scoundrel! I'll soon sort it out.'

But their conversation had alerted Madame Escolier who bustled up to them in her nightcap and nightgown. 'What's going on here?'

Allegra explained and the woman's face dropped with dismay. 'I cannot believe it,' she cried. 'This is a respectable place. Respectable women come here. Oh, if they were to find out! No. It must be stopped.'

'Listen, I will pay a call on our prying friend – me and some of the others. I'll wake them up.' Quickly, the youth called on some of the other men and soon a group of four or five had assembled in nightshirts and breeches. Some carried sticks and one had a pistol in his belt.

'You, run to the Piazza for the nightwatchman,' Madame Escolier instructed one of the younger men. Then they all disappeared quietly down the stairs.

Later, Allegra slipped her fur cloak around her shoulders and followed them downstairs. A sickening realisation had occurred to her. Celina and she had blithely tricked Alexei and Phillipe without a second thought. Was it not just as likely that they in their turn might have tried to trick the girls? What better joke, in their estimation, than to follow them both and spy on them from the next building?

As she reached the doorway, Allegra was appalled to see a group of men wearing the shining helmets of the Doge's guard gathered beneath a flaming torch. For a moment, she huddled in the shadows, berating herself for not having guessed earlier. What if Alexei lost his commission? All of Phillipe's attempts to work secretly to undermine the French king would be thrown into the open. They might both be thrown into the Inquisitor's gaol. She was stupid, stupid, stupid.

It was with a squeezing pain twisting her heart that she saw the guard seek her out.

'Signorina. Do you know this man? He says he knows you.'

Grimly, she prepared herself to face the recriminating eyes of both men. What a fool she had been. A coy, priggish fool. All that had been taught her, she had ignored.

She followed the guard but still could not see Phillipe or Alexei.

'Where are they?' she asked, looking wildly amongst the torchlit faces.

'This is the man.'

Incredulously, Allegra looked at the wretch hanging between the arms of two guards. He was as pale as a ghost, with dark rings beneath his eyes and loose red lips. 'Allegra. Speak for me.'

She peered at the voyeur more closely. Dressed in unkempt clothes he may have been, unshaved and untidy and a little older – but still, she could just recognise Leon.

'It is Leon di Rivero,' she exclaimed. 'Leon, how dare you watch me like that!'

'So it was this man who spied on you?' asked the guard.

'It certainly was.'

In an instant he had been hurried away, dragging his feet and imploring Allegra to speak for him. With him went Madame Escolier and a few of her men, eager to press charges against Leon. For a few moments, Allegra paused in the cold air, pulling her cloak tightly around her naked shoulders. The guards and their captive disappeared into swathes of mist at the end of the *calle*. The morning light was getting stronger, illuminating the little square with misty, greying light. All around her, behind the stone facades of houses, churches, convents and schools, the citizens would soon be rousing themselves from dreams to face another day. It was time to wake up Celina and go home.

Half a year passed. The snows melted and the lagoon once more splashed and danced across the ancient stones of the quayside. The sun shone in skies of sapphire blue to illuminate the Doge and his company casting a golden ring into the sea, once more to celebrate the age-old wedding of the Serene Republic to her capricious spouse. Visitors glided into the lagoon with heavy purses and danced and made love and played cards and left in the Autumn with lighter purses and even lighter hearts.

In the Palazzo Raffi, a letter was a rare occurrence. So when a boy called with a message for Signorina Allegra di Vitali and pushed a large, red-sealed document into Celina's hands, curiosity made her inspect it with the utmost care.

'Allegra,' she cried, scampering up the stairs to their chamber. 'Look! A letter from the Office of the Inquisitors. Open it quickly.'

Allegra was seated by the window, mending her Columbine gown in the evening light. The rich fabric had been badly used; there were stains and tears all about the hem and in places the stitching gaped at the seams.

'I have no idea,' she began, pulling apart the crimson seal. She unfolded the thick paper, read it and then began it again. 'Oh,' she said quietly, as she read the paper a third time.

Celina tried her best to sidle behind her and read it. As she did, her eyes widened. 'Allegra!' she squealed. 'You will be rich. The whole of your guardian's inheritance. My goodness. Leon is dispossessed.'

That was indeed the import of the letter. That Leon had been deemed unfit to hold the title of a nobleman and as a consequence of his being dispossessed, all of his material goods and inheritance were to pass to his only living relative.

'What will you do?'

Allegra was dazed, reading and rereading the letter, trying to understand the enormity of changes this would mean to her. Turning to Celina, she suddenly threw herself, weeping, into her arms. For a while she stayed there, sobbing into the soft fabric of Celina's dress.

'Ask rather what will the pair of us do?' she said, finally raising her tear-stained face, half-laughing and half-crying. 'Though Leon left me penniless, I will give him an allowance. But the rest? Celina, we will have such a time as this city has never seen!'

The time of carnival again spun round. Now Allegra sat at her mirror in a new costume, draped in white satin as the goddess Diana, her hair set with a chaplet of jewelled oak leaves and a golden belt at her waist. Phillipe was returning in a few days. Both he and Alexei would occasionally travel away, to Poland or the courts of Saxony or Bohemia. It was sad for Celina and herself to see them leave, but this pain was soon replaced by a delightful mixture of tender loss and exciting freedom once they were away. In truth, their absence made their returning all the sweeter.

Allegra could hear her friend singing softly in the next room as she bathed. It had been such a pleasure to indulge Celina: to buy clothes and furniture and jewels and books to amuse her. For herself, Allegra had indulged herself in only one large commission. It hung above their bed now, a large painting which the artist Signor Guidi had been pleased to work on all these last three months.

The subject of the painting was naked, her sumptuous flesh revealed to the observer in all its sensual detail. Diamonds and pearls studded the woman's throat, navel and the artfully painted centre of her sex. Dark, luxurious hair cascaded down past her shoulders, studded with strings of pearls and a diamond coronet. In her outstretched hands was a set of fine chains, proffered to the viewer. Yet the expression on the subject's face was not submission, rather it was an offer, made thoughtfully, as a gift of pleasure. Allegra smiled as her eyes met those of the woman in the painting.

The face of the subject was Allegra's own.

In a heady cloud of musk, Celina swept into the room. This carnival she had chosen the costume of a priestess of the vestal virgins. Dressed in a white gauze vest and skirt, her long hair falling in braids set with a silver crown in the shape of a diamond-eyed asp.

'I have had an idea,' Allegra confided, still gazing at the painting. 'It is a second commission for Signor Guidi. He is a very good painter, don't you think?'

'I am sure it was a delightful subject for him to paint. How could it not have turned out well? You look beautiful.'

Allegra turned to the window, where the first flurry of snow was falling past the glass, glittering whitely in the reflected light of their lamp.

'How cold it must be on Santa Agnetha tonight.'

'I thought you had been thinking of that place. There is something solemn in your features.'

'I know you will think me a fool. And I know the Prioress took my dowry. But still – do you not think Signor Guidi would paint a wonderful Philomastrix?'

Celina stopped coiling her hair and looked at her closest friend and lover.

'He would, but I think there is more to this.'

Placing her palm against the cold glass, Allegra stared into the snow-flecked darkness. She remembered the long stairs down to the sister's chapel, the pain of the birch and the exquisite bonds at her ankles and wrists. She recollected too, the beautiful awakening of her own, ecstatic sexuality.

'I would like to make a gift to the sisterhood. That is all. At Santa Agnetha I received a gift which is beyond value. And I should like you to be his model for the goddess.'

'Thank you. Of course. It would please me very much.'

'There is an old Venetian saying, "For a gift, return a gift". I am obliged to them for all I have – including you.'

She looked at her friend with such an expression of sweetness that Celina too felt a teardrop collect in her eye.

'Come along, these are too serious thoughts for such a night.'

Suddenly Celina was swinging her in her arms, kissing her lightly on the lips. 'We shall see Signor Guidi in the morning and arrange it all. I am very honoured to be asked. But for now, where is your mask?'

Together they slipped on the fur cloaks and a pair of pretty, lace-trimmed masks. Then descending the stairs in a great rustle of silks and taffeta and lace, they disappeared out into the snowy night beneath the silver disc of a hunter's moon. It illuminated their way through all the byways of that great serene city, in search of new, undiscovered loves and the age-old rites of pleasure.

LOOK OUT FOR THE ALL-NEW BLACK LACE BOOKS – AVAILABLE NOW!

All books priced £6.99 in the UK. Please note publication dates apply to the UK only. For other territories, please contact your retailer.

WICKED WORDS 9
Various

ISBN 0352 33860 1

Wicked Words collections are the hottest anthologies of women's erotic writing to be found anywhere in the world. With settings and scenarios to suit all tastes, this is fun erotica at the cutting edge from the UK and USA. The diversity of themes and styles reflects the multi-faceted nature of the female sexual imagination. Combining humour, warmth and attitude with imaginative writing, these stories sizzle with horny action. **Another scorching collection of wild fantasies.**

FEMININE WILES
Karina Moore

ISBN 0 352 33874 1

Young American art student Kelly Aslett is spending the summer in Paris before flying back to California to claim her inheritance when she falls in lust and love with gorgeous French painter, Luc Duras. But her stepmother – the scheming and hedonistic Marissa – is determined to claim the luxury house for herself. Still in love with Luc, Kelly is horrified to find herself sexually entranced by the enigmatic figure of Johnny Casigelli, a ruthless but very sexy villain Marissa has enlisted in her scheme to wrestle the inheritance away from Kelly. Will she succumb to his masculine charms, or can she use her feminine wiles to gain what is rightfully hers? **A high-octane tale of erotic obsession and sexual rivalry.**

GOING DEEP
Kimberley Dean
ISBN 0 352 33876 8

Sporty Brynn Montgomery returns to teach at the college where she
used to be a cheerleader but, to her horror, finds that football player
Cody Jones, who scandalised her name ten years previously, is now the
coach. Soon Brynn is caught up in a clash of pads, a shimmer of pom-
poms and the lust of healthy athletes. However, Cody is still a wolfish
predator and neither he nor his buddies are going to let Brynn forget
what she did that fateful night back in high school. **Rip-roaring,
testosterone-fuelled fun set among the jocks and babes of the Ivy
League.**

Coming in April

HOT GOSSIP
Savannah Smythe
ISBN 0 352 33880 6

Suzy Whitbread packs in her job and returns to the village where she
grew up. She was frowned upon as a teenager for the close friendship
she had with Clifton McKenna, a successful horse trainer with an
overbearing wife. Now, Suzy finds that Clifton has recently been
confined to a wheelchair after a riding accident, and she is determined to
help him recover. But with Clifton's son Jem also having designs on Suzy,
father/son rivalry becomes the catalyst for some very hot gossip. **Sizzling
sexual tensions in small-town England as a secret affair becomes public.**

LA BASQUIASE
Angle Strand
ISBN 0 352 32988 2

The lovely Oruela is determined to fit in to a lifestyle of opulence in
1920s Biarritz. But she has to put her social aspirations on hold when she
falls under suspicion for her father's murder. As Oruela becomes
embroiled in a series of sensual games, she discovers that blackmail is a
powerful weapon that can be used to obtain pleasure as well as money.
**An unusual, erotic and beautifully written story set in the heady whirl of
French society in the 1920s.**

Black Lace Booklist

Information is correct at time of printing. To avoid disappointment check availability before ordering. Go to www.blacklace-books.co.uk. All books are priced £6.99 unless another price is given.

BLACK LACE BOOKS WITH A CONTEMPORARY SETTING

☐ IN THE FLESH Emma Holly	ISBN 0 352 33498 3	£5.99
☐ SHAMELESS Stella Black	ISBN 0 352 33485 1	£5.99
☐ INTENSE BLUE Lyn Wood	ISBN 0 352 33496 7	£5.99
☐ THE NAKED TRUTH Natasha Rostova	ISBN 0 352 33497 5	£5.99
☐ A SPORTING CHANCE Susie Raymond	ISBN 0 352 33501 7	£5.99
☐ TAKING LIBERTIES Susie Raymond	ISBN 0 352 33357 X	£5.99
☐ A SCANDALOUS AFFAIR Holly Graham	ISBN 0 352 33523 8	£5.99
☐ THE NAKED FLAME Crystalle Valentino	ISBN 0 352 33528 9	£5.99
☐ ON THE EDGE Laura Hamilton	ISBN 0 352 33534 3	£5.99
☐ LURED BY LUST Tania Picarda	ISBN 0 352 33533 5	£5.99
☐ THE HOTTEST PLACE Tabitha Flyte	ISBN 0 352 33536 X	£5.99
☐ THE NINETY DAYS OF GENEVIEVE Lucinda Carrington	ISBN 0 352 33070 8	£5.99
☐ DREAMING SPIRES Juliet Hastings	ISBN 0 352 33584 X	
☐ THE TRANSFORMATION Natasha Rostova	ISBN 0 352 33311 1	
☐ SIN.NET Helena Ravenscroft	ISBN 0 352 33598 X	
☐ TWO WEEKS IN TANGIER Annabel Lee	ISBN 0 352 33599 8	
☐ HIGHLAND FLING Jane Justine	ISBN 0 352 33616 1	
☐ PLAYING HARD Tina Troy	ISBN 0 352 33617 X	
☐ SYMPHONY X Jasmine Stone	ISBN 0 352 33629 3	
☐ SUMMER FEVER Anna Ricci	ISBN 0 352 33625 0	
☐ CONTINUUM Portia Da Costa	ISBN 0 352 33120 8	
☐ OPENING ACTS Suki Cunningham	ISBN 0 352 33630 7	
☐ FULL STEAM AHEAD Tabitha Flyte	ISBN 0 352 33637 4	
☐ A SECRET PLACE Ella Broussard	ISBN 0 352 33307 3	
☐ GAME FOR ANYTHING Lyn Wood	ISBN 0 352 33639 0	
☐ CHEAP TRICK Astrid Fox	ISBN 0 352 33640 4	
☐ ALL THE TRIMMINGS Tesni Morgan	ISBN 0 352 33641 3	

- ☐ THE GIFT OF SHAME Sara Hope-Walker ISBN 0 352 32935 1
- ☐ COMING UP ROSES Crystalle Valentino ISBN 0 352 33658 7
- ☐ GOING TOO FAR Laura Hamilton ISBN 0 352 33657 9
- ☐ THE STALLION Georgina Brown ISBN 0 352 33005 8
- ☐ DOWN UNDER Juliet Hastings ISBN 0 352 33663 3
- ☐ THE BITCH AND THE BASTARD Wendy Harris ISBN 0 352 33664 1
- ☐ ODALISQUE Fleur Reynolds ISBN 0 352 32887 8
- ☐ SWEET THING Alison Tyler ISBN 0 352 33682 X
- ☐ TIGER LILY Kimberley Dean ISBN 0 352 33685 4
- ☐ COOKING UP A STORM Emma Holly ISBN 0 352 33686 2
- ☐ RELEASE ME Suki Cunningham ISBN 0 352 33671 4
- ☐ KING'S PAWN Ruth Fox ISBN 0 352 33684 6
- ☐ FULL EXPOSURE Robyn Russell ISBN 0 352 33688 9
- ☐ SLAVE TO SUCCESS Kimberley Raines ISBN 0 352 33687 0
- ☐ STRIPPED TO THE BONE Jasmine Stone ISBN 0 352 33463 0
- ☐ HARD CORPS Claire Thompson ISBN 0 352 33491 6
- ☐ MANHATTAN PASSION Antoinette Powell ISBN 0 352 33691 9
- ☐ CABIN FEVER Emma Donaldson ISBN 0 352 33692 7
- ☐ WOLF AT THE DOOR Savannah Smythe ISBN 0 352 33693 5
- ☐ SHADOWPLAY Portia Da Costa ISBN 0 352 33313 8
- ☐ I KNOW YOU, JOANNA Ruth Fox ISBN 0 352 33727 3
- ☐ SNOW BLONDE Astrid Fox ISBN 0 352 33732 X
- ☐ QUEEN OF THE ROAD Lois Pheonix ISBN 0 352 33131 1
- ☐ THE HOUSE IN NEW ORLEANS Fleur Reynolds ISBN 0 352 32951 3
- ☐ HEAT OF THE MOMENT Tesni Morgan ISBN 0 352 33742 7
- ☐ STORMY HAVEN Savannah Smythe ISBN 0 352 33757 5
- ☐ STICKY FINGERS Alison Tyler ISBN 0 352 33756 7
- ☐ THE WICKED STEPDAUGHTER Wendy Harris ISBN 0 352 33777 X
- ☐ DRAWN TOGETHER Robyn Russell ISBN 0 352 33269 7
- ☐ LEARNING THE HARD WAY Jasmine Archer ISBN 0 352 33782 6
- ☐ VALENTINA'S RULES Monica Belle ISBN 0 352 33788 5
- ☐ VELVET GLOVE Emma Holly ISBN 0 352 33448 7
- ☐ UNKNOWN TERRITORY Annie O'Neill ISBN 0 352 33794 X
- ☐ VIRTUOSO Katrina Vincenzi-Thyre ISBN 0 352 32907 6
- ☐ FIGHTING OVER YOU Laura Hamilton ISBN 0 352 33795 8
- ☐ COUNTRY PLEASURES Primula Bond ISBN 0 352 33810 5

☐ ARIA APPASSIONATA Juliet Hastings	ISBN 0 352 33056 2
☐ THE RELUCTANT PRINCESS Patty Glenn	ISBN 0 352 33809 1
☐ WILD IN THE COUNTRY Monica Belle	ISBN 0 352 33824 5
☐ THE TUTOR Portia Da Costa	ISBN 0 352 32946 7
☐ SEXUAL STRATEGY Felice de Vere	ISBN 0 352 33843 1
☐ HARD BLUE MIDNIGHT Alaine Hood	ISBN 0 352 33851 2
☐ ALWAYS THE BRIDEGROOM Tesni Morgan	ISBN 0 352 33855 5
☐ COMING ROUND THE MOUNTAIN Tabitha Flyte	ISBN 0 352 33873 3

BLACK LACE BOOKS WITH AN HISTORICAL SETTING

☐ PRIMAL SKIN Leona Benkt Rhys	ISBN 0 352 33500 9	£5.99
☐ DEVIL'S FIRE Melissa MacNeal	ISBN 0 352 33527 0	£5.99
☐ DARKER THAN LOVE Kristina Lloyd	ISBN 0 352 33279 4	
☐ THE CAPTIVATION Natasha Rostova	ISBN 0 352 33234 4	
☐ MINX Megan Blythe	ISBN 0 352 33638 2	
☐ JULIET RISING Cleo Cordell	ISBN 0 352 32938 6	
☐ DEMON'S DARE Melissa MacNeal	ISBN 0 352 33683 8	
☐ DIVINE TORMENT Janine Ashbless	ISBN 0 352 33719 2	
☐ SATAN'S ANGEL Melissa MacNeal	ISBN 0 352 33726 5	
☐ THE INTIMATE EYE Georgia Angelis	ISBN 0 352 33004 X	
☐ OPAL DARKNESS Cleo Cordell	ISBN 0 352 33033 3	
☐ SILKEN CHAINS Jodi Nicol	ISBN 0 352 33143 7	
☐ EVIL'S NIECE Melissa MacNeal	ISBN 0 352 33781 8	
☐ ACE OF HEARTS Lisette Allen	ISBN 0 352 33059 7	
☐ A GENTLEMAN'S WAGER Madelynne Ellis	ISBN 0 352 33800 8	
☐ THE LION LOVER Mercedes Kelly	ISBN 0 352 33162 3	
☐ ARTISTIC LICENCE Vivienne La Fay	ISBN 0 352 33210 7	
☐ THE AMULET Lisette Allen	ISBN 0 352 33019 8	

BLACK LACE ANTHOLOGIES

☐ WICKED WORDS 6 Various	ISBN 0 352 33590 0
☐ WICKED WORDS 9 Various	ISBN 0 352 33860 1
☐ THE BEST OF BLACK LACE 2 Various	ISBN 0 352 33718 4

BLACK LACE NON-FICTION

☐ THE BLACK LACE BOOK OF WOMEN'S SEXUAL   ISBN 0 352 33793 1   £6.99
     FANTASIES   Ed. Kerri Sharp

To find out the latest information about Black Lace titles, check out the
website: www.blacklace-books.co.uk or send for a booklist with
complete synopses by writing to:

> Black Lace Booklist, Virgin Books Ltd
> Thames Wharf Studios
> Rainville Road
> London W6 9HA

Please include an SAE of decent size. Please note only British stamps
are valid.

Our privacy policy
We will not disclose information you supply us to any other parties.
We will not disclose any information which identifies you personally to
any person without your express consent.

From time to time we may send out information about Black Lace
books and special offers. Please tick here if you do <u>not</u> wish to
receive Black Lace information.   ☐

Please send me the books I have ticked above.

Name ....

Address ....

....

....

....

Post Code ....

Send to: Virgin Books Cash Sales, Thames Wharf Studios, Rainville Road, London W6 9HA.

US customers: for prices and details of how to order books for delivery by mail, call 1-800-343-4499.

Please enclose a cheque or postal order, made payable to Virgin Books Ltd, to the value of the books you have ordered plus postage and packing costs as follows:

UK and BFPO – £1.00 for the first book, 50p for each subsequent book.

Overseas (including Republic of Ireland) – £2.00 for the first book, £1.00 for each subsequent book.

If you would prefer to pay by VISA, ACCESS/MASTERCARD, DINERS CLUB, AMEX or SWITCH, please write your card number and expiry date here:

....

Signature ....

Please allow up to 28 days for delivery.